THE EYE OF THE DAY

DENNISON SMITH

THE EYE OF THE DAY

DENNISON SMITH

periscope

www.periscopebooks.co.uk

THE EYE OF THE DAY

First published in Great Britain in 2015 by

Periscope
An imprint of Garnet Publishing Limited
8 Southern Court, South Street
Reading RG1 4QS

www.periscopebooks.co.uk
www.facebook.com/periscopebooks
www.twitter.com/periscopebooks
www.instagram.com/periscope_books
www.pinterest.com/periscope

ISBN 9781859640616

A CIP catalogue record for this book is available from the British Library.

Typeset by Samantha Barden
Jacket design by James Nunn: www.jamesnunn.co.uk

Printed and bound in Lebanon by International Press:
interpress@int-press.com

for my father

Amos Cobb wrenched his boots from the trainyard mud, and the earth gave a sucking sound. Everything was slowed by the weather. The freight train full of tractors was late moving out and the commuter train hadn't come in. Over the passengers waiting on the platform, the lamps sizzled and buzzed, while hailstones drove at a hard angle under the tin roof. The weather was nothing new: it was terrible or beautiful, and usually it was terrible when there was outdoor work to do. There was always outdoor work for Amos.

He lifted a thigh-high boot; he put it down in the muck. Doing one thing at a time kept things under control. Felling for the lumber companies and blasting in the granite pits had taught him to take his tasks slow and not let his thoughts crowd him. Otherwise, there were accidents. He was rutty and bearish and marred already, one half-finger lopped off in a sawmill, and he was only twenty-five, though to other people he didn't seem to have an age. Vermonters said he was like a rock – strong, big and sturdy, nothing to look at – and no one had met a young rock. Now sulphur from the coal dust lined his nostrils. Soot and slush commingled on the ground. But Amos, working for the railroad tonight, wasn't distracted by the weather.

Tomorrow he'd be up in the hills, dredging the cold lake for the float-away parts of the Shaw Browns' dock, which had surely come apart in the storm. He could see the family, the kid and his dad, waiting on the platform for the late train from Princeton to arrive and deliver the mother. Of all his jobs, caretaking their summer cottage was the softest. Summer, even on a night like this, was a cushy season, even when he had to shovel-feed a freight train because June hail had clogged up the chute.

A stale wind blew from the coalhouse, which stood on stilts twenty feet high and spanned the length of the spur track. Climbing the ladder on a fine night, Amos would have seen the valley carrying away the Lamoille River through the quartzite foothills of the mountains and the railway tracks edging its banks. But he might not have noticed, because the scenery was always there. Vermont never changed much, which was one of its graces and the principal reason that, despite the weather, the cottagers travelled north. Vermont moved slower than the human mind, and educated people like the Shaw Browns got sick to death of their minds. Vermont didn't change except in storms, when the mountains disappeared. When the weather passed, it changed right back again. Halfway up the coalhouse ladder, in the driving hail, he could see only the fouled yard and the freight train steaming up, and beyond it the kid and his dad, who looked grey underneath the lamps.

Amos was still like any other man, except that he was big. The kid looked up to him because he was big, but that would pass, and one day Aubrey would look down on him; it was a subtle but inevitable divide between summer and winter folk.

Amos had paused on the tenth rung. Under him was the locomotive. The hail played on the train like a toy monkey on a tin drum. Like any other man, Amos couldn't see inside things. He couldn't see the conductor complaining of the weather while screwing down the pop valve hard – too hard, because the gauge was busted. Or the arrow that pointed to one hundred and fifty-five pounds, though in reality the pressure had topped three hundred. He couldn't hear the conductor mutter to himself, "If it says it, you better believe it. Give it another yank. Goddamn summers in Vermont ..." Like anyone, he couldn't see much, till under the mounting load the locomotive blew up.

The conductor died in an instant: he had his head sliced off. The train's steel skin burst like a pickling bottle, and sheets of metal shucked like cornhusk. The firebox end of the engine rocketed into the coalhouse; the cab end disappeared. Black hail and iron, coal dust and coal chunk and disfigured steel tore across the yard, and a hundred thousand rivets shot out of the train's iron body and into the nearby woods. One low-flying spike pierced Amos's jaw and carried on through the back of his head; a searing darkness entered his skull, and the light in his left eye was snuffed. An awesome force threw him off the ladder to the ground, but equally strong and mysterious, the earth stood him up again.

Blast followed blast. The engine's coal stock exploded, then the tractor oil in the freight car ignited, then the coalhouse went up in flames.

The first blast propelled Aubrey, who was slim and fragile and only eleven years old, right past his father's arms. He landed hard on the concrete platform. A bulb shattered above him and cut him just over his eye. As he lifted himself, the second blast brought him down again. He reached out his hand to break his fall, and a glass shard sliced his thumb.

His father leaned over and said, "Your head is bleeding." He offered a hand to help him up, but Aubrey was too distracted to see it.

"It's not. I'm not," he said, his heart pumping so hard it wouldn't let him feel anything else.

His father withdrew his hand.

Aubrey pushed himself up alone. Across the tracks, the coalhouse was burning. The night was bright with fires. He tried to open his eyes wide, but the slanting rain and hail, mixed with drips of blood, stung his eyeballs. "I can't see Amos," he said.

"Amos?" asked his father, as if Amos were insubstantial. Everett Brown wasn't thinking of the handyman. He was already concerned for his wife.

"He was there. On the coalhouse ladder. Is he dead?"

"I don't know."

"Go help him, Father."

"You're bleeding. And your mother –"

Everett turned round in circles like a weathercock in a cyclone. His wife had stayed behind to convalesce in Princeton and was now travelling north to join her family for the holidays. The slightest exertion could put her back in bed for weeks. He looked past the inferno towards the darker valley, expecting to see the lamps of her train twisting along the river. There they were: two dim lights gleaming in the distance. They grew brighter and bigger, then stopped and then diminished. The headlamps were pulling away. Ruth's train had been radioed and diverted to Montreal; she would cross the border to Canada, leaving her husband and child behind.

"I'll find us a car," he said.

"A car?"

"To take us home. Your mother's not coming. And this is no place ..." He didn't finish his sentence as he started to walk away.

"Don't go," said Aubrey.

Father called back, "Wait here."

Aubrey leaned over the platform and spat. Soot had stuck in his throat. His tongue – he had bitten it hard – was bleeding too. He wiped his mouth and pulled his shirt sleeve, no longer white, across his forehead.

Beyond the tracks, the coalhouse, which resembled an Iroquois longhouse on stilts, was burning fast. Already the volunteer fire department had sounded the horn and a ring of villagers, wielding buckets of water, had gathered around the nearby sawmill to stop it igniting. It was too late for the coalhouse. The big log braces on the south end had given way – the fire eating quickly to the heartwood – and the house bowed on its knees. The ladder, detached from its moorings, lay blazing on the ground. Near it, something moved. Even in the jittering shadows, Amos was unmistakable.

Aubrey lowered himself onto the tracks. The heat on his face made his skin contract, and his dried eyes stung with rain. As if hell-bent on self-immolation, he ran towards the burning coalhouse. Meeting a wall of heat and light, he felt his head could break in two. He half-closed his eyes and kept running.

"Amos," he called.

It couldn't be anyone else. He'd risen to his feet. He was standing up. He was giant.

Amos placed a hand on Aubrey's head to steady himself – if he'd given him his weight, he'd have crushed him. The two of them, weird in the firelight, resembled some grafted and newly made thing.

Everyone transformed in the firelight. Like a dwarfed drunk, a toddler slumped against a wall. Two ladies in wide, long dresses were pitched like tent poles, one against another. A frenzied boy called his border collie's name, then stood pointer-like with hand to his ear, trying to hear a dog's whine over the human crying. Down on all fours, a man groped through broken glass, feeling for his spectacles in the dark until someone led him, blind, off the platform. A policeman's lips appeared to stretch into his megaphone as he pleaded with the panicked or stupefied people to step away from the fires.

The fire horn was audible in the hills, and farmers and doctors and veterinarians – because there weren't enough doctors – were rushing through the weather in their one-horse buggies and Fords. From every town with a weekly paper, reporters and their cameras arrived. Headlights and lanterns stretched down the road and the parking lot overflowed. Burly farmers were rounding up the injured. Their tough wives stood on the porch of the railway hotel, waiting to wash and stitch wounds. There were people on the move everywhere now, not just train workers and passengers; the hills had emptied, the population descending into the small village of Greensboro Bend. The police chief, taking the megaphone from the junior policeman, spoke to the crowds: there were body parts to find amongst the rubble.

Aubrey stood by Amos. Beside them, the burning longhouse. Coalhouse. Aubrey struggled to remember where he was. So near the fires, his brain was lava, and the hard rain seemed to burn. Hailstones matted in his hair, then melted. He imagined hell was a railway station, but he was wrong to imagine that Amos thought so too, or that Amos was thinking anything.

"Can you speak?" asked Aubrey, who believed if someone could move it proved he was alive – that was obvious – but if he could speak, it meant he would stay alive.

As Amos nodded, he lost his balance and his hand slammed down on Aubrey's head. The two of them stumbled but didn't fall. Aubrey dug his feet into the mud and Amos steadied himself.

"Can you walk?" asked Aubrey.

Amos put one foot in front of the other, and they walked heavily across the yard towards the railway hotel, where the injured were gathering. Pausing on the porch, Amos leaned hard against the banister. Then he stood erect again, and, with Aubrey's help, walked in.

Men, women and children, tribal with mud, sat on the lobby floor with their backs to the walls. Behind them, soot blackened the wainscotting. With a sewing needle and cotton thread, a large woman was pulling together the flesh of a child's arm. A man rising from a chair left small red berries on the pale upholstery. Red tassels hung from an overhead shade, a single extant bulb not shattered by the blast aggravating the coal dust in the air. Everyone was hurt and wet and scared, but when Amos entered, people crossed themselves and looked away. They must have felt spared. Amos was huge, and the red tassels grazed his hair. The light shone down through a hole in his skull and poured out an opening in his jaw. There was a strange absence of blood.

From the outer dark, Aubrey heard his father shout, "Taxi! Taxi!" as if this were New York City. Then Father called his name: "Aubrey! I've got a ride!"

Aubrey, being an obedient boy, stepped away from Amos, and as he did, Amos fell. The tumult of camera bulbs, like a nightmare of morphine syringes, glassed the tiled floor.

A mos had worked for the Shaw Browns every summer as far back as Aubrey could remember. Each June, Aubrey's father retreated from the marbled halls of Princeton University, and the family – father, mother, grandmother, son – took up residence in the cottage on the northern lake. Vermont was unimaginable without Amos, and that summer after the explosion passed slowly in his absence. He was only convalescing – a word Aubrey had heard repeatedly, as his mother was always sick – though the *Hardwick Bulletin* reported Amos had died. "Tragedy in the Trainyard" was the headline on the slushy morning in June: the conductor, the lineman and the labourer, Amos Cobb, had been killed. Then in July, on a sunny day, "Monster Defies Death." Aubrey pasted the newspaper clippings in his photo album and read them often enough to commit the words to heart.

Over the winter in Princeton, he overheard the grown-ups talking. Greensboro neighbours, cottagers whose summer camps dotted the lakefront that had once been farmers' fields, sent numerous appeals to his grandmother, pleading that Old Mrs Shaw decline to take Amos back into her employ. Handymen were a dime a dozen, they wrote, and the disfigured man had changed. Mrs Shaw, having read the philosophers, found no fault in their argument. Aristotle believed that an ugly man could not be truly happy, while Hume determined that ugliness was a cause of pain, not to the ugly man himself but to the innocent observer. How could Amos not have changed for the worse? her neighbours asked. Though Aubrey wasn't consulted on the subject – being a child, no choices in his life were his – his existence bolstered their argument. The Irwins and the Smiths were concerned for their children; weren't the Shaw Browns concerned for him? The family should take care lest their employee strangle them all in their sleep.

For a week or two in the early spring of '39, the decision, like the spring itself, hung precariously in the balance. Also like the spring, it could not be put off indefinitely. Father, who avoided becoming embroiled in family matters, showed ambivalence, but Mother was uncharacteristically insistent, exhausting herself in Amos's defence. Grandmother, fearful for her daughter's health, acquiesced to her wishes. "However," said Grandmother, "if I wake up one morning with a rope around my neck, I will hold you entirely responsible."

Aubrey was happy, and his mother, though she was too tired to show it, seemed happy also. The family was eager to get to Vermont, where Ruth could rest. The whole family slept a good deal in Vermont. Every year, when the hibernating bears awoke, the family arrived to replace them in their sleep. Due to clean air and altitude – the lake was near the Canadian border, in one of the coldest elevations in the state – the family couldn't keep their eyes open. Amos would have plenty of time to kill them, Aubrey said to his mother, and his mother laughed.

He thought it more likely he'd die from swimming in the frigid lake. He loved Caspian Lake, but in early summer, as the yawning trout rose from the fallow depths, the water had warmed only enough to avoid hypothermia. He knew all the warning signs of hypothermia – difficulty speaking, puffy skin, numbness and, his favourite, terminal burrowing, where the victim undressed and buried himself – and in all weather but thunderstorms, he jumped in and risked a few cold strokes. He loved Greensboro, Vermont – summer Vermont, which was the only Vermont he knew.

His mother, who understood his reckless happiness (understood it deeply, despite her illness or because of it) said her son was unshackled by the summers. His grandmother called him unruly. With schoolboy legs skinny and pale from a winter of books, he'd run whooping into the water and re-emerge blue and shivering, crying out for a towel. The maid, Delia, would bring him one. And Amos, carrying a box of tools, would walk out onto the dock to chisel the rot off the decking while the sawhorses trembled beneath him.

Aubrey sat in the back of the LaSalle sedan, wedged between his grandmother and the extravagant picnic basket. It was the first of July, and they were heading north. Though the family had taken the train up every year, this year was different. Father claimed his decision to drive had nothing to do with the previous year's railway accident; it was only because the roads between the historic town of Bennington and the capital city had been paved over that winter. There'd been progress in the world: this was the summer of the car. It was, however, a slow, two-day journey.

Aubrey watched the land scroll past the window. He counted electricity poles or slept to make the time go faster. He read *Around the World in Eighty Days* and thumbed through the pictures of gemstones in *The World of Rocks*. When he was done, he dropped his books under his feet and ate graham crackers, one after another. His grandmother scolded him sharply. Clucking and fussing, she swept the crumbs off her travelling suit. He coughed in the air grown stewy with Father's cigarettes, and opened the window and dangled his hand in the wind, but Mother worried that he'd lose his hand on an electricity pole. Though her voice was faint, it was full of space and tolerance, so he played with her long red hair, something he'd always done. It fell in front of him around the back of her seat. At last she looked weakly and sweetly towards him and told him she'd had enough.

Father said, "You don't know when to stop, Aubrey. Can't you see your mother's tired?" He refrained from saying, "You're getting too old for such nonsense."

Mother never let on how tired she felt. She pulled her hair between her fingers and smoothed out the knot he'd made.

At the gas station – the smell of fuel and chewing gum pleased him – Grandmother demanded he run around the pump to expend his excess energy, commanding, "Again, young man!" until he was puffing. He wanted a piece of Bazooka bubble gum, so Mother bought it, but when her own mother complained that gum-chewing turned people into cows, she tucked it into her sleeve – the same place she kept a clean handkerchief – and whispered in his ear, "Later."

At the overcrowded hotel where they stopped for the night, he was compelled to share a room with his grandmother, because everyone in the world, it seemed, was driving somewhere for the summer. Thankfully, there were two single beds, but his grandmother's ancient odour – starch and talc from the faded nineteenth century – overwhelmed even the scent of stale sheets and borax. He tossed about and buried his face in the pillow. Neither of them could sleep, and as the hours passed, Grandmother sighed indignantly.

They set out before dawn. He loved the darkness in the car, and in the back seat Grandmother slept at last. Aubrey half-slept, dreamt of the lake, the loons, the tire swing over the drop-off where submarinal cliffs had been carved out by glaciers, and listened to his parent's voices, hushed and intimate.

"What will you do first?" whispered Mother.

"Take the sailboat for a spin. You?"

"I'll be watching."

Mother was always watching. Whenever he read by her bedside – which he always did when she napped, though now perhaps he was too old for that – he imagined even in her sleep she was watching.

By the tedious afternoon, Aubrey was wide awake. He peered over the seat at the wooden dashboard, nagged his father to drive faster, cheered when the quick LaSalle honked at a tractor, and for the final fifty miles asked every twenty minutes, "How long till we get there?"

As if in answer to his question, and to his extreme dissatisfaction, the car stopped at a Revolutionary War memorial rising in a cow pasture, and the family set out across the field.

"My socks are wet. Can I get back in the car?" he complained, touching the edge of his shoe to the edge of a cow pie to test its stiffness.

"Aren't you interested in history?" asked his father, already knowing the answer.

"He just wants to get to the lake," said his mother, who was leaning against the memorial. Her lips looked pale beside the granite slab. Her skin except her cheeks was ghostly white – in all seasons, her cheeks looked sunburnt.

Grandmother was agitated. "Ruth, you should have stayed in the car. And you, young man, should appreciate artefacts like this. Your father will read the inscription."

"Birthplace …" the professor began, but, accustomed to the acoustics of crowded lecture halls and the hollow vibration of ancient tombs, he read poorly.

Grandmother reassigned the task to Aubrey – he was staring into the distance as if the miles would shuck away and there, at the end of the pasture, he'd see the lake. "Wilson Aubrey was your namesake," she said. "You owe it to him to read his monument."

"Birthplace of Wilson Aubrey, Brigadier General in the Revolutionary War, who commanded the American forces in the Battle of Crooked something."

"Crooked what?"

Aubrey squinted at the rock. He'd read *The World of Rocks* cover to cover. He liked rocks, in the same manner he liked the ancient ferns that grew under the porch: he liked them for their simplicity and longevity. The history of men was fleeting, but even at twelve years old, it pleased him to know the air he breathed had first become breathable two and half billion years ago. He inhaled deeply, puffed out his cheeks and held his breath and swallowed – what he called eating air.

"There's too much moss to see it," he said.

"Skip it and read the rest," said Grandmother, not noticing his foolish behaviour, for she was inspecting the farmer's fields for signs of the past.

But there was no further inscription. "That's all," Aubrey told her.

Though Grandmother did not have her spectacles, she glared at the memorial, insulted. "Well, it *should* say that General Aubrey was a great man who unfortunately had to hang his uncle for not giving horses to the cause!"

"Didn't he like his uncle?" asked Aubrey.

"I'm sure he did."

"How could he hang him, then?"

"It was wartime."

"How did he know he was doing the right thing?"

His grandmother looked askance and ended the conversation. "Suffice it to say, he did what he did, and history took care of the rest."

Old Mrs Shaw was a pragmatist. She was, as well, an atheist, which was why she liked Vermont. Vermonters did not indulge in phantasmagoria, religious obsession or romance. While across New England, Shakers had fulfilled their ecstatic mission of dancing and cabinetmaking, notably only their cabinetry had travelled north. And though Joseph Smith and Brigham Young had once milked cows in a Green Mountain pasture, when the spirit moved them they'd been led away to the salt lakes of Utah. Even the French-Canadians who emigrated south with their native Catholicism had abjured cathedral building and thrown in their lot with barn raising. Vermont was a state of red barns with weathercocks and white farmhouses with laundry frozen on the line, where the land was served before the Lord, and what had to be done was done. Old

Mrs Shaw forgave the war memorial's brevity, calling it "succinct."

Back in the car, she complained of wet stockings and Aubrey felt vindicated. He removed his own damp shoes and socks and picked the lint off his feet. He thought about his namesake confessing to his mother that he'd killed her brother, and tried to imagine his own uncle choking in a noose. Raised to believe in the Great Man theory, in which one man was capable of changing the world, Aubrey felt uneasy about the way that great men died, their faces turned away from everything they'd conquered, as if everything they'd conquered was a lie.

He thought of the great men he knew. His father, at the top of the list because he was his father, probably didn't belong there. People said Mother was the beauty and Father the brains, as if they were two sides of a street, while, in fact, Mother was the centre, and sometimes Father was seated in the centre with her, and sometimes he was just a fellow running around in circles, trying to find his way in. It was Amos, whom even a train couldn't kill, who belonged at the top of the list. As to Uncle Jack, Aubrey hadn't seen him in years. All he knew was Jack lived like a king in Mexico City and every Christmas sent a crate of pomegranates, though nobody in the family actually liked the fruit.

"Stop fidgeting," said his grandmother. "Go back to sleep; it will make the time go faster."

Though he wasn't tired, he laid his head in her solid lap – there was nowhere else to put it – and looked up through the speeding window.

"My petticoats are damp," she warned, readjusting herself beneath his head. Under her skirts she still wore petticoats, though they were hopelessly out of style.

He turned on his bed of starched cotton and stared at his mother's auburn hair falling over the seat in front. He loved her hair, whose colour changed with the hour of the day – now horse-chestnut, now rust, now brilliant red. It was full and lush its entire length.

"Third Reich," the car radio said.

Aubrey sat up. "Is Adolf Hitler going to take over the world?"

"Please try to sleep," Mother said.

"You should ask your Uncle Jack," answered Father, flicking an ash out of the window. "Of Standard Oil," he added, and the corporation's name sounded oily in his mouth. It was a thin mouth, though he was a handsome man. He had Romanesque features with high cheekbones, often softened by a cloud of smoke. His physique was manly enough to make up for the ivory cigarette holder held permanently between his lips. His mother-in-law would never have allowed him to smoke a hookah, so the cigarette holder substituted as a more modest reminder of evenings spent amongst Bedouins reclining on blood-coloured rugs. He'd picked up odd habits while digging in Iran and Egypt, habits he wanted to keep to himself. If the cottage walls weren't riddled with knotholes, his son would never have known he squatted on toilet seats. Squatting was an efficient practice, and his digestion had tormented him ever since the Great War, while an American diet of steak and milk made it worse. He dreamt of an escape to foreign lands, and sometimes at dinner, in mind of the uncluttered expanses of the Mojave Desert, he forsook his fork and knife and used his fingers on the scalloped potatoes.

"Don't talk nonsense," Grandmother snapped at Everett. She bristled at the mention of her son in the same breath as Adolf Hitler. "And keep your eyes on the road."

"Greta Garbo is on the lake this summer," Father said to change the subject.

"Is it true?" Aubrey asked his grandmother, the authority on all things real.

"Bad news travels fast enough without your help, Everett Brown," Grandmother said.

"Yes, it is true," said Mother.

When Mother turned in her seat to look at Aubrey, he saw yellow flecks like chamomile blooms in her fair blue eyes.

"When are we going to get there?" he asked her.

"The more you ask, the longer it takes," Grandmother answered for her.

"Is it *really* true Greta Garbo's on the lake?"

"You are to leave that woman alone! No doubt she's looking for a little happiness like the rest of us." Grandmother pushed his head back into her lap, but between Greta Garbo, Adolf Hitler and the lake getting closer every mile, Aubrey could not sleep.

Like the Germans, he loved Greta Garbo. The Germans had fallen in love with her first, but the Americans had won her. Her rags-to-riches story was an American tale: working-class girl with a ninth-grade education rising to become the highest paid actress in Hollywood ... demanding and dark, always more money, always black curtains draped behind her when the camera zoomed in for a close-up. So it wasn't that Aubrey had something in common with Hitler that made him squirm; it was the weirdness of lying on Grandmother's lap while remembering Mata Hari. She was seducing her lieutenant in front of a Russian icon of the Virgin Mary. The Swedish Sphinx. The vamp. She both beguiled and disdained the camera, and seemed to hold the answer to a question her audience didn't even know to ask.

"I saw her in *Mata Hari* at the Bend," he said, though Grandmother's hand held him firmly in place.

"You didn't," she insisted, as if she knew everything about him.

"I did. Amos took me last June, before –"

"I knew the real Mata Hari," Father interrupted. "I met her at a party in Paris during the war. She claimed to be a Javanese princess, but she was really just a Dutch girl who gave herself a fanciful name. It's Javanese for the sun, literally 'the eye of the day.' She was a very unhappy woman."

"Why?" asked Aubrey.

"Ours is not to reason why," said Grandmother, who thought her grandson's habit of always asking why was rude.

"Because she lost everything she loved," said Father. "Her husband, children, home, even her identity."

"It's no wonder she became a spy," said Grandmother.

"Actually, it's not certain that she was a spy."

"Everyone knows she was a spy," said Aubrey. "She was hung for it."

"She was shot by firing squad," Everett corrected his son. Aubrey had no memory for history, though he was good at science and maths. "But that doesn't make her guilty," he continued. "She was a powerful woman, and in a horrible situation we all look for someone to blame. The Javanese believe there were cosmic reasons for her bad luck and her sadness. She always performed at night, but she named herself after the sun, and the Javanese have a myth about a child of the sun. They say, when the sun's in the sky, the child shares all its godly qualities: he is happy, bright, energetic and giving. But when the sun goes down, the child feels like dying."

"Oh," Aubrey said. He didn't particularly care about the real Mata Hari. Only *Mata Hari* at the movie hall in Greensboro Bend mattered: he imagined her stepping off the screen and climbing the hill to Greensboro.

"It's a curious coincidence," Father said, "that *mata-mata* means 'spy' in Malay. Did you know there's no Hebrew word for 'coincidence'?"

"Is it *really* true Greta Garbo's on the lake?" asked Aubrey.

"Aubrey Brown," Grandmother cried, "you are to leave that woman alone!"

In the unchangeable haven of Greensboro, where celebrities appeared sporadically, special rules of decorum applied. A star could hike Barr Hill, with its view of the lake and the mountain range, past picnic sites where youngsters played croquet through obstacle courses of cowpat and bramble, and the young might look up from their mallets, and the mothers and fathers from their gin and tonics and roasting corn, but no one would call out to the goddess of screen, no one chase after the salubrious Garbo; they would lift their heads like curious cows in a field and then return to grazing. Aubrey felt trapped between expectation and desire.

"How long till we get there?" he asked again.

"We'll get there when we get there," Grandmother answered. Disturbed that her grandson had seen *Mata Hari* with Amos Cobb and without her permission, she added, "You are not to go sneaking off *anywhere* with Amos this summer. *Everything* has changed. We don't know who he is anymore. Do I make myself clear?"

Father took his eyes off the road, turned his head towards the back seat and whispered, "Aubrey ... Mother ... quiet ... Ruth is sleeping."

The family drove in silence.

The clock on the dash moved slowly, but time rushed past the window frame. Though the world would soon go to war again, and what had not been ploughed under by the last onslaught would shortly be ravaged by a worse one, a current dragged on the family that buoyed them nostalgically in the past. And yet in the name of progress, though the train had taken one day whereas the car took two, when the Green Mountain Flyer pulled into the station in Greensboro Bend, the Shaw Browns with their picnic basket were not on board.

Amos looked up at the clearing sky while hawks, circling on the updraft, stared down at the one-eyed giant. Though the railway had taken one of his eyes, Amos reckoned it left him the better one. Dropping his chin to his square chest, he said to the dog at his side, "More rain tonight. Don't let the sky fool you." The green land squelched under his hide boots, and wetness oozed through the split in the sole. Whether from snow melt or summer rain, it was always wet in the valley.

Stepping onto a grassy hummock under which lay the granite foundation of his ancestral farmhouse long subsumed by crabgrass, he looked back at his rented shack. This land had been Cobb land even before the Revolution, but after Runaway Pond it was sold away, and other than Amos there were no more Cobbs in these parts. He was lucky even to rent these days. The shack door flapped in the breeze, the lower half rotting on its hinges. A stream ran under the house and straight on through the paddock. His cow and workhorse were mud-spattered.

"What'd I tell you?" Amos asked the dog as another shower passed, a flat, grey ghost floating across the fields. "And that ain't the end of the weather," he said, hitching his horse to his cart.

They were on their way to the station. Amos, his horse and cart and dog were meeting the train from New York City to lug a summer's worth of clothes and books and sporting equipment back to the Shaw Browns' camp – up the steep hill road between Greensboro Bend and Greensboro proper, then around the lake road and down the diminishing lane. It was a shame the luggage was arriving alone – he'd always liked having the kid ride in the rig beside him while the older folks went by taxi – but he was lucky to have his job back. It was the only one he had now.

"Come on, let's get a move on," Amos said to the dog.

Compared to the dog Amos was a talker, but in human company he wasn't. His jaw hurt since the accident, and he'd never been fond of chatter. He was less fond of it now than ever, as there were noises enough in his head. He lifted a boot and put it down on a maple stump smothered in mosses with a sucker tree growing out of the pulp. The dog sniffed at his big ankles and then stuck its nose in the mud.

"Go catch yourself a snake," said Amos. So the dog chased a smell around.

Pale forget-me-nots bloomed in the mire, fed by underground streams. Black water like an oil seep in the blue flowers was all that was left of a pond. The dog returned panting, his breath making visions in the cold air. Amos turned up the dirty collar of his lumberjack jacket. In the highest reaches of Vermont, also called the Northeast Kingdom, mountains rose to the east, west and south but not to the north, so when the wind blew from the Pole, Vermonters said weather was king. Even in July, it was cold in this valley forged by a glacier, dug by a river and drowned by a pond.

"Runaway Pond. It's a long story," Amos said to the dog. "I ain't gonna tell you now."

He kicked his sodden boot against a railway sleeper, stepped over a rusted sugaring bucket and a hunk of quartzite, picked up a sharp-edged flint, imagined it might be an arrowhead, and stuffed it in his overall pocket. He could hear a car tear down Route 16. He could hear the tumult of the railway beyond the woods. His dog racing behind the horse and cart, he followed the track towards Greensboro Bend, where the roads intersected and the trains refuelled.

The Bend owed its existence to the railway. A one-horse byway in the eighteenth century, by the end of the nineteenth it had grown into a three-horse village as a sawmill emerged, then a pool hall, a school and a hardware store with a millinery shop in the rear. The Bend had continued to prosper, growing on the back of its neighbour's success. The next stop down the line, the town of Hardwick, where granite was quarried and chiselled into graves, had boomed through the Great War, while in Greensboro, in increasing numbers since the war's end, holiday-makers sunned themselves on the granite outcrops of Caspian Lake. The valley allowed the trains to bore through, battling the weather, snow in May, hail in June, while a cold snap frosted the radishes, and summer came, as the summer folks came, briefly. A new boarding house served travelling salesmen peddling phonographs and dioramas; a movie hall provided visions of the goddesses of screen; and the railway hotel (its couches newly upholstered since last summer) offered refreshment to the better-heeled. An ancient Model-T taxi shuttled ladies in hats and summer whites, like Old Mrs Shaw and beautiful, frail Mrs Ruth Shaw Brown, up the hills or down. The trains had ushered in the telegraph, followed by mail-order shopping and day trips to the capital city or longer adventures to real cities, Boston and Manhattan, from which cultured metropolises the summer inhabitants hailed. The wilderness had inched away to accommodate human pleasure and industry. The wolves and bears were gone. Up the hill, Caspian Lake had become a destination, and down in the valley, Greensboro Bend was the place of disembarkation.

Amos's dog barked at a snowshoe hare whose summer-brown paw was stuck in a trap made from two tin cans. Pulling the horse to a stop, Amos said to the dog, "Dinner," and slit the hare's throat with a pocketknife, peeled off the skin in both directions and pulled the soft flesh from the tail. He squeezed under the ribs, then slid his hand down to the rump till out popped the entrails. He hung the carcass off a tree limb to cold-dry and heard the blast of the whistle between the hills.

When the train pulled into the Bend, Amos was there to meet it. Flags flew over farmhouse and cottage alike – the village preparing for fireworks day – and there was little evidence of the inferno the previous summer. No evidence except his own body, some half-charred trees that survived the fire and a bronze plaque on the reconstructed depot showing the names of the conductor and the lineman. A new coalhouse stood on its stilts.

Amos piled golf clubs and tennis racquets, suitcases packed with shorts and gauzy dresses and old liquor boxes heavy with books into his hay-damp rig as railway workers prepared the freight cars and passenger cars for the return journey. Cows and crates of raucous chickens were shoved on board. Tins of maple syrup and buckets of cream were loaded on the empty seats, the large steel cans rattling and clanging. And, under the din, the quiet sloshing of milk.

Amos worked with his head down so as not to look at the woman lounging on a bench amidst a circle of gin-soaked boys.

"There's Amos," whispered Donna, leaning on her plump hip.

"Uglier than sin," said one of the boys.

"He don't know nothing about sin," she snarled. "That's his whole problem. Too dumb."

Her painted lips gave a false sheen to her pale skin and black hair. A gold coloured wedding ring curled around her finger like a halo around an albino snake.

"You'd know. You married him," said the boy.

Donna Cobb glared at Amos. Though he went about his work as if he couldn't see her, with one eye open and one stitched closed, he always seemed to be winking at her. His smooth, satiny eyelid was soft enough to line a coffin, while the rest of him was rough and veined as a lump of granite. She shuddered to think what time would do to those horrible silky scars. She forced down a wave of nausea. If only that spike had killed him; she would have looked beautiful in black.

"By what insanity did you ever marry Amos?" asked a red-haired boy with a bottle in a paper bag. He spat tobacco juiced with liquor, then casually touched her leg. "A beauty like you coulda done better. Still could."

Donna let him finger her thigh. "Life only lasts so long anyway," she said.

Her reasons were no one's business. First of all, unlike any of the pawing boys on the bench, Amos never drank so much that tables and chairs got broken. He didn't fight when he didn't need to, or hold back when he did. He'd slugged her daddy so hard, Daddy had never come near her again. *That* was reason enough to marry. Even before the accident, he wasn't exactly handsome, but he was the strongest and sturdiest man in the state. He could do the work of twenty men, and every employer knew it. His sheer size had promised to lift her out of adversity, and when she got pregnant the first time, he was gentle enough not to ask how. They might have been a happy little family, like the ones she'd seen in the movies, if, soon after their visit to the justice of the peace, the baby hadn't dropped out dead. That wasn't a tragedy; that was destiny. Donna had read the word a million times in the women's weeklies. She had one, a destiny – she was sure of it.

The facts of her miserable life threatened to rise up with her breakfast. Life had broken all of its promises. Amos was a monster, or he looked like one, which was tantamount to being one, and either no one wanted to hire him or he didn't want to work for them. The exception being one stuck-up family: the Browns, the Shaws, the Shaw Browns, whatever they were called. The village had pooled some money together to see the two of them through his convalescence, but that was long spent. This winter, increasingly broke, they'd moved from a half-decent rental on Main Street to a shack in a dried-out swamp, where Amos said he felt he belonged. He rightly belonged in the grave. His strength had come back tenfold, but what did he do with it? Nothing except rise up like a zombie in their bed and fill her with his seed. Her belly was getting bigger again, and now in the mornings she couldn't keep down her food. Hoping the condition wouldn't stick, she'd told him she was getting fat on cheap lard because he couldn't afford butter – and this in a land of cows! She hated even to lay eyes on him, but she wasn't going to let him ignore her.

"Hey, Amos!" she called across to him. "Looks like the Browns got you hard at work. Where are they?"

"Driving up this year," Amos called over his shoulder, still not looking. She was drinking and flirting again.

"I want a car!" she purred to the boys. "Which of you men wants to buy me a car?"

"My grandpa says girls shouldn't drive cars," said one.

"That's 'cause he's old and dotty!" said Donna. "Don't he know girls drive in the movies all the time? You know Greta Garbo's summering on the lake? I saw her in the flesh, right here in the station. She had the nattiest luggage. The postmaster says she calls herself Harriet Brown." She screamed across to the hay rig, "Wonder what the Browns think of that, hey, Amos?"

Donna took a swig from the red-haired boy's paper bag and said, "I bet Greta Garbo can drive a car."

Now the coal chute opened and drowned out the racket of the animals shipping south to slaughter and the iron-toothed raving of the sawmill across the road.

"My pa sold her some milk," said one boy. "Said she was thin as a deer in winter."

"Which of you thinks I look like a dark Mae West? Tell me, don't I look just like a really dark Mae West?"

The fellows on the platform looked Donna up and down and right through her dirty dress. She'd played Annabelle West in a performance of *The Cat and the Canary* before she dropped out of school to tend to her drunken dad. She did look a little like the film star. But though she was pretty and easy, everyone knew she was crazy, widely cracked, like two legs. The boys grinned at Donna, because a guy can enjoy crazy when he gets it for fifteen minutes and isn't the one stuck with it for life.

Amos carried his load into the cottage. With three boxes in his arms and two suitcases on his head, he looked like the sketch of a sherpa that hung in the study. The family's arrival was imminent. Already a package had come by post from Sears and Roebuck: some contrivance for making coffee. Delia, the housekeeper, stood in the kitchen, shaking her head over the new contraption.

Every summer, Delia opened the Shaw Brown camp. She cleaned the larder of mouse droppings and the rafters of cobwebs, washed dishes left spotless the year before and grown grimy from a season of disuse, made up beds and aired quilts, sneezing as the dust scattered. In the study, she cleaned the stains off the inkstand and dusted the sketches on the wall: the professor's renditions of tombs and temples and a print by someone – Escher, the professor had said. It was a strange print: identical men, smiling inanely, running in their nightcaps down an unending, twisting, shrinking stairway, until the men were nothing more than splotches.

She forced open the sticky windows, then hung rag rugs over the lowest branches of the large pines and beat them out with a broom. After cooking a meal of early spinach and ham on the wood stove and covering it with a lid, she laid out a swim towel on the porch, because Aubrey was bound to dash into the lake the moment the car pulled in. She still had the coffee contraption to assemble.

"Donna was ..." said Amos, stacking boxes on the kitchen floor and heading back out the screen door before returning with more, "... at the station again." His voice was low and resonant, his chest like an oak cask.

Delia snorted, her hands in her peppery hair. "What in heaven's name am I supposed to do with this?" She turned over a cup-like thing that didn't appear to fit anywhere. "Mrs Shaw buys some gadget to make work in the kitchen easier, and half a day is spent just taking the thing out of its box!" She beat two metal pieces together in the hope of making them fit.

"Glad it ain't my job," said Amos, who had sweated out the pits of his lumberjack jacket.

"Just you wait," she said. "It won't be me tinkering under their car when it won't start up."

She rolled up her sleeves past her thick tan lines to better thump the one thing against the other. She was a capable woman – a farmer's wife, she worked a hardscrabble farm up Barr Hill, the best but coldest view in the county, and tended thirty cows, fifteen chickens, an irritable rooster, twelve sheep and a pig while cleaning and cooking for the cottagers in summer and in winter teaching every grade at the one-room schoolhouse above the graveyard – but for the life of her she couldn't figure out how to assemble the percolator.

"Why do they need a car anyway, except to carry more no-good contraptions into the country and whiz back to the city when something breaks? Soon they'll be driving to the city to get cream for their coffee, or ordering it from Sears and Roebuck! Even the cows will be out of work!" She put the damn bits down and went to the stove to make coffee in a saucepan to sooth her nerves.

"Where they want these golf clubs?" Amos asked.

"In the closet under the stairs. You know Mrs Irwin?"

"Nope."

"Sure you do." She added the grinds directly to the water. "Mrs Irwin needled Farmer Jacobsen into letting the summer folk play golf on his pasture. If a ball hits a cow, it's still in play! I wouldn't like to be a cow in the twentieth century."

"You got too many opinions to be a cow. Where they want the books?"

Delia looked up at the man she'd known since he was a boy, his massive hands round a crate of books he wouldn't read. He was alone in the world, the last of his name on an impoverished acreage, with a wife sick in the head, and his own head skewered by a railway spike. If he was alone always, he'd become doubly alone since the accident.

"In the study," she said. "Well, if it makes them happy." She was back to talking about cars again. "But seems to me they should be happy if the sun decides to shine and we don't get a month of rain. You want coffee?"

"What's wrong with trying to be happy?"

"Amos Cobb, Tom Jefferson was an idealistic fool!" The small woman stared up at the giant man at the top of the stairs in the same manner she'd stared down on him when she was his teacher years ago. "The pursuit of happiness

– my foot! People have got no godly idea what makes them happy!"

But Amos, his arms full of books, wasn't interested in philosophy.

While her grinds boiled in the saucepan Delia pondered the pursuit of happiness, which was the degrading cornerstone of the Greensboro economy. Winter folk were employed by summer folk and summer folk were shameless happiness seekers, devoting their days to swimming, golfing and picnics. On Sunday mornings, white-frocked ladies boated to chapel, even in thunderstorms, even if they couldn't swim, hymn books under their arms and tennis racquets stowed in the hull in case the courts dried out. Piety was a front for idleness. There was no God above nature, no matter what happy folk claimed. Nature wasn't nice to humans. Nature didn't care for happiness. Nature wasn't summer. Though Delia bit her lip to keep her job, a true Vermonter – a winter person – could stomach neither God nor sloth.

"Flatlanders," she muttered into her coffee cup and, remembering she had a hammock to hang between two trees, got back to work. She did not dislike her employers, but in a way, after so many years, she hardly knew them. She knew Ruth Shaw Brown was an invalid, Everett Brown was a scholar and Mrs Shaw, often called Old Mrs Shaw because of her impressive age, was refreshingly, unlike so many of her kind, an atheist. Aubrey Brown … who could say what he was, for he was only a twelve-year-old boy who looked no older than ten.

"Tennis racquets in the closet too?" Amos bellowed from upstairs. His voice carried effortlessly through the cedar hallway, down to the landing with its large window, into the porch-darkened room. The American flag that hung off the porch flapped hard in the wind and wrapped around its pole.

A car could be heard charging the hill and speeding around the lake. Here they came, the summer folk; here they came, up over the mountains, churning up dirt on the dusty roads, in pursuit of a receding horizon.

When the family's car finally arrived at Caspian Lake, Delia rushed into the driveway with doughy fingers and planted a kiss on Aubrey's forehead. Grandmother walked about, prodding the shingles, inspecting the house that had sat sorry and empty through a pyrotechnic autumn, an interminable winter and what the winter folks called mud season. Mother, tired from the journey, accompanied by Father, prepared to remove herself to the porch to rest and admire the lake. But when Amos appeared in the driveway, the grown-ups looked down at the dirt. His ugliness was brutal, as if acquired from years of killing men.

"Welcome home," said Delia. "Nothing's changed. I'm a year older. Too old to make head or tail of the coffee machine, Mrs Shaw. You'll have to come in and instruct me, Professor Brown." As she returned to her place in the kitchen, she called back to Aubrey, "If you're going swimming, don't forget your towel."

Though he'd been instructed not to stare, Aubrey couldn't take his eyes off Amos, who was as solid as granite shot through with mica, yet should have been a ghost. Aubrey had seen him fall and had thought he'd seen him die. But Amos couldn't die, because a rock can't die.

It can't speak, either: Amos hadn't said hello. Maybe he hadn't had a chance. In previous years, in Amos's cart, they'd have talked from the Bend to the lake, but this year, coming up by car, all things had happened at once. The car had parked, the lake had appeared, and now Aubrey pretended not to stare by preparing for a swim. As Amos unloaded the back seat, his big hands fumbling about in the wells for cookie cartons and books, Aubrey sat on the bumper, frantically undressing. Under his shorts were his swim trunks. He dropped his clothes on the car, which, having laboured up the hills, produced heat ripples in the cold air.

"Slugs!" Amos warned him. The slimy creatures lined the path after every rain.

Aubrey was happy to see Amos could talk.

"Water!" Aubrey called back, tearing down to the lake.

His skin twisted at the touch of it; his blood rushed home to his organs, and his testicles shot up inside him. He jumped up and down in the waves in excited agony, then threw himself onto the dock, shivering as loudly as he could. He didn't have a towel until his father joined him on the dock.

"It makes me cold just to look at you. Delia said to give you this," said Father, dropping a towel on his blue offspring.

The distant mountains purpled in the sunset. The sun struck the wings of swallows hunting invisible insects, and the windows of cottages on the eastern shore flashed like signal lamps.

Father said, as he did every year, "This is what we come a thousand miles to see." Though the mileage was an exaggeration, it was one of the many rituals by which the family knew they'd arrived. A camera hung around his neck. Father, though proud of his drawing skills, considered his new Retina II to be progress: reconnaissance artists in the Great War had been limited to paper and pencil, and in their rush to interpret what they saw from their planes they'd made dangerous mistakes. As an ambulance driver in France, Everett had sped down a mined road to a reported battle, and found a rugby game.

Father shot a picture of the mountains. "Amos says it's going to rain." He said the name strangely, as if it were a secret. "But he promised it'll stop by morning."

Wrapped in the towel, his shivers subsiding, Aubrey contemplated the fickleness of weather that could storm tonight and change tomorrow. He yawned from the thinness of oxygen that would soon result in what summer folk dubbed the Great Greensboro Sleep, which fell yearly upon the seasonal arrivals.

Aubrey looked up towards the cottage, its cedar shingles greyed by weather, perched on the western bank halfway up a hill of blackberry brambles. On either end grew massive pines that were regularly hit by lightning, and the eaves showed burn marks where the strikes had travelled. Once, when he was a baby, a lightning bolt had forced a nail out of his bedroom wall, and the nail had shot across his cradle and shattered the glass over a photograph of his mother. Luckily it was only a photograph. There was Mother now, resting on the porch amidst butterfly nets and raincoats.

"Can I borrow your camera?" asked Aubrey.

Father gave it to him and turned up the path. But now Aubrey thought better of shooting his mother. The dark was growing rapidly; her face had vanished and only her shadow remained. Amos stood behind her, doing something, but Aubrey couldn't tell what. Grandmother's hand closed the upstairs window. Or maybe it was Delia's.

Aubrey coughed to clear what was left of the car in his lungs, and the cough echoed against the cloistering hills and echoed again in his father's receding cough. Father was always coughing, but nobody blamed cigarettes. The gas of the Great War still lingered in his chest.

Somewhere a gun was fired, and the farther hills answered the singular clap. Aubrey looked towards the far side of the lake. Out there was the camp in which he knew Garbo would be staying. Everyone in Greensboro knew who lived where. While most cottages belonged to bankers or academics, there was one – it didn't look different from the rest – whose owners were acquainted with Hollywood. That's where the star would be found. The mountains were turning black. A squall skimmed the inlet, and the rowboat moored beside the dock scraped against its rope. Desire overcame obedience. Tomorrow, he would row to her, unable to imagine what harm a glimpse could do.

The next morning, the air was brisk and the green fields and dark pines that graced the shore gleamed with last night's rain. Aubrey scooped up the worms floating in the mud puddles and dropped them into a rusty coffee can. As he now had nothing with which to bail the rowboat, he splashed the icy water out of the hull with his hands. Amos, out of nowhere, stepped out onto the dock.

"You running away?"

"Going fishing."

"Yup," said Amos, meaning the opposite.

"You're here early," Aubrey said. He suspected Amos hadn't gone home last night. Hunting for worms, he'd noticed a flattened patch the size of Amos in the long grass.

"You got a good memory?"

"Why?"

"You're gonna want a camera." He was holding the Retina II, which Aubrey had returned to his father's desk the previous night.

"My dad says there are Indian tribes who think a photograph steals your soul," said Aubrey. "Do you think that's true?"

Amos thought a moment, then said, "If a window's real clear, birds don't see it. Or if it reflects good, they think they see another bird and fly at it. The big window on your stairs kills a lot a birds. Robins and cardinals, mostly. They're always flying at it, trying to chase themselves away. That's kind of the same."

"The same as what?"

"Photos stealing souls."

"Kind of."

"You want the camera?"

"Yep."

When Amos handed it over, Aubrey pointed it at him.

Amos said, "Good thing I got here early this morning," and smiled a toothy smile.

Whether or not he was telling the truth, whether he'd come from the Bend or slept in the field, either way, it was hardly morning. The sun was elsewhere, hidden behind the mountains in someone's else sky.

Aubrey coiled the rope into the hull with numb fingers. A straw hat shading his freckled face, camera around his neck, white shorts exposing the goosebumps all over his skinny legs, he took his seat at the oars.

Amos pushed the boat into the deeper waters and watched the boy floating away. He liked the kid for his loneliness. It was the loneliness of a cornfield in the winter, though the kid didn't know it yet, his loneliness not having come upon him fully. Amos watched for a while as Aubrey rowed towards the centre of the lake and abruptly turned his boat in the movie star's direction.

He was rowing harder than usual. Typically the wind stayed low before dawn, so the crossing should have been easy, but this morning a motorboat whose driver had risen early to take advantage of the glassy conditions roared back and forth, tossing the little rowboat on artificial waves. In the middle of the lake, Aubrey gave up the fight, held onto his oars and, lurching to and fro, enjoyed the violent ride, hoping the momentum would move him closer to his destination. When the waves passed, before the motorboat could circle back again, he put what little muscle he had into rowing hard. He wasn't strong – a fast and enthusiastic runner, but in baseball games he still used a junior bat.

On the far side of the lake, he dropped his anchor, a rock knotted to a rope tied to the rowboat bench. Biting his lip, he speared a worm in the bucket and cast his line, then secured the rod tightly between his thighs. His hands now free to hold the camera, he snapped the sun rising on the cow fields, and snapped it again as it mounted the hills. He liked the sheer fields and the round horizon – loved everything about Vermont – but Amos hadn't brought him the camera to capture the pastoral views. He might actually see Greta Garbo lit fiercely by the slanting sun, one eye hidden by the shadow of a broad-brimmed hat. And because Amos had thought to bring him the camera, he felt somehow more hopeful that he would.

In the women's magazines that his mother sometimes read, he'd pored over Garbo's pictures: stark black-and-white photographs, her face always lit from the side, her strong jaw and cheekbones catching the darkness, and often only a head, as if her body existed merely in films. But it was in motion pictures – isolating moments strung together – that Garbo came alive for him. Movement was everything, movement was life, according to his mother, who was always still, sat quietly in her chair, and yet she had told him that.

The bobber in the water lolled like a little head. Nothing bit his hook, and the sun kept rising. In the distance, a sailboat, running with the wind around the racing buoys, unfurled its yellow spinnaker. As he recognized his father's sail, his heart accelerated. There was no good excuse for fishing where the lake was shallow – everyone knew the big fish swam in the deeper waters around the submerged islands. If he was caught near the camp where the star was staying, Father would punish him with coldness, Mother would smile through her disappointment, and Grandmother would talk of it for weeks. But to his relief, Father was speeding away in the opposite direction. The sail was quickly shrinking.

If he craned his neck, he could just glimpse the corner of the house shielded by a turn in the bank. Rocky outcrops cowled the shoreline. Long before anyone's memory, magma had torn through the earth's crust and cooled here into solid granite. If it weren't for the granite, he would have had a perfect view of the cedar porch, sash windows and Dutch door, where the top opened separately from the bottom. As it was, Garbo would have to come down to the water to be seen. He was, he thought, hoping against hope. He wondered what that expression actually meant: how could you hope against hope?

Aubrey heard the tinny voice of a radio coming from the turn in the bank. The radio gave him hope. He imagined she'd unlatched the upper half of the Dutch door; she was leaning through the opening, soaking in the morning sun, still in her bathrobe, listening to the day's news. He could hear it. The Third Reich was destroying degenerate art, and the expressionist painter Ernst someone had killed himself. Then, the woman herself walked down the path and onto the rocks.

Aubrey stood up and instantly sat back down again as the boat lurched beneath him. It was Garbo, and Garbo was naked. She was naked, and her nakedness was imprinted in his brain forever. Nothing, no future, no sadness could erase it. Everything else was wiped away: morning, fish, motorboat, the rising wind, even the danger of his father's sailboat returning.

He watched her empty her coffee cup into a rock pool and put a toe into the water and shiver. Then, sitting on her rump, she slid down the slimy rocks into the cold lake.

He watched her swim. He no longer had ears or mouth or nose; his entire body was an eye. She swam straight towards him. He expected her to swim past him, but she didn't. Relentless as time itself, she was swimming up to him. Even under his mounting excitement, he wanted to know why.

"Have you caught anything?" she asked.

As if she were dressed in a gown made of water, she neglected to cover herself. Panicked, Aubrey reeled in his fishing line for fear of catching her nipple.

"Have you caught anything?" she asked again.

Aubrey failed to speak. He stared at his bucket and the auburn haze on his worms. His hands on the fishing rod were clammy with a cool sweat. He felt as if his head had been dunked underwater, and the roaring in his ears was the motorboat's engine about to chop it off. He shook it: no.

She hung on to the red rowboat, and it tipped slightly under her grasp. Instinctively he leaned away to counterbalance her weight. Her naked weight. Her fingers around his oarlock were a lengthy prelude to her alabaster arms. Her sculpted eyebrows and lashes were almost white, while her eyes were so dark blue that in the shadow of the boat they were an inky black. But the beauty of her face was nothing: it paled in the presence of her breasts. They floated on the water's surface, and a prismatic glaze of gasoline coloured them in blues and purples.

He did not dare look up. He did not dare move. He thought if he moved, *it* would move too: his penis would inch up like a worm from a mud hole. His freckled skin was as red as his boat. His veins burned – the way nitrate film catches fire. He thought he'd never be cool again. Summoning his courage, he raised his eyes to her floating breasts and looked directly at them, but the gasoline caught the sun and hid them, and he dropped his gaze back to the fat worms.

"Okay, goodbye," she said, for he did nothing but shake his head, as if he were shaking water from his ears. She dipped below the surface of the lake in which, at a depth of twenty feet, he could still see the sandy bottom.

"Wait!" he cried and lifted the camera.

He saw her turn underwater.

She liked children. He remembered that. He had read it once in a magazine: though Greta Garbo didn't like adults and "wished to be alone," the innocence of children made her happy.

She reached out her endlessly long naked arm towards the rowboat. If she scribbled her autograph with a wet finger onto the side of his hull, he'd capture the moment forever. Nothing would take it away.

Greta Garbo emerged smiling, then her photographic face contorted. As Aubrey shot the picture, she splashed water on the lens.

"Damn you!" she cried.

Ruth Shaw Brown had watched as her son set off at dawn in his rowboat with his fishing gear, and she'd watched as Everett rigged up the sailboat and took it for a spin in the sunrise. She had watched as the sun roused the placid lake and the waves began to build, so her child's return would be arduous and her husband's, soaring. The father, sailing untraceable patterns between the sunken islands, speeding past the son, the two of them rushing off in opposite directions.

Since he was a toddler, Aubrey had raced around the shore with dirt on his face and twigs in his hair. He reminded Ruth of a passage from the *Song of Solomon*: "Be thou like to a roe or a young hart upon the mountain of spices." The passage was not really appropriate, as the rest of the song was lustful, but she couldn't help what she was reminded of, and he was like a young hart. She had watched and given thanks.

From her great elevation on the porch, she was always watching. The heart condition that kept her stationary showed in her flushed cheeks, so that she appeared to have just dashed up a hill or been caught in the act of love. But even seated in a rocking chair, she didn't move. What moved, you saw; what was still, you missed, unless you were equally still. Near the dock were the lakeside marshes. Cattails with long, thin, musical leaves, home to the double-winged dragonflies. How long had it taken before she saw the two white water lilies, half-hidden in the ovular leaves? *Mine are the only eyes to see you, for no one else waits so long.* She had watched and given thanks.

Not being a properly religious woman, rocks and water and sky-blue oxygen made Ruth Shaw Brown give thanks. The delicate movements of seasons and the fierce creativity of skies. The echo of nature in the dream of a person: the way thought rose upward like the wind rising, gathering and scattering and lifting off again. Or how the shape of human bones was like the granite outcrops of glaciers that carved the hills. What arose fell away, and if there was sorrow it might be unbearable, but its counterpart was joy, the two set so close together that man might split the atom but would never successfully tell these two apart.

Her heart pressed against her breastbone and she struggled to catch her breath. Her son was a flash of red by the submerged islands and her husband was a plain white sail. Her heart missed a beat. She loved them both, and suddenly she felt afraid she'd never see them again.

"Give me a sign that you love me," she whispered to her husband's sail.

The boat changed course, sped with the wind, and the bright yellow stripes of the spinnaker blossomed. Ruth smiled in the shadows of her summer hat.

The morning had progressed, and the dark corner of the garden glowed in the light. The housekeeper arrived with lamb shanks from her farm. The unfortunate maimed handyman appeared with his toolbox to mend a weak joint in the porch rail. Her husband returned to sequester himself in his smoky study, and her son was tying his rowboat to the dock and running up the path.

Aubrey didn't notice his mother on the porch. He was unaware of having tied the boat to a peg on the dock and stowed the oars, and oblivious as he hurried up the wet hill and a slug squished between his toes. Though he saw Amos slam a nail into the railing, he strode past him without saying a word. His mother said, "Come sit with me, Aubrey," as the screen door slammed behind him.

Inside the house, he stopped. He couldn't ignore his mother. He returned to the porch and perched on the edge of the railing, knocking something off into the underbrush below.

"Hammer," Amos said, and walked off to retrieve it.

"Did you catch anything?" asked Mother.

"No," said Aubrey. His answer was unusually terse. He added, "I think it's still too cold. The fish are slow. Now I'm wet." He hoped his wetness would get him sent upstairs to change. But it didn't, for his mother knew he enjoyed being wet.

"Did you take any good pictures?" she asked, glancing at the camera around his neck. Its lens was fogged with lake water.

"I have to pee," he lied. He spoke unashamedly to her, as he always did, even though he was lying. But saying he had to pee made him blush, because he thought of his penis and what he was going upstairs to do. He was not a child anymore.

"Nature calls," Mother said, smiling at him.

Turning around, he slammed into Amos and his hammer.

"Slow down," said Amos, cheerily enough. "You'll crack your head open." Then he said, "Mrs Brown, you got creatures living under your porch."

The screen door slammed again. Not waiting for his eyes to adjust to the dim light, Aubrey navigated the house blindly. Cool and damp, perfumed by raw pine and cedar, the cottage smelled good to him, and he usually paused to sniff, but today he didn't. As he ran up the stairs to his bedroom, he felt his childhood ending. Hurrying towards its finale, he closed the door, opened his fly and grabbed himself.

"Aubrey!" It was his father's voice.

He yanked his hands from his trousers and clumsily buttoned up his fly, putting the wrong buttons into the wrong holes. He left his room and followed the trail of cigarette smoke that drifted down the hall. Before stepping through the doorway, he lifted the camera off his neck and held it behind his back. In the study, he found his father seated upright in a straight-backed chair, his posture successfully disciplined but his mind having dissolved into another world. Father was studying the temples and gods of Egypt, or maybe Italy or India today – it was always somewhere far from here, mysterious and holy.

Everett turned his head just enough to acknowledge his son's arrival but didn't lift his eyes from his book, except to tip the long ash of a cigarette into an ashtray made from half a geode. Though he'd called his son into his study, he felt invaded nonetheless. Taking his time, he exhaled and observed the fumes. He considered smoke his thinking-breath, imagining his musings rising up to the heavens, though in fact the smoke caught in the rafters and drifted through the gaps in the walls that made privacy in the cottage nonexistent.

Father's world was dizzying. Smoky light flickered over vanished worlds: there were perspectival drawings of a domical vault in Tolemaide, floor plans of a church in Kalb Lauzeh, a longitudinal section of Kharab Shem, a martyrium in Resafa, the western view of the Duomo in Florence, the eastern view of the Dome of the Rock in Jerusalem, and the Temple of the Gods in the Heaven of Indra, copied from an ancient book Father had found in a dark bazaar on a hot day in Calcutta. Meticulously executed by Father's hand, and yellowed by smoke, a copy of the bust of Nefertiti looked remarkably like Greta Garbo. As Aubrey inhaled the cigarette air, he imagined the unrendered parts of the Egyptian queen and wiped his hands on his shorts.

"Mmm-hmmm," said Father, holding up his index finger to signal his son to wait. At long last, he placed his pen in its tortoiseshell inkstand and asked, "Did you take my camera somewhere?"

"I was fishing."

"Catch anything?"

He didn't answer.

"Aubrey Brown ..." His father suspected something.

Aubrey hated his name. He shuffled his feet in silence a moment. Then suddenly – the bust of Nefertiti was to blame, or the half-finished business begun in his room, or the confusing shame he felt by lying to his mother about peeing – he feverishly blathered "Garbo" and "naked" and "water" and produced the Retina II. "She got it wet," he said, "but I wiped it off."

"Give me the camera," said Father.

"I didn't take a picture of her," Aubrey said, trying to take control of himself.

"Didn't you?"

He was hopeful still. "If you take out the film, can I use the camera?" He was thinking quickly. He would row across the lake tomorrow ... he would take another photo of her ... everything would happen exactly as today ... she'd swim to him ... surely she swam every morning ... couldn't tomorrow be identical to today?

"Hmmm?" Father had set the ivory nub of the cigarette stem back into his mouth. "No, I don't think so."

"Without the camera, fishing is boring. Even Amos thinks so." It was another lie: he didn't know what Amos thought.

"What Amos thinks is irrelevant," said Father.

"But it is. It's boring."

"Cultivate stillness or learn to draw." Father had picked up his pen.

Ruth watched her son burst from the dark house; he was storming back to the dock. She saw him chew viciously on a stalk of grass and flap his arms like plucked wings. She noted how tall he looked. He was small for his age, but his shadow, which seemed to follow him around relentlessly today, made him taller. His spine looked unusually stiff, and there was defiance in the thrust of his shoulders. Grass stalk in his teeth and eyes fixed on the distant shore, he appeared unhappily transported. She followed his gaze, expecting to see a hawk in the sky ravishing a songbird, but there was nothing there.

"Amos," she said, "go see what's bothering Aubrey."

Amos put his tools down and lumbered along the same path the boy had charged down minutes before. Though Amos's step shook the dock, Aubrey was lost in his thoughts. Then Amos laid a hand on his shoulder, making him almost fall in the lake.

Amos caught him by the scruff, chucked him fondly in the arm, and laughed as Aubrey rubbed the spot more than was needed. He said, "You look like your blood's run away like Runaway Pond."

"I guess."

Aubrey didn't know what Runaway Pond was, and right now he didn't care.

"I ain't ever told you about Runaway Pond?"

"You ain't," Aubrey said, and though he liked to say *ain't* when his grandmother wasn't listening, he didn't enjoy it now.

"Another time," said Amos. "I gotta fix the pump in the pump house. Delia don't got any water pressure." He plucked two crayfish out of the lake, one having ripped the claw off the other. "They're hungry or mean, hard to tell the difference," he said, throwing them back, but in opposite directions. "Can't keep them out too long or their gills dry out. They can't breathe and die. People think crayfish are red, but that's only if you boil them, and they're not much of a colour at all if they die for other reasons." It was more than Amos had said to anyone in weeks. He kicked his boot at the waterlogged planking and watched the rotten scrag ends floating away on the waves. A tired leaf fell from a young maple overhanging the water. "Leaves turn early if the tree is sick," he said. "Your ma –" he began to say, then thought better of it. "*Garbo*," he said, trying the word like an unknown food, "sounds like a kind of fish. You get a picture of her?" When Aubrey nodded, Amos said, "Donna saw her in the train station. Women won't make you happy." And he trudged off to the pump house.

Nursing his arm, Aubrey looked back across the waves. The lake was at one moment the substance that transmitted the star's flesh like an electrical current from shore to shore, the next it was only the distance between his body and his desire.

"Aubrey!" Delia was calling from the kitchen window, a strong voice that could endure the winters. "Can't you hear me? Lunch!"

"Grand Central Station," Aubrey said to himself.

Cream of leek soup was served with spinach salad. Cheese pie would be followed by ice cream. Amos had carried the ice to the kitchen on his shoulder, a jug of cream sloshing under his arm, and Delia had groaned and sweated an hour over the gummed-up crank. There were more cows than humans in Vermont, and the family's diet reflected the fact.

"Delia," scolded Grandmother from her place at the head of the table, "you are fattening me up and intend to butcher me along with your pig in the autumn!"

"First I'd have to catch you, Mrs Shaw," said Delia. "And that's not very likely."

The powerful old woman swelled with the compliment. This cottage was hers, as was the house back in Princeton. Everything – money, ideology, a home in the country and social standing – came through Old Mrs Shaw, descended from General Aubrey, right-hand man to George Washington himself. She had standing in society – she was *born* standing, she claimed – and knew how to use her weight. A large woman, there was nothing spongy about her weight; it was solid, stiff and chalky. One of her eyes had a cataract, and glassy and dim as it was, it had only increased in transfixing power. When she squinted, the world narrowed to a razor's edge. Now she inspected her grandson and, leaning her head towards her daughter, whispered, "Ruth, your son is dirty."

Mother said to Aubrey, "After lunch, why not go for a swim to get clean?"

"He must wait an hour to digest," said Grandmother. Then she waved a fly away from her face and announced a picnic was in the works. The Irwins and Smiths were planning the pleasant outing, which would be more pleasant than ever, for the Shaw Browns could take Barr Hill by car. "By storm!" she said, delighted.

"Did you know," said Father, "Seth was not only the god of the desert but of storms? In later myths, he was also the god of darkness and chaos."

"Boom, boom, speaking of nothing," Grandmother objected, and continued to expound on the wonders of Barr Hill as reached by car. They would park round the back of Delia's three-story barn and briefly admire that massive architectural folly before taking the short walk to the picnic area, with its fire pit and view of the mountain chain. Too large for the difficult land it stood on, its paint peeling off in the pitiless climate, nonetheless a good Vermont barn rivalled the best European cathedral. The nineteenth-century farmers who'd built them had imagined an ever-increasing congregation of cows, and so built big. When sunbeams poured through the cupola, in the vast interior of Delia's barn even an atheist like Grandmother thought of God.

"Delia will permit us to park beneath her hay elevator," she said. "Won't you, Delia?"

"Yes, ma'am."

"Aubrey," Grandmother insisted, "name the mountain peaks for us."

"I want to be alone!" Aubrey wanted to say, but didn't.

He'd never heard Garbo say those words in *Grand Hotel* – he'd only read about her saying them. He imagined *Grand Hotel* playing at over a thousand cinemas in over a hundred countries, Garbo's face consumed by a hundred thousand eyes, and felt a wave of jealousy. He'd felt jealousy before – whenever his father banished him from his mother's room while remaining there himself – but this, he thought, was different.

"Go on," Grandmother prompted.

He mumbled into his soup: "Signal, Spruce, Killington, Buffalo, Breadloaf, Hunger, Mount Mansfield, Camel's Hump."

"And ..."

"Madonna Peak."

"But everything," Grandmother declared, "depends on whether or not it rains. Ah," she said, being a fan of philosophy, "summer is a respite, never a reality; that is, if reality means a thing has consistency. Summer is inconsistent."

Everyone had to agree.

"But today is perfect," said Grandmother. "This is a true Vermont day!" She often commented on the weather, though she had a habit of sitting with her back to the view.

Aubrey had his back to the window because that was his designated seat at the table. He squirmed in his chair and glanced over his shoulder at the lake, hoping against hope that Garbo would rise amongst the whitecaps.

"Aubrey," Mother asked, "did you catch anything this morning?"

Aubrey turned back to the table. She had asked him that already. He glared at his father, who was testing the heat of his soup spoon against his lower lip. Aubrey felt certain he'd betrayed him.

"Fish," Father intoned. He never told his wife anything that might possibly upset her.

"No," answered Aubrey, and he tortured a spinach leaf with his fork.

"Ah, I forgot," said Mother. She looked tired. "I already asked you that."

"Perseverance," Grandmother said. "Try again tomorrow."

"Tomorrow and tomorrow and tomorrow," teased Father, knowing that tomorrow Aubrey would not be fishing on Hollywood's side of the lake.

Mother looked uneasily from husband to son, not knowing whom the joke was on. "What was it Shakespeare said ..." she said, but she did not finish her sentence. There were days when her voice trailed away and the clatter of dishes overcame her words.

"Good God!" cried Grandmother. Despite her habit of neglecting the view, she was looking out the dining-room window. A boat was manufacturing waves, competing with those more perfectly produced by nature. "The Pearsons have brought up a motorboat!"

"I hear their chauffeur drives it," Father said.

"It's the end of the world," said Mother. Aubrey didn't know if she meant it.

Mother and Father stared at each other. When their minds wandered, they often wandered together, and Aubrey felt excluded.

"Wittengenstein says that at the end of the world we must ..." Grandmother began. But now her son-in-law looked at her sideways so that she doubted she'd pronounced the name correctly. She devoured philosophy and quoted it commandingly, but as a woman who had come of age in the nineteenth century, she had never sat in a university lecture hall. "Eat your beets," she said to her daughter. "They are very good for the blood."

Finally, there was a gap in the grown-up conversation.

"Can I be excused?" Aubrey asked.

"May I," answered Grandmother.

"May I be excused?"

"There is ice cream to come," said Grandmother. "Stop slumping over your food."

"If I don't want any ice cream, can I – may I – leave the table?"

"Where are you going?" Grandmother demanded.

"I'm going out to the woods. I'm going to look for chanterelles." He spoke into his empty plate, not daring to look up and see who knew he was lying.

But Grandmother only said, "Silly boy, it's far too early for chanterelles."

"It doesn't hurt to look," Mother said indulgently.

Grandmother corrected her. "It always hurts to waste one's time doing what can't be done."

"The joy is in the doing," Mother protested.

"And the folly is in the getting muddy, and the finding of no chanterelles! Go, Aubrey, go!"

As Grandmother waved him off, Mother smiled, expecting her son to return the smile; but Aubrey, without a backwards glance, ran out the kitchen door. She'd wanted to whisper to him, "What's out there, Aubrey? Why are you lying to us about the chanterelles?" but she didn't have the chance. Ruth felt a wave of loss. These waves were breaking more frequently, which was the lot of mothers.

Delia brought out the ice cream. As the kitchen door swung open, a radio could be heard: a newscast reminded everyone that one year ago today Amelia Earhart had risen into the skies and disappeared. In the kitchen, Amos was visible. He was holding a wrench, his head underneath the sink.

After Old Mrs Shaw had eaten her ice cream, pushing back her chair, she removed herself to a more comfortable one in the corner. She took out her spectacles and a pair of her grandson's socks from a sewing basket of woven willow reeds. Though she regularly entertained atomic scientists, Nobel laureates and presidential candidates in her Princeton home, now she prepared to darn socks. It was a matronly exercise, but needle and sock in hand, the old lady looked masterly.

"I can do that, Mrs Shaw," said Delia.

"No, I do what I enjoy. By the lake, I get away from it all. By the lake, I remember priorities: socks."

Everett stood up from his place at table. "Well, I must get back to work." He lingered awhile at the dining-room window. He hated to turn his back on the day. He wanted to be out with his watercolours – ultramarine-blue pigment could have captured the sky – or racing his sailboat against the one traversing the lake just now. But he was a disciplined man, a virtue his mother-in-law applauded.

"Staunchly towards all things," she said, quoting the family motto carved in Greek over the fireplace.

"You don't want to sit so you can see the view, Mrs Shaw?" asked Delia as she wiped the crumbs from the table and straightened the doily.

The mountains stood crisply in the sun, and beneath their rocky majesty, smaller worlds roiled with bass and trout. Around the sawhorse legs of the dock, schools of minnows swarmed. A heron crooked its marvellous neck and with a few slow flaps of giant wings crossed the rippling lake. The spire of the village church and the cupola of a barn rose over the pines on the eastern shore. A sailboat let out its spinnaker, and its red stripes made the blue sky bluer and the whitecaps whiter. It was a perfect day on Caspian Lake.

"I know what it looks like. It isn't going to change."

"I shall lie down now," said Ruth.

Her mother agreed she should, and her husband nodded politely.

Everett watched his wife climb the stairs, glance back at him one last time, and then complete her ascent. Though he loved her dearly, he was not a man for daily demonstrations of affection. There were no goodbye kisses between breakfast, lunch and dinner, when Ruth went to her rocking chair on the porch or up to her room to rest. From his study, his tobacco fumes seeping through the holes in the wall, he'd send her domestic smoke signals communicating remoteness and intimacy. That was all.

In the room at the far end of the corridor, where Ruth took her afternoon nap, there was only a view of a pine tree. As the room did not catch the morning or evening sun, it was cold, but nonetheless Ruth was hot. She felt inordinately tired. Drops of sap had dripped onto the window ledge and formed a seal, and she struggled to lift the sash. She wanted to stand with her head in the clear air, drawing in the mountain breezes and the infallibly beautiful view, visible only if she leaned out far enough to see beyond the tree. But though the window had opened for Delia, it refused to open for Ruth.

She gave up and went to bed. Knowing better than to trust her internal heat, and thinking she might have a fever, she covered herself with a patchwork quilt. It still smelled of mothballs from its winter in a trunk. The quilt was made from tattered frocks, which someone in a sewing bee had used all over again. Ruth thought about death that way. *Someone will use me all over again.*

It was not an ideal life, but she had loved it, which was more than most could say. She'd conceived a baby, carried him to full term and survived the birth, but had never been the same. She'd nursed her son on goat's milk. When she went upstairs to sleep, it wasn't the sleep of too-rich lunches. When she said, "I'll lie down now," a hush fell over the family, like floorboards smothered by rugs. Ruth had been born dying; she'd had a heart attack at three minutes old. The doctor had diagnosed an enlarged heart, which would continue to grow until one day it ruptured. It was suicide, he said, to marry and bear a child. But with a heart that had grown beyond the size of the most passionate woman's, no one, least of all a doctor, could tell her whom to love.

Aubrey would return from the woods and describe to her the cinnamon ferns and the mountain laurel and the bee queen mating with her drone, dropping a hundred feet out of the air onto the mossy floor. He'd describe to her the beauty of the world beyond the view from the cottage. She closed her eyes and saw him. Her young hart. He worried her, as he ran over the hills of Zion and over the Green Mountains, lit by the rising heat inside her breast. When she slept, she was no one's mother. When she slept, she was neither person nor thing, but a luminous whiteness, its substance withdrawn.

Aubrey followed a deer path through the forest where the moss made a fertile carpet and lichen ashed the granite slabs thrown helter-skelter by the glaciers. Boulders and shale and quartzite glimmered in the undergrowth, pollen glistened in the botanic rays, small blue forget-me-nots burst into miniature sky blooms, and a rusty bucket poked from a cluster of weeds. But he didn't see the beauty of the woods.

"Greta Garbo, Greta Garbo, Garbo, Greta," he said, over and over, until the alliterative words sounded weirdly like *gumbo* and *regret*. Her name had conjuring power, and if he narrowed his eyes he could pretend to see her in the flickering light. "Greta," he said. Then he listened to the silence, though in summer, silence was scored by the racket of birds and the hum of bluebottles. Other than flying creatures, no sentient being was there.

He lay down in a clearing beneath the maple canopy, once his favourite spot for hide-and-seek. His limbs were thin and his knees and elbows bony; his face was a pale watercolour of his father's – at least that's what people told him. Though he looked younger than he actually was, he didn't feel like a child as he loosened his belt and reached into his shorts.

His free hand gripped the root of an apple tree which, overhung by the forest roof, grew little knots of fruit that could never reach maturity. He closed his eyes and the forest vanished. In the darkness, the star appeared. In the watery darkness she appeared, naked, hanging off his boat. He squeezed his penis with determination.

For a moment he thought he'd never get there, but he was wrong. His face contorted. His thin spine twisted like a tortured snake. He left his white jet on the emerald moss and, spent, he fell asleep.

When he woke, the moss bed had blackened with drab and consuming shadows. It was later than he expected. The heat having sucked away from the earth, the lustre had vanished from the forest. He shook the browning pollen from his shirt.

He followed the fading light out of the woods, and then the dirt road home. Though he knew he should hurry, the twin releases of orgasm and sleep slowed his walk. He suspected he was late for dinner, but pleasure made him careless. Swayed by the scent of wild roses, he stopped and stood like an idle cow. He picked up a birch branch that the wind had dropped and drew it along the ground a while, imitating the trail of a garter snake. He watched as the last light emptied from the trees. The forests on either side of the road were interrupted only by fields where hay or corn or cattle eventually gave way to forests again. The sky went quickly black, and in response he walked a little faster. He was relieved when he passed a barn where an electric bulb buzzed and the hum of a milking machine gave a sign of human life. From a one-room schoolhouse, a lone black window stared at him. Worst of all was crossing the graveyard in the dark. He held his breath and ran from the ghosts, from the north gate to the south.

When he at last threw open the back door, Delia was brushing the flour off her apron and preparing to go home.

In the living room, his father was leaning against the liquor cabinet with a whisky in one hand and his cigarette in the other. Mendelssohn's minor piano chords were drifting through the open window from a distant gramophone on the far side of the lake: a weekly summer concert broadcast over the ambient water. Grandmother was pouring herself a port. "You're late; wash your hands," she commanded.

His father was irritated too. All afternoon, Everett had toiled over a certain passage, writing and rewriting it but gaining no satisfaction. In the end he had sacrificed the day to nothing. The evening's music, one of the pleasures of the recent arrival of electricity, was only a further nuisance, for he was not a fan of Mendelssohn. Dinner had been waiting and growing cold for a half-hour. His son was late, his wife still asleep. There was not a chanterelle to be seen in the child's pockets, and the boy stood before him, breathless, afraid and guilty. Ragged, unbrushed and pollinated. Everett preferred not to think about it. "See to your mother, would you?" he said.

Aubrey looked at the clock on the wall, then at the scrubbed floorboards. With mounting guilt, he climbed up the stairs to his mother.

Because of the pine tree outside, her room was darker than the others in the house. The white moon was rising, but the tree blocked its light, as if to shield the sleeper. The room smelled, as always, of pine needles and his mother's vanilla perfume.

He sat on the bed beside her. Sleeping, she was even more beautiful. Her face looked more still and perfect than ever, as if it belonged to a statue she'd left behind for her family to worship while she ran off to wander in a foreign world. He imagined her running through forests.

"Mother," he said quietly. She did not stir. "It's dinnertime." His words sounded small and wrong and unworthy. She should sleep right through the night if she wanted, for she couldn't have been more perfect. "The concert's playing." That sounded nicer; he should speak to her of music, or tell her what he saw in the woods. But he hadn't seen anything.

Touching her cheek to wake her, Aubrey felt himself rushed into the shadows. Her skin was cold.

"Aubrey!"

It was his father. An irritated step on the stairs slowed as it reached the door. Father's figure appeared in the door frame like a lonely god beneath a baldachin as Aubrey looked up in terror.

Death went on for hours.

She was his mother and not his mother, something gelid and hard that had never been anything but supple and warm before. He stared at the thing, not knowing whether to love it or run from it, believing somehow that he was the cause of it. He had turned her into it. He was guilty for it, for everything, or for nothing, because she was only sleeping. With a small movement, she'd return to life: she'd done so many times in the past. She'd smile or lift a lock of hair from her eyes. He sat at her bedside, waiting for it. Forgetting and remembering, every half-instant, that his mother was dead. He picked up the hairbrush from the bedside table. He loved her hair, and he was brushing it now.

Delia walked down the lane to the Irwins' cottage, where there was a phone to ring the coroner.

Grandmother lost all colour and declined to enter the room.

Everett looked hopelessly on. This was nothing like he'd imagined. He had studied death. It was, he knew, the terrifying epicentre around which culture was built. Ruth had envisioned this day; knowing it would come, she had said, "You need to prepare Aubrey."

"Don't be silly. You'll live forever."

"Everett, please, you need to prepare Aubrey."

So he'd explained to his son that, due to her health, his mother should not have had a child. Therefore she wouldn't live forever; therefore he should be a good boy and take advantage of every moment.

"Did you talk to him?" she'd said.

"I did, but you're better at those things."

Everett had studied death. He'd crawled into Queen Nefertari's grave to copy the paintings of her journey to offer milk to the Lady of the West, and he'd witnessed death every day, en masse, in the trenches of France. But his insides were splattered against the walls; he was completely unprepared. And he had nothing to say to his son.

Aubrey would not, even by the command of the coroner, stop brushing his mother's hair.

The coroner took the brush from his hand and tucked it in his own pocket. "Be a good boy," he said. "Go sit with your father. Let me do my job."

Aubrey asked Father, "Is Amos still here?'

"He finished his work hours ago."

So Aubrey sat alone at the end of the bed.

But when the undertaker arrived with his horse and carriage, someone needed to carry the corpse down the stairs. Everett expected to lift his wife lightly in his arms, as he had on their first night together when he carried her over the threshold to their bedroom, but when he put his arms around her, he found his own life running out of him. As he struggled beneath her spiritless body, her head turned in the winding-sheet and her long red hair cascaded over his hands.

Aubrey shouted, "Leave her alone! I hate you!"

Delia said, "I'll get Amos."

"He's gone," said Father.

Delia said, "He's outside."

As Amos came into the house, the night was bright with a perfect moon, and the Milky Way streamed like silver-backed salmon through invisible rivers. Aubrey heard his footsteps. They couldn't have belonged to anyone else. He was coming slowly up the stairs to carry down the dead.

"The weather's wrong," Amos said to Aubrey, as he lifted him gently out of the way. "Tonight should be all black."

Aubrey's body, almost as rigid as his mother's, softened in Amos's hands. He did not resist as Amos placed him standing on his feet.

Father stood by the window and turned his cheek to the glass. "I want you to cut down that tree," he said to Amos.

Amos didn't answer. He picked up the lovely dead mother.

As Amos walked from the room, Aubrey followed him. At the picture window on the stairwell landing, they paused a moment. A sourceless rain pounded hard on the cottage roof. Where it had come from, no one knew, but the heavens had opened and would not close. The lake vanished in a sky-water shroud. Flash floods overtook the valleys. The mountains were obscured, and the sweetness of flowers and grasses subsumed by greater powers.

The summer residents, all of them, attended the funeral and the gathering that followed. There was general agreement that the eulogy – *We have lost the gem around our necks, the light above our tables, the sweetest fruit of our seasons* – was not only well said but true. Everyone appreciated Ruth Shaw Brown, and many even claimed to love her, though under the exposing blue sky, no one felt free enough to weep. Everyone was dressed appropriately in black, and in true Victorian fashion, Mrs Shaw had ordered the mirrors in her house to be covered with dark crêpe. As dusk fell in the living room, the mourners, like American crows in a seeded field, became less and less visible, though their voices, hushed at first, were gradually raised by liquor.

Everett appeared to drink frugally, his head bent over his whisky tumbler, as if mesmerized by the sluggish melting of his ice cubes. But the impression of moderation was deceptive: he'd already filled and emptied his glass five times. His son had counted.

Now Father said to Aubrey, "I'm taking you to see *Mata Hari* at the Bend."

"It's not playing there," said Aubrey, who didn't want to see a Garbo film ever again. But he made the mistake of saying, "*Anna Karenina* is."

"I'm taking you to see *Anna Karenina,* then."

"You don't need to."

"I'm taking you," Father said, adding loudly enough that everyone could hear, "Let it be known: I'm taking my son to see Greta Garbo in *Anna Karenina*, because that's what he wants more than anything. Anything!"

Until that moment, Aubrey didn't know loss had fangs – it was the first sign of the future. And though he wasn't surprised or disappointed when, two days later, his father reneged on his offer, it was the second sign.

Father called Aubrey into his study and said, "Anna ..."

Taking forever to finish a sentence, he returned to drawing a copy of *The Healing of the Paralytic* and left Aubrey waiting in the fermented chamber stinking of turps, tobacco and liquor. On the desk was a lock of Mother's hair, displayed in a butterfly case. Father had asked the undertaker to clip it for him.

Not wanting to look at his mother's boxed and disassembled hair, Aubrey stared at the graphic-granite paperweight, its mock cuneiform writing like an unintelligible code.

Father, finally finishing his sentence, ruined the end of the movie: "... Anna kills herself in a train station. She throws herself under a train, because Tolstoy hated trains and thought they were destroying the world. Tolstoy wrote that railways are to travel as whores are to love. I just thought you should know that."

Aubrey thought he knew why: Father wanted to show him that people other than Mother died too, or that they died more violently. Father wanted to punish him for letting her die. Aubrey hadn't read his book by her bed to keep her awake, hadn't tugged her finger or slapped her face (whatever it was you had to do in the nick of time to stop a person from dying), hadn't shaken her awake when she slept so deeply she died (wasn't that how people died?), hadn't

done anything. Instead, he'd lied about the chanterelles and
gone to the woods to unbutton his shorts. He was born: that
was why Father ruined the ending.

"If …" Father said, and paused again.

"Can I go now?"

"Don't interrupt," said Father. "I was saying that *if you
must* see Garbo, I'm afraid you'll just have to row. And you'd
better go now – before Amos brings in the boat. We don't
have time for the movies, not with our leaving early."

The room was unusually dim. The mirror that should
have reflected light from the window was covered in black
cloth.

"It doesn't matter," said Aubrey.

"It seemed to matter a lot to you."

"I didn't want to go anyway."

"I hope you're not lying again."

"I didn't think there'd be time to go."

"I don't know how you imagined we'd actually have time!
My God, your mother just died!"

Father had become like an alder, the tree Amos called the
widow-maker because you couldn't see the hollow inside,
and so, when you cut them down you never knew which
way they were going to fall.

"Can I go now?" Aubrey asked again.

"You might as well."

On the way downstairs, Aubrey met Amos coming up,
carrying an axe.

"Your dad in his study?" Amos asked in his deep-water
voice.

Aubrey lingered on the stairs to hear their conversation.
He heard Amos say he was going to cut down the pine tree,
and Father say, "Good." He heard Amos say that cutting it

down in summer would bring a heap of toadstools, whereas if he waited for winter, toadstools would never grow. And Father, who knew nothing about living things, believed Amos's lie.

Father said, "As long as the tree is gone when we come back next year. As long as I never have to see it again. It stole the air and the view from Ruth's window. I blame the tree for bringing miasma, Amos. Do you even know what miasma means?"

"Nope. I don't know that word."

Aubrey hurried down the stairs, but Amos's stride was so much longer than his, he caught up to him on the porch. They stood side by side, Aubrey all in black, Amos in overalls that were almost black with dirt, the two of them watching the ants navigate a highway of sap that ran down the pine's trunk. Amos, who had so much work to do, stood there next to Aubrey as if he had nothing to occupy his time.

"You can take an axe, turn it round and use it like a hammer if you want," he said to Aubrey. "Swing from the wrist for aim, but you gotta swing from your elbow for power. Like this." He took a nail from the bib pocket of his overalls and, leaning over the porch rail, drove the nail into the tree. The ants scurried away up the sap.

"Won't be long before the bark grows round it," he said, "and anyone who didn't put it there wouldn't know it was there at all." For a man who hurt whenever he spoke, today he had a lot to say. "I was a kid about your age, working with my dad for Copper Matches – maybe it was some other lumber company, the past gets scrambled up. I was just a kid, and kids never know the whole story. The bosses stopped paying or started paying peanuts or something. A man got turfed out 'cause he complained. The men were mad as hell at the bosses, but shut up about it, 'cause they needed their jobs. Then someone said we should spike the trees and break the saws. So we hammered nails into trees all over. Hemlock, white pine, red pine. Deep enough they disappeared. Then we cut the trees down, 'cause that was our job. Those nails in the trunks broke the saws in the mill. Each tree stopped work for a week and cost the bosses a bunch. We were happy, for a moment anyway, 'cause we'd done something, even if it weren't much, and was gonna put us out of work. Copper lost so much money, it went out of business and sold the land. I don't know if what we did was right or wrong. Some things ain't either one. You can still see the trees standing on Stannard Mountain."

He pointed with his sawed-off finger to the low range beyond the lake, which at dusk turned purple and at night black, but in the daylight was a blend of blue grass and conifer green. "No one's cut them down yet. I been thinking about that since your ma died. I ain't gonna bring down this tree for your dad. It didn't do nothing to hurt her. You didn't, neither," he said.

Mangled and ugly, Amos descended the path to the beautiful lake. Tomorrow, he'd lean a ladder against the house and affix wooden shutters to the upper windows, making the family's final nights in the cottage pass undisturbed by dawn. But now he had to take in the dock.

He heaved the rowboat, then the sailboat, out of the water and onto the hill, crushing the ferns under the sailboat's keel. He'd carry the boats up later, stow them under the porch for the winter. He needn't have bothered to roll up his overalls before wading out into the water: the lake was deep from the recent rain, and his sodden denim clung to his thighs. As he floated the last section of the dock in to shore, the sawhorse that had supported it, weightless now, drifted out into the deeper waters. Amos followed, and stepping over the drop-off was suddenly up to his neck. He was lucky to catch the horse when he did, since he didn't know how to swim.

Remains of the summer were scattered on the hill – the boats, lifejackets, folding chairs, sawhorses, planking, hemp rope, and the rock anchor. Purple with cold, and wet through, Amos filled up his arms. A tiny insect flew into his only eye and instantly died. He lay down the anchor and rubbed it out, then picked up the anchor again. On the porch, where the mother had so often sat, he saw Aubrey, standing still where he'd left him, watching.

Mrs Shaw pried open the tiny cardboard door on the Advent calendar propped against the poinsettias and, through the peephole, spied a miniature family at prayer. Considering hope superior to prayer, she hoped her son's visit would at last bring the Christmas mood to her Princeton home. The time of mourning was over: she'd set aside her black damask gown and dressed in her smart navy blue. She had commanded her family to do similarly. She placed the Advent calendar back on the mantel and plumped the sofa pillows, which her housemaid had failed to plump, then went hurtling up the stairs with stiff-limbed power.

Everett, in black, was bending over a bookcase in the second-floor hall with his nose in *The Liturgy of Funerary Offerings*, also called *The Book of the Opening of the Mouth*. His face still handsome, his eyes still blue, but the tenuous blue of ancient tombs that could rub off on your hand. He pushed the book towards his mother-in law and told her, "It's the oldest known Egyptian text."

"I need you to see about the drinks, Everett, not oblations to Osiris! Is Aubrey in his room?"

As she reached for the doorknob, Everett said, "You'd better not go in without knocking. He's not a child anymore.

Anyhow, he'll be out soon and glad to see his uncle. At the very least, Jack will make him feel tall. Napoleon was five-foot-one, Mussolini is five-six, and Franco in field boots is a total of five feet."

Mrs Shaw's hand tightened on the doorknob, for not only did she take offence at the insinuation towards her beloved Jack, she had forbidden all talk of war in her house. The newspapers wrote of nothing but the mounting Nazi threat, and the great Albert Einstein lived nearby with a bounty of five thousand dollars in German marks on his head. War was near, but Old Mrs Shaw, self-schooled in the philosophy of structural linguistics, regarded the withholding of a word as a defence against its incarnation. She had, in the same breath, banned the word *war* and declared an end to the family's term of mourning.

She pursed her lips, and her lipstick cracked along the vertical age lines. "My son is travelling all the way from Mexico City to visit me! Though you have never been a fan of his – Everett, it's Christmas!"

"It's just a bit of trivia in the *New York Times*," said Everett, speaking with the entrenched belligerence of the chronically unhappy. "The Indian Vedas show an astrological correlation between shortness and the war planet, Mars. The *Times* didn't say how tall Hitler is, but no doubt Jack can tell us."

Mrs Shaw's petticoats rustled and her cataractous eye narrowed. She saw no sign of Everett recovering from what was done and could not be undone and hence must become, like all sorrowful things, an unquestionable fact of life. And furthermore, if anyone was to blame for Ruth's death, it was him. He had seduced her into marriage despite her doctor's warnings. Everett was the reason her beautiful Ruth wasn't alive for Christmas.

To avoid being heard through her grandson's door, she whispered what she wished to shout: "You knew Ruth would die when you married her. Don't take it out on the rest of us – particularly not her brother!" Then, releasing the doorknob, she said, "If Aubrey is really as grown up as all that, I'll have to buy him some trousers. Shorts will no longer do." And she rushed back down the stairs to tend to the ritual lighting of the tree.

Everett stood alone by his bookshelf. Loss was supposed to become easier; instead, it became more complete. As each day followed the last, each day was as miserable as the last, and if the human heart must believe in progress then each day was worse than the last. Day after day in his lonely room, he'd awake at the crack of the weak sun then fall back to sleep and endure another senseless hour dreaming of his wife – only to have her die again when the maid brought in the coffee tray, at which time he'd dress in black and go about his day, waiting for night to come.

Now it had come, and he could pour himself a cocktail. He would see about the drinks. He closed *The Book of the Opening of the Mouth* and returned it to its place, coughed and lit a cigarette. Knocking on his son's door, he called, "Your uncle will be here any minute."

He was unable to hide the disdain in his voice. Though he hated Jack, he couldn't say why, and he told himself he hated no one. He'd pass on to his son that gulf between intuition and knowledge. Everett begrudgingly followed his mother-in law down the stairs.

Aubrey took his ear from the door. His father was gone, but not far enough away for safety. He wished his father was digging things up in Egypt or – he ran his finger along the tin globe on his bedroom desk – Japan. He spun the globe in its harness. If the Earth had a beginning, he couldn't find it. Unable to tell the difference between fear and hatred or sorrow and hatred or self-hatred and hatred, he believed his father hated him. Aubrey couldn't explain the sick feeling in his own heart, let alone why his father drank and yelled and cried. It was easy to think his father hated him; it was the obvious answer, which was easier than the right one. That Father now allowed him to use the camera wasn't a sign of love, only regret that there were so few shots of Mother.

Next to the globe on the desk sat a skull, which Father had dug up in Egypt and Aubrey had stolen from the study. Unearthed alongside a female figurine that had proved a forgery, the skull was not much older than Grandmother, and Father, disappointed, had stashed it away in a closet. Aubrey had drilled a hole through the jaw and another through the top of the cranium. Modelling the lobes of a brain from balled-up paper, he'd glued them to the inner skull. A stick, representing the railway rivet, poked through the jaw and cranium holes. On the desk, a book from the school library was open to a page describing the brain's right hemisphere. Aubrey had circled several words – *intuitive, nonverbal, fantastical, holistic, random* and *concrete* – and in the margins he'd written, "What does Amos see?"

Winters in Princeton were long. The plane trees on the way to school had been pruned, and they lined the road like blotchy amputees. The young rose bushes were wrapped in burlap sacks. The leafless oak out his bedroom window reminded him of himself: it was comfortless except for a layer of snow. When he closed the book and hid the skull underneath his bed, the room felt empty.

But Uncle Jack was coming. Coming all the way from Mexico, from where the warming waters of the Gulf Stream flowed north to Florida, ran parallel to the Jersey Shore then departed the Eastern Seaboard for Europe. The Gulf Stream was not a stream, but a powerful ocean river. Aubrey had been a toddler the last time Uncle Jack came to town, and he didn't remember him. But Grandmother had described him. Jack had Mother's face. Jack's coming made Grandmother happy, and Aubrey wanted to be happy too, so he obeyed her wishes, stripped off his black wool shorts and pulled on his light grey ones.

Mrs Shaw was concerned. If her grandson was so mature that her coming and going from his bedroom was no longer appropriate, surely he would consider himself too grown up to hunt for the Christmas pickle. Yet this year, like every year since the boy could read, the pickle had been hidden, treasure-hunt clues written and an early gift set aside to present to him upon the vegetable's discovery. But the boy's apparent maturity threatened to spoil the holiday tradition. Christmas without a mother was difficult enough, and Mrs Shaw determined that it should not be attempted without the pickle. Breathing harder than usual, she sat down on the velvet couch beside the Christmas tree, which appeared to be asphyxiating under its burden of garlands.

Collapsed there on the couch, she felt decidedly Victorian, a relic in a modern century, which had begun well enough with fireworks and parades but had progressed – at the speed of light – onto one world war and was hurtling towards a second. She was unable to fully grasp the implications of Dr Einstein's physics, but she found them resonant all the same. She liked Albert Einstein, and as many of her circle disliked Jews and blamed them not only for the death of a god-man in whom she herself did not believe, but for the current unrest in Europe, she had already begun to take personally the threat of another war. Thus she had, in the last few months, particularly since the Night of Broken Glass (the newspaper's name for that violent night that sounded like a Christmas carol – *kristallnacht, heilige nacht, alles schläft; einsam wacht* – sung door to door down the Jewish quarter by Hitler Youth in a landscape of bloody snow), found herself for the first time in her life at odds with her environment. Her mournful family on one hand, the Daughters of the American Revolution on the other. But she was hopeful for the visit of her son.

Now a maid brought her a bourbon from the copious holiday supply, and Everett crossed the room to the liquor cabinet, ostensibly to inspect the beverages on hand for Jack's arrival. Tonight, everyone was an animal making for the waterhole. With a sigh, she said to her son-in-law, "The Christmas stockings still stink of mothballs. Does the smell attract mice? Aubrey's stocking has a hole in the toe the size of a Florida orange!"

Aware that mothballs were used in the Punjab as snake repellent, but knowing nothing about their effect on mice, Everett didn't feel compelled to answer. Silently, he poured himself a drink.

When the cook came into the living room with a large green pickle in her beefy hand, Mrs Shaw stood up immediately. "What are you doing? Put it back! Put it back *exactly* where you found it!"

"Did you want me to serve it with something, Mrs Shaw?"

"No. Oh, my goodness, no!"

The old woman waved away the cook, who scuffled off to the kitchen while the maid proceeded down the hallway to open the big front door. The doorbell was ringing.

Mrs Shaw clutched the banister and shouted up the stairs, "Aubrey, come down at once! Your uncle!" As her grandson emerged on the landing, she hastened down the hall and threw her arms around her only living child.

The man who stood haloed by the portico was strong and attractive with a short body and tightly knit bones – where the shortness came from, no one knew. He did indeed have his sister's face.

Everett gathered up his brother-in-law's luggage and looked out towards the darkened taxi. "No Ethyl?" he asked. "No children? I thought you were bringing the children."

"He never said he was bringing the children," Mrs Shaw corrected him. "But no Ethyl?" she asked her son.

"Good God, Mother! Do you expect me to take the children's mother away and leave them behind to torture the maids?" He laughed. After a long day of travel – plane from Mexico to Miami, another from Miami to Trenton, and taxi from Trenton to Princeton – he wasn't even tired. "I'm joking, Mother! Ethyl's still in the taxi. She's nursing a terrible headache. And I think she's changing her shoes: she forgot there would be snow." He passed his remaining luggage to Everett and lifted his mother up in his arms.

She squealed in her blue apparel. Having folded and set aside her black, in her son's arms she felt like a debutante again. Light-hearted and virile, her boy was a charm. He erased the horrors of the summer and the further horrors of the world. She felt the bourbon tingle on her lips. She kissed Jack on the forehead, and then on either hand.

Aubrey came down the stairs.

His uncle shouted to him, "My God, you're thin!" and the friendly loudness of his voice made the insult a form of intimacy. "Put some meat on the boy, Everett!" Jack taunted. Then, tossing his arm over his nephew's shoulder – for adults remember children even if children don't remember them – he swept Aubrey instantly into his magnetic field. "Come visit me in Mexico and I'll stuff you with beef tamales! I bet you don't even know what a tamale is. I'll get your cook to make one. Now, show me the Christmas tree!"

Mrs Shaw looked proudly on the two generations – son and grandson, almost the same height, stood shoulder to shoulder staring admiringly at the tree – and unlike her son-in-law, stationed in the distance like a charred stump, neither was dressed in black. Though her son was known to drink – who didn't? – unlike Everett, Jack could handle his liquor. He never turned angry or mopey and did not suffer from hangovers. He laughed loudly, spoke freely, and his amiable manner overshadowed all past ambiguities. He'd been dismissed from a career in the military for reasons unknown to the family, but as is often the way with the charmed, trouble was merely a precursor to bounty: so began his stellar rise in oil. Jack Shaw had become Mr Jack Shaw of Standard Oil of New Jersey, who lived royally in Mexico City, spearheading Central and South American interests. Or something like that, Mrs Shaw concluded, for her son was needed all over the world, and though she tried to understand it, she didn't actually know why. "Just look at that Christmas tree!" she declared.

It stood twelve feet high, and its atheistic angel scratched the ceiling with its halo, while around its trunk was laid a miniature train track. Despite the new trend towards electricity, candles graced the tree in a gesture to a faded century. Hand-cast leaden fruits and gingerbread hearts recalled Christmases of earlier years in which the pears and sugared plums were edible. The gingerbread hearts still were, and because mice had been known to climb up the tree to eat them, the hallway was equipped with bowls of water in case a mouse toppled a candle and set the room on fire. The candles were a hazard, but no one could say they weren't beautiful. In their radiance, blue-glass icicles sparkled with internal stars, and reindeer turned on the updraft. Tin and glass ornaments glistened. There were gilded tin bugles and seraphim, egg zeppelins and a woven basket suspended from a hot-air balloon. There were glass fish swimming in airy rivers and glass birds perched on the highest boughs, legacy of the dead woman who had favoured natural forms.

As he thought of his mother, a wave of sadness broke over Aubrey and quickly gave way to anger. Trinkets acquired on Father's travels, not officially ornaments, had been tied to ribbons and hung from the tree: a Star of David, an Egyptian scarab, a diminutive Buddha on a gilded throne, a Tibetan eye of spiritual enlightenment and a Turkish evil eye bead, as well as a tiny Tutankhamen sarcophagus – a coffin, which Father should not have hung, not this year, not if he had any feelings.

"Come visit me in Mexico, Aubrey," Uncle Jack was saying. "I mean it." He was fingering a red paper flower. This being an educated and historically minded family, there hung red and white paper flowers – red for knowledge, white for innocence – as on the first paradisiacal tree in the now-snow-covered garden of Eden. "I'm not being polite. Am I ever polite? I hope not. Come to Mexico, and I'll show you a Christmas tree the likes of which you've never seen."

"Are the Christmas trees wonderful there?" asked Aubrey.

"I don't think he's talking about something that grows in a forest," answered his father, who, unlike his son, was not comforted at finding Ruth's face replicated in her brother's. The two faces could not have been more similar, nor more contrary. Having handed off the luggage to a maid, Everett poured himself a second drink. Though he waited religiously for the evening hours to imbibe, it was a custom he felt collapsing within him, and he was glad that the winter sun descended by half past four.

"A Christmas tree's part of an oil well," Uncle Jack explained. "It's called that because the valves and fittings line up to look a little bit like a tree. But where there's oil, there's not always Christmas: Persia, Iraq, Saudi Arabia. We're on the lookout for oil in Egypt these days. Your dad's been digging in all those places, but what Standard Oil's after is at least a million years older than anything your father's ever found."

"I haven't been to Saudi Arabia," objected Everett.

"They're all the same. Hot. Arab."

"They're actually not all Arab."

"Never mind, Professor! It's Christmas!"

Uncle Jack threw Father a marvellous smile, and then turned the same smile on Aubrey. Compact and powerful, he could create a new world where Christmas trees weren't trees.

"In the Mexican desert there's Christmas but no trees," Uncle Jack told Aubrey. "So someone was probably a little homesick when he named the thing. A Christmas tree is used to stop oil from spilling onto the land."

"Does it make a great mess when it spills?" asked Grandmother.

A voice in the hallway surprised them. "Let's just say it would take more than a couple of your maids to clean it up, Mother," the other Mrs Shaw answered.

Aunt Ethyl, who had sat in the taxi for a good ten minutes, entered the room in an ermine coat. Now she complained of a raging headache. She would excuse herself from socializing, for her headache, she said, was splitting her head in two. Apologizing, though not profusely, to the elder Mrs Shaw, she kissed her mother-in-law's cheeks with a coolness that could only be warmed by the Mexican sun. Aunt Ethyl wore ice-blue silk, and to match she had painted her eyelids blue, her lips pink. She had done herself up to perfection. Nursing her headache and whatever grievance had mounted between Mexico City and Princeton, she bristled beneath her husband's shining eyes. She never, when sober, punished the man directly. Words hovered at her lips, a perfect pink, and seeped away. She said to him only, "Goodnight. I'm sure I'll be asleep before you come up to bed."

Jack's wife departed in sublime composure – a pug nose, small chin and light, sharp eyes – but there was a certain unsightly tightness in her jaw, for she did not smile freely. Nonetheless, she was pretty and had weathered well the birth of her three sons. After each gruelling event, the Mexican midwives had bound up her belly in warm linens and massaged it every day, and their ministrations showed in her meticulous preservation. She was somewhere in her thirties, but Jack had lost count and Ethyl had stopped telling. Her blonde hair, like most blonde hair, had moused down with the years, though when she applied lemon and sat in the sun it yellowed up again. Though she wore her hair in a tight coronet bun, winching back her temples, she walked with a weary and sensual listlessness and had a perplexing habit of shrugging in answer to every question. When she slept, her loose hair wrapped like golden ropes around her face. Her husband enjoyed her particularly when she slept: he liked how her breasts fell after every in-breath, and how her exhale smelt of tenderloin from supper. Such secrets about his aunt, Aubrey didn't know, but he would learn eventually.

Aubrey was watching Aunt Ethyl ascend as Grandmother pressed the first clue for the pickle hunt into his sweaty hand. He noticed how the light of the Christmas tree merged with that from the chandelier and muted his aunt's features. He thought of running upstairs to get the camera, but of course if he did, he'd miss the moment.

"Well, go on," said Grandmother. "Read the clue."

He didn't want to play the game; he wanted to follow Aunt Ethyl up the stairs. But he also wanted the early present, which he couldn't have without complying, for Grandmother maintained that all good things demanded effort and a child should have something to do other than eavesdrop on grown-up conversations. He didn't feel like a child anymore, except that he had no power over his life, and except that it was childish of him to want his early present, especially as he already knew what it was. It was the same thing every year.

"Hup to," said Grandmother, shooing him along. "I expect you to have found the pickle before dinner."

Old Mrs Shaw, being proud of the difficulty of her clues, was soon displeased by the speed with which her grandson deciphered them. He found the first clue in the linen cabinet and the second taped to the bottom of a whisky decanter. Of the dozen clues, there was only one that forced him to ask for help.

"You shall have to think very hard on this one," Grandmother said, and quoted Henry Ford. "Thinking is the hardest work there is, which is probably the reason why so few engage in it."

Aubrey read it aloud: "'The moon gazed on my midnight labours while, with unrelaxed and breathless eagerness, I pursued Nature to her hiding-place.'"

"It's from *Frankenstein,*" said Father, already dangerously slurring his words.

"You're thirteen years old," laughed Uncle Jack. "You should know where nature hides things."

"The attic?" Aubrey asked him, certain his guess was wrong.

"Look in on your aunt," winked Jack, "if you're going by."

He had only meant to pop in his head, but Aunt Ethyl invited him into the room and dipped her fingers into her cocktail, pulling out a light-green olive. Accepting the olive, and sucking the gin off, Aubrey could see her cleavage beneath her dressing gown. A freckle pointed towards the scarcely hidden nipple.

Light from a gooseneck lamp struck the bedroom vanity, and several martinis intended to ease her headache replicated themselves in the mirror. Knowing she could see him in the mirror, he was careful not to stare at her breasts. Her eyes were red and watery, and though he should really have left her room, he felt compelled to stay. He offered her his handkerchief. She touched the cloth to the clotted powder on her pug nose and smiled strangely, as if she were trying on her husband's face as her own. She looked him up and down with a listless curiosity.

He stuck his hands into his blazer pockets, then pulled them out again and shoved them in the back pockets of his shorts, uncertain why his aunt had invited him into her bedroom and feeling something was expected of him.

"Do you need something?" he asked, but she only shrugged. When he glanced again at her breasts, the freckle seemed to twinkle, like a star in a hidden constellation. "Shall I ask the maids to bring you another martini?" he suggested.

She turned in the white swivel chair at the vanity and pulled him closer by his empty blazer pocket. She whispered, "I'm very sorry your mother died. The sooner you learn that life isn't perfect, the happier you'll be." She added, "Your uncle is going to hell. Do you believe in hell?"

He didn't know how to answer that. He was uncertain about almost everything. He couldn't even say which he wanted more: to curl up like a child in her lap, or to touch her breasts. Her motherly lap, too slim to be truly motherly, was only inches from her breasts. And her hand was in his pocket.

"No," he said. It was a decisive answer, being his grand-mother's, not his own.

Ethyl raised her tweezed eyebrows at his apparent self-assurance, but all the same agreed with him. "I don't either," she said.

She let go of his coat and Aubrey stepped away. Though his feet shuffled back and forth, they refused to take him out of the room. Embarrassed by his feelings, and by the way his hand kept twitching through his hair, he put his forehead to the window to touch the cold, hoping it would calm him down. Looking out the window was almost like leaving the room without actually having to do so. Out there in the dark in the neighbour's yard grew an enormous oak, the same one he could see from his own bedroom window.

"Oh!" he said.

"What is it?"

"I think I know where nature hides things."

"I should hope so."

"In a tree."

"A tree? Your tree?"

"Our neighbour's, Dr Eisenhart's tree."

"You mean Dr Einstein's tree?"

"No, but Dr Eisenhart's in the maths department too."

"There are too many great men in Princeton," she said, sipping her martini, "while I feel like I just crept out of the primordial bog." What she said and how she looked appeared vastly contradictory.

Wanting to make her happy, Aubrey said, "Princeton's not all that great. Dr Einstein called it 'a quaint little village of puny demigods on stilts.'"

"He's a great man with a great tree."

"It's not Dr Einstein's tree."

They had confused each other, and neither knew what they were talking about anymore, which was strangely intimate. Ethyl gestured to Aubrey to sit, and as there were no other seats, he sat down on her bed. He could see the indentation of her pillow where her blonde head lay crying moments before; he could smell the rosewater in which she'd bathed. He would have liked to take her picture, but a photograph wouldn't capture the way she smelled – rosewater, gin and something else. One day he'd learn that his aunt smelt like gin at night but warm milk in the morning. Now she leaned forward in her chair, and a breach opened up in her bathrobe.

"How old are you?" she asked.

"I just turned thirteen," he said. He saw into the breach.

"How awful."

A knock on the door and Aubrey's father called his name.

"He's with me!" answered Ethyl as she sank back into her chair.

Nudging open the door, Father said, "It's no use hiding in here, Aubrey. Your grandmother wants to know why you haven't found the pickle."

Aubrey glanced towards the withdrawn invitation in his aunt's bathrobe and then out the window at the oak tree in which a hole gaped dark in the moonlight.

"Grandmother calls," Aunt Ethyl said.

Heat rose off the Christmas tree candles. The room had grown increasingly stuffy. Jack, with a hand draped over the sofa, waved at Aubrey and asked, "Ethyl's happy?"

He answered yes, not even noticing he was lying. Aunt Ethyl happy, smiling, laughing, running through fields of buttercups with her hair down: for a fraction of a second, a picture of cinematic bliss had appeared before him.

He let the front door slam behind him and the mistletoe on the lintel shook. He held his blazer closed against the cold, ran across the road and looked back at the house. A light shone in his aunt's bedroom. He wanted a reason to go up there again, but didn't have one. His deeper reasons were hidden from him, like carp wintering at the bottom of a lake.

The cold was a relief: it made his fingers numb and shrunk his organs. The big oak had a large hole where squirrels hid their acorns. He knew that holes often formed in a tree's early childhood: a lower branch, starved for sunlight, would break off and fall to the ground, then the sapwood, exposed on the wound, would grow infected, fungus eating away at the bark and bore beetles burrowing into the heartwood. As he'd suspected, the next clue was stuffed into the hole in the tree. He held his grandmother's writing up to the streetlamp, the ink smeared by snow.

"And all who heard should see them there, and all should cry, Beware! Beware! His flashing eyes! His floating hair! Weave a circle round him thrice, and close your eyes with holy dread, for he on honey-dew hath fed, and drunk the milk of Paradise."

Aubrey was startled by a figure coming around the corner, but it was only a man in an overcoat arriving home late from work. Berry-sized clumps of snow adhering to his woollen knee socks, Aubrey ran back to his own front yard and round to the kitchen door. The pickle hunt was over. The word *honeydew* in the poem was a giveaway, as was the milk of paradise. He entered the larder and there, beside the cook, who was impaling toothpicks into yet more finger sandwiches, a large pickle sat on a gallon bucket of Vermont maple syrup.

"Look, Daisy," he cried, "I found it!" She turned towards him with toothpicks in her meaty hands.

In the living room, announcing to the grown-ups that he'd found the pickle, forgetting he was a full thirteen years old, he felt as proud in his finding-skills and as excited about his early present as he ever had.

"Bravo!" Grandmother clapped, a strained applause. "Well done, Aubrey! Bravo!" She was clearly unhappy, for due to her son-in-law's inebriated sullenness, conversation had been veering towards the forbidden subject of war.

Father said to Jack, "You haven't mentioned Ruth since you got here. Is her name banned from this house too?" and Aubrey laid the pickle on the mantel. Before Jack could answer, Father continued, "I was in Verdun in 1916 when my dissertation on early Christian iconography was published, and Ruth, who was so happy for me, arranged for the book to be sent to the front. Do you remember, Mother?" he asked, but gave her no time even to open her mouth. "Our French interpreter offered to read the book and took it away with him to his tent, but the next morning he returned it and said in perfect English, 'I have discovered how France will win the war! We will print a hundred thousand copies of this book, and drop them on Berlin! We will *bore* the Germans to death!'"

Jack laughed, as he was supposed to do.

Everett fell silent. There was so much he could have said, but didn't. Jack had never been to war, though he'd made a career – however brief – in the military. Ten years older than Jack, Everett had postponed college to volunteer as an ambulance driver even before America joined the fighting, and for nine months he'd dragged the dead and nearly dead out of the trenches in France. By Christmas, a quarter of a million were corpses. The Mincing Machine of Verdun. "We are humbled by war, Jack," Everett whispered – drunk on whisky, grief and memory in equal measure. "Sometimes in the strangest ways."

"Well, open it, Aubrey!" ordered Grandmother, thrusting a package into his hands.

Aubrey peeled back the tape so as not to rip the paper on which tiny printed children tobogganed on snowy hills.

His father was saying loudly, "Ruth didn't look like you, Jack. Everyone thinks she looked like you, but she was a beautiful woman."

"God, yes," said Jack, with great equilibrium. He patted Everett on the back as if to say *poor man*. "She was gorgeous, and you were a lucky fellow. So what's under all that wrapping?" he asked Aubrey.

Displaying his new train carriage, Aubrey told his uncle apologetically, "I get one every year."

All bad things had become his fault in the months since his mother's death. The way he accepted his aunt's olive out of her glass, his father's drunken speech, the stupid pickle, all made him feel guilty. But Uncle Jack didn't seem to care. Like the Babylonian sun god whose portrait hung on Father's wall, his uncle seemed perfectly sure of himself.

A maid arrived to announce the dinner. Already there'd been finger sandwiches and cheese and crackers and devilled eggs, too much to eat and too much to drink, but dinner, according to Grandmother, simply had to be served.

Each sat in his usual seat. Uncle Jack sat in Mother's. Grandmother sat down in a much-needed chair at the head of the table, tumbler in her hand. Father pulled his legs up into his Queen Anne chair and left his shoes empty on the Oriental rug. As he reached for his food with his fingers and tore the chicken from the bone, Grandmother – her son-in-law having exhausted her spirit – sat uncharacteristically mute and closed her eyes.

Aubrey watched his father crack a bread roll into two tattered halves and dip both simultaneously into the chicken, though neither half arrived at his mouth.

Father said, "If you don't want to eat, Aubrey, you can be excused from the table."

"God knows why I'm eating this," laughed Jack, scraping the sticky glaze from his honey-glazed chicken, the oversweetened meat shining up at him. "Your father's right

– God, why eat? Go look in on your aunt instead. I bet she's the only one who's actually hungry."

As Aubrey rose, desperately grateful to leave the table and retreat into the queer warmth of his aunt's company, his father asked his uncle, "So what do you think of Hitler?"

"Boom, boom, speaking of nothing, as Mother says," Jack laughed again.

"You think the Night of Broken Glass is *nothing*?"

"Picking a drunken argument, Everett?"

"I want your expert opinion, Jack."

"Okay, then. Hitler's up to the job, and as far as I can see, he's not a bad guy. He's rebuilding Germany from the ground up. He has a sense of the future. As for the Broken Glass stuff – believe me, there's only so much one man can do in the face of an angry mob."

"So are you a fascist, Jack?"

"I'm an American, for God's sake!"

Uncle Jack laughed, always laughed, and the angel on the Christmas tree laughed with him, and the face on the Tutankhamen sarcophagus opened its mouth and chuckled too. Aubrey wanted to laugh; he hadn't laughed in months.

"I believe in progress, Everett! Progress, exclusively! Is this chicken supposed to be so sticky, Mother?"

But it appeared that Mrs Shaw was sleeping.

For the second time tonight, Aubrey visited his aunt, sat on her bed and sucked on olives from a line of empty martini glasses. Aunt Ethyl had progressed to schnapps, having procured a bottle and a shot glass. She had reapplied her lipstick – changed from pink to red – and smoked a Guinea

Gold cigarette with a rouged tip designed to match. The flame at the tip, the filter and her lips were an equal red. Smoke filled the bedroom and mingled with her jasmine perfume. Aunt Ethyl, who wasn't hungry for food, asked him, "Have you ever eaten oysters?"

"No. Lobster, though, and lots of crayfish."

"It's not the same. I once ate monkey brains," she said, "which reminded me of eating a child. Not that I've eaten a child."

Her conversations had no boundaries. She appeared to share secrets with him, even while talking nonsense. She told him she didn't particularly like children – her own were a disappointment – but that she liked him. He didn't ask why, and she didn't reveal how already he was giving her something her husband did not. Unlike Jack, Aubrey was transparent in front of her, and with him as an audience she could, for better or worse, indulge in being herself.

"*Skol!*" she said, lifting her shot glass and opening her throat.

Aubrey asked what *skol* meant.

"'Cup.' It's asinine, but traditional. My Scandinavian father used to raise his cup and shout, 'Cup!' It literally means 'skull,' because the Vikings drank liquor out of their enemies' skulls. Jack likes it when I say it." She paused, then added blackly, "I'd like to learn how to drink out of my own head." Despite her blonde hair, she was dark inside; despite her nonchalance, dramatic. And despite the contours of her naked body under her robe, her cigarette fixed her to the room; without it, she might have disappeared. "If you could run away, would you?" she asked.

"From home?"

"No, that's too easy." She thought and smoked a moment. "From truth. That's a lot more daring."

"I don't know."

"Why don't you believe in hell?" she asked.

He hesitated. Most nights this winter were hell. So to claim he didn't believe in it felt like a lie. Also, the reasons for things were difficult. He could give no good reason for his mother's death or his father's cruelty, though the obvious conclusion was that there was none. That life had no reason was his worst fear. He knew his mother had died of a heart condition, and in calmer moments he even knew that his father was broken-hearted, but knowing the cause was not the same as the reason.

"Because Grandmother says Christians made up hell and heaven to get people to be good," he answered. "She says they made up God and the Devil in order to have someone to blame."

"Well, *I* don't believe in hell," Ethyl said, "because if there were one, we'd all be there. Which means, of course, I don't believe in heaven, either. But the real secret is I don't even believe in Earth, because if this place is real, *it's* hell. Which I don't believe in." She laughed coldly and explained, "I'm a little drunk."

But Aubrey thought he understood her: she knew that the way out of terrible places was to believe they were not real.

Now Aunt Ethyl looked towards the door and said, "I keep expecting your father to knock, but they must be having a good time downstairs."

"My father's being rude to Uncle Jack."

"Really?" It was clear she was not displeased. "Why?"

"Because he's mean."

"Jack?"

"No! My father."

She frowned into her schnapps, then smoked in silence. Finally, she said, "My father was in the war too. He was a military man, so though he was really too old for the front, he went anyway. He had his face shot off in the trenches. A lot of men did, and because they came home looking like monsters, painters were hired to make them masks. My father's was held on by glasses, even though he didn't need glasses. From across a room, the mask looked real, but it couldn't smile or blink or cry or anything, so up close, to a child, it was terrifying. The mask was based on a photograph taken before the war, so my father always looked happier than he was. He was actually an extremely unhappy man."

Her words lay on the bed between them like someone stripped naked. It was such a personal thing to have told him – he felt like an adult. And he felt obliged to confess in return.

"There's a man in Vermont named Amos whose head opened up to let a nail go through. Then it closed again. I have a skull in my room that I pretend is Amos's, so I can understand what happened. What kind of brain damage he has, though there doesn't seem to be any. But maybe there is – nobody checked – or maybe it's the opposite of damage. I don't know. The *Bulletin* thought he was dead, but he wasn't. I thought he was dead. When the *Bulletin* said the area of bone loss was only half as big as the width of the nail, I asked my father how that was possible. He said he didn't know. He said he wasn't a biologist. No one made Amos a mask."

Aubrey stopped talking. He was staring at Aunt Ethyl's breasts. On her bathrobe, where her left nipple hid, was a wet mark.

"Oh, that!" she shrugged.

With long, buffed fingernails, she flicked open her silky robe to uncover her small and lovely breast. Aubrey turned his eyes away, mortified and excited. And there it was again, reflected in the vanity mirror. It was leaking milk, though she'd stopped breastfeeding her youngest years ago. She took the miraculous thing in her hand and wiped the pink disk of her nipple with Aubrey's dirty handkerchief.

"It happens sometimes when I'm feeling sympathetic," she said. She gave him back his hanky, left her bathrobe gaping and sent him down to dinner.

When Aubrey walked into the dining room, Father screamed at him, "Your mother was far more beautiful than goddamn Greta Garbo!"

Aubrey felt his breath snag in the base of his neck. Instinctively, he took a step backwards. He looked up the stairs towards his aunt's door, but that solace was too strange to help him. There was no refuge in his mind either, for he had used up his mother's image by conjuring it too often. And though he didn't know what to do, what he did was of no consequence anyway, because whatever he said or did or didn't do, his father was going to scream at him.

"Did you know, Aubrey," his father said – his voice quiet now, but thin and sharp as a wire about to break – "I've been doing some research in the university library, and I've learned that it takes twenty-four stills per second to make a film star move her body. Multiply that by a ninety-minute feature, then by sixty seconds, and what does it come to? That's one hundred and twenty-nine thousand, six hundred stills of Greta Garbo in one single film, and yet there are only two photographs of your mother. Two! One is a goddamn daguerreotype! Do you understand me? Your mother will be forever as her photograph – do you think that's some kind of compensation, Aubrey? Do you?!" Father was screaming again. "That she will never suffer the betrayal of her face in the mirror, and she will never quietly weep at the lines creasing her lips? Her beautiful auburn hair will never turn grey, then brittle, and have to be cut. She will never grow unrecognizable to herself. Never will the body we loved be a leaky and vermin-ridden house that anyone with the wherewithal would leave! Oh, yes, she will be forever like her photograph! While everything else around us goes to hell, nothing about your mother will change, except that like her goddamn daguerreotype, she will fade completely!"

"Grandmother's dead!" yelled Aubrey. Maybe for a moment he actually believed it, or he just wanted his father to stop. As his father stared at the corpse in horror, Aubrey added weakly, "She looks dead."

Grandmother opened her eyes. "I'm not dead. I'm sleeping." She overarticulated every word, and she planted her stone-turning gaze on Everett. "Because I'm sick and tired and ancient!"

Uncle Jack rose and walked to the liquor cabinet to indulge in a nightcap. Passing Aubrey, he joked, "You want one?" He poured himself a brandy and said, "Why don't you go play with your new train now?"

As Aubrey was leaving the room, the door to the kitchen opened and a maid appeared.

"Well?" Grandmother asked her.

"Will you be having dessert, Mrs Shaw?"

"Of course we'll be having dessert. When do we not have dessert?"

The maid retreated to the kitchen to fetch the pudding, Father pressed his eyes against his fists and wept, and Aubrey closed the dining-room door behind him.

Jack waited until Everett had wept himself out. Then, smiling amiably, he said, "Send Aubrey down to live with me in Mexico for a while. Ethyl's a decent mother. He'll have the company of his cousins. And frankly, Everett, you're not up to this." Then he turned to the matriarch: "Permission granted, Mother?"

Aubrey refused to cry. He could not control anything around him, but he could pretend to control himself. He drew himself in tightly, so tightly he could hardly breathe.

Under the Christmas tree, he hitched the new passenger car to the team of other cars attached to the Lionel engine. Turning the lever on the black box, the electricity buzzed and lights shone in the carriage. From the little windows miniature families with picnic baskets waved. From one window peered a boy. As the train charged around the Christmas tree, Aubrey felt a terrible ache: he imagined the train going up to Vermont. In Vermont, he'd been happy and carefree. In Vermont his mother lay. In Vermont was Amos. He wanted to go back to Vermont. He wanted to be as small as that boy gazing out of the window. He willed himself into the train.

Snow fell over Greensboro Village. Snow fell over Greensboro Bend. The Lamoille River, coiling through the valley, was eyeball-white from one river twist to another.

Snow fell over Barr Hill. Snow fell white on a Great War rucksack, as his little train sped through little towns in which he'd arranged tin soldiers. Snow fell on the once Green Mountains. Snow fell over Caspian Lake, named Beautiful Lake before it was renamed for the far-off sea, its sunken islands like a buried treasure where, beneath its ice, the fish slept. And when the snow stopped and the clouds lifted, the cold fell down like an angel's corpse, and the birds no longer sang, their breathing made laborious and troubled.

There were record lows in Vermont that night, though the locals claimed it was not as bad as the year eighteen-hundred-and-froze-to-death, and like their fathers before them they knew they would get by. On Barr Hill, Delia curled close to her farmer husband and three farm cats beneath a pile of patchwork quilts. Her glass of water on the bedside table was stiff with a layer of ice. In Greensboro Bend, Amos chopped wood for the fire while his furious wife cursed the monster who liked to chop wood in the moonlight. Lying alone in her bed, Donna's gaze climbed up her pregnant belly as if up a burial mound. In the soil, the worms froze hard as rabbit droppings. And the snakes, sleeping off the winter somewhere down in the rocks, drew their blood in deeper, protecting their patient lives with the semblance of death.

Snow fell on an unmarked grave. And when the snow stopped falling, cold fell on the untouched snow.

"**S**now's stopped," said Amos, talking to a dead dove in his hand. The thick scars on his head and cheek ached in the heartless weather. The iced sky was a pale vermilion, and the earth blanched as if it'd never green up again. Last night having been unspeakably cold, this morning Amos counted his doves. There were gaps in the shoddy barnboard dovecote that were large enough to pass a fist through, and he'd lost birds before to fisher cats and foxes and more than once to a hobo who came through the Bend on a train, but today he'd lost one to the most common cause: the weather.

Leaning his back against a tree and holding the dead bird under his chin, he rubbed his hands together to put some life back in them. His scars hurt in the cold air and his head hummed like wind in a railway tunnel. And in the wind he heard things. He didn't think he was brain-damaged, like Donna claimed, just that his senses were busier than other men's and were especially alive in the cold. He heard the faraway snow whizzing across the distant plains and rising upon the mountains. He felt the hunger of a white-tailed deer in a young woods where the snow lay deep beneath the pines. He smelt old roots of long-felled forests decaying into the next thousand years of coal. He even saw the shadows of vanished trees, white pine two hundred and forty foot tall, black oaks thirty foot thick, the ghosts of bounty-hunted wolves, extinct eastern elk, heath hens and carrier pigeons, all of which men's industry had killed.

Now a clatter rose from the sawmill and the rail yard in the Bend. The labour of the day had begun, but he didn't hurry to join it. He'd done more than his share in his twenty-six years, being only a kid when he started work in the pits. He'd worked granite mines and marble quarries, asbestos, copper, soapstone, limestone, dolomite, quartzite and slate, whatever he could put his big hands on and sling out of the earth. He'd brought down forests to raise them upright as electricity poles lining the streets of cities he'd never seen. His entire life he'd been sending his homeland south. He'd shipped pulpwood downriver to Massachusetts. He'd helped fix up the Connecticut River dam so the Dalton Power Company could turn what was left of Vermont's virgin forests into the *Boston Post*. The product of his labour was the news of the world, kraft paper bags, rug backing and gummed tape, and the Searsburg and Harriman dam, which extracted the juice from the Green Mountain snow-melt to light up the chandeliers of Harvard.

Extraction is the means of thieves that make us kings, plunder rewritten as productivity, economy and growth. What Amos knew he couldn't articulate, but nonetheless, he knew it. He knew it or he heard it, the hole in his head carrying sound like any empty pipe.

"Dammit, Amos! Dammit, dammit! I said you coming in?"

Amos looked up to find Donna standing in the door to the ramshackle house, thrusting her giant belly out the threshold.

"If you ain't going to answer me, I ain't going to talk to you! I *said* you coming in?"

"Yup," he answered, but didn't move, even when she slammed the door.

She had skin like the snow, but the snow was better: it fell without anger, and its silence staggered the soul. He lingered a while longer outside, for though his hands swelled up, he felt at ease when he breathed cold air. Man hadn't tampered with weather at least.

He leaned against a maple and stared up into its leaflessness. Railway rivets were lodged invisibly in the branches, the bark having grown right over them. Except where squirrels hid nuts in the autumn, all the holes had healed. Amos hadn't – his scars became infected. He could still feel his jaw shattering, his skull bulging like a mushroom and the fontanelle opening to its great surprise as the rivet soared up and out. He could still see the vision of a thousand rivets like a thousand stars sailing outward as far as the forest. One day the lumber companies would try to clear-cut the forests, and the rivets in the trees would stop their saws for months. He hoped so. Ever since the lady's death, he'd spent his days out in the woods. He let Donna believe he'd been hired as a tree feller.

"What makes a man not an animal?" he remembered Delia asking her classroom when he was no older than Aubrey – something about the stubble in the snow, twitching in the wind, made him think of the boy. She'd answered her own question: "When he picks up a rock and does something ingenious with it. When a man takes a rock and beats open a nut, he's invented a tool, but when he knocks open the head of another man, he's invented a weapon. Stop looking out the window, Amos, and maybe you might learn something!"

Amos dropped out of school the next week in order to go to work. Not because Delia was wrong, but she *was* wrong: all tools were weapons, only the victims weren't men.

Amos carried the frozen bird into the kitchen, where Donna was stirring a pot.

"Don't walk through here in your wet boots! Can't you see I only got socks on!" She wouldn't look at him – too ugly to look at first thing in the morning – so she appeared to speak to the stew. "Think it might thaw back to life, do you? Don't leave dead things by my fire!"

He laid the bird on the slate by the hearth and took a large spike from the pocket of his backpack, which hung on a hook by the door. If their love, or whatever you called it, had been bad in the past, it was awful now that she was pregnant, and worse since he'd stopped bringing home any pay. Intending to make a wood stove and chimney for his dovecote, he strode into the tool room around whose frame hung shabby Christmas tinsel.

He pounded a hole into a bucket, hammered the spike into the bottom, and with the claw wrested it out again. Using pliers to grab hold of the curls of tin, he peeled back the metal to widen the hole, then found a long length of iron pipe to fit it. With a pair of metal shears he cut a rectangle out of the bucket's side. He grabbed a handful of twigs and the legs of a broken chair from out of the kindling pile, scrunched up the headlines of the *Hardwick Bulletin* and, shoving the paper and a box of matches into his pocket, he picked up the bucket, pipe and some wire and walked back through the kitchen, past the thawing dead dove and his seething wife perched black-faced over the stove.

"What're you dreaming, Amos?" she asked the thickening pot of canned tomatoes, hoary onions and tough meat.

He shut the door against the cold and trudged through the snow to the dovecote, where he jammed one end of the pipe into the bucket and the other end out a gap between the planks. So as not to set the walls on fire, he brushed away the sawdust from the floor around the makeshift furnace. His hands were so swollen and inflamed with the weather, he took several minutes to light a match, but at last the kindling caught and the newsprint released a thick blue smoke. He squatted like an Indian to keep his rump off the frozen ground.

Smoke poured out of the pipe into the wider world. The doves choked slightly but gathered near the fire in twos and threes, drawing inward where it wasn't warm but it wasn't the killing cold either. No more would be dying today. Amos placed his hands in the air above the burning bucket, and a dozen doves alighted on his massive arms.

Coming back into the kitchen, he returned the iron spike to his backpack. Heavy with thick nails, the pack dragged on its straps as he slung them over his shoulders. His wife cussed into the stew, and Amos saw her black-eyed fury.

"Tea's hot," she hissed. "Guess you don't have time, huh?"

"Nope." He saw her baby inside her like a bulb beneath the ice.

"Don't smile at me when you ain't got time for me. And don't leave that dead thing by my fire, I told you!"

"Cook the pigeon up for your dinner, Donna."

"I'm making mutton stew, if you ain't already noticed."

"You'll keep the fire going in the dovecote?" he asked. He saw how she carried her child like a knot in her stomach.

"When hell freezes, I'll keep it going."

"That mean you'll keep it going or not?"

"What time you home?" She slammed a teacup into a saucer. "When you planning on getting paid?"

"Usual time," he said, his eye on the door.

"I ain't seen nothing usual about your pay, excepting there ain't been none."

"Usual time I'm coming home."

"And when you getting paid? They got some plastic plates in every colour at the village store. Even you could afford them, if you ever get paid."

"No reason to afford nothing new, when the old is still around."

She spat into the stew.

"Why'd you do that for?"

She spat into the stew twice more.

Amos reached into his pocket. "I got an Indian-head penny in my pocket. You want it?"

"A penny? You giving me a penny?"

He was always giving her things – a smooth river stone or a polished acorn – but an Indian-head penny was rare. Delia had told him the government put an Indian face on a coin just about the same time the last of them was being killed out West. "Says 'Liberty' on the Indian's hat," he said, as he leaned down to pat the dog.

Donna stomped her feet. "You don't speak two words to me all week, and when you do, you say something stupid! Asinine imbecile, free of brains as a toad is free of feathers, idiotic monster about as smart as a box of rocks, stupid one-eyed goddamn dunce, stupid, stupid –"

"Stop it, Donna."

"Why?!" she screamed. "You got plastic plates in that stupid pack of yours?"

"Nope."

"I want plastic plates!" She banged her fists on her belly like she might bang on the hood of a car. "You're probably hoping I'll drop this one dead like I did the last one."

"Jessum Crow," said Amos, "you better shut your mouth."

Watch your head. Watch your head. It was all he could think as he laced up his ski boots and threw his axe over his shoulder.

"When you coming home?!" she demanded.

Watch your head.

"When I come home," he said slowly.

"Cause you're out in the woods screwing she-bears!" she shouted. Donna was jigging about the kitchen, thrusting her hips forward and back, her eight-months pregnant stomach leading like a pig on a rope. "And when in the hell are you getting paid for screwing your sexy she-bear?"

Amos opened his mouth to say something, and shut it again. Silent as the fallen snow resting shin-deep out the door, he stepped outside to strap on his skis.

Donna picked up her teacup, decorated with a skater in muff and bonnet traversing a winter scene, and as the door closed behind the man she threw it at his absence. The shattered form of a miniature Currier and Ives child fell amongst the tattered skirts of nineteenth-century farm girls woven into a rag rug on the floor. The dog whined in the corner.

Wearing two pairs of woollen socks and lopsided with pregnancy, Donna stormed to the door, threw it open and screamed at the plaid of her husband's lumberjack jacket receding into the whiteness. "Damn you, Amos! I hope you die for real this time! I hope you die in your stupid woods! Don't you damn ski away from me! Say something!"

The dog whined louder. Then, with its wet black lips, it smiled, as far as dogs smile, at the cold freedom of the open door and tore out after the disappeared man, its dark hinder-legs tearing up the snow.

Donna slammed the door shut. She cried to herself by the wood stove, warming her angel-cake face sorely blotted with the rosacea of pregnancy. Through the early touch-and-go months, she'd hoped against hope that she'd drop this one dead like the last one, but the thing inside had clung on to spite her. She swept the pieces of broken china into a dustpan. She licked her fingers and ran them along the floorboards to pick up the smaller flakes. Then she dumped the pieces in the trash. Amos would want her to keep the cup and mend it with hide glue, so she threw it away.

"Can't afford nothing new," she mocked him in a low voice, while with one eye closed and her arms stuck out in front of her she marched about the shack, her knees locked, like Boris Karloff in *Frankenstein*. She might as well have married the monster. She should have married the handsome storekeeper with his plastic plates that didn't break every time a husband and wife fought. The storekeeper had just bought himself a shiny yellow Ford. As soon as she got back her figure, she'd let him hump her in the car.

Suddenly her housedress and socks were drenched and hot. Her hand scuttled through her skirt and froze at her crotch, then slid slowly up to her belly. She let go one horrible sob and swung the door open to the cold. The horizon fell off into woods over hills, and no man or dog to be seen.

The baby was expeditious. There was no time to call for a midwife and no phone in the shack anyway. Wave upon wave wrecked inside Donna as she battled unstoppable forces. "Why is this thing coming out?!" But there was no one to hear her, and the thing came forth alone. A form, the shape of what it might become, came premature but perfect, pale as the daytime moon, with wet black hair and its deep blue eyes blinking at the air around it, so ideal a miniature female that the cows in their pasture might kneel down, but Donna turned her face away. The beautiful newborn baby dropped from her reluctant mother onto the floor.

Donna cut the cord with the meat knife, then staggered to her feet. When she dragged herself outside for a gulp of water, another wave hit as she leaned into the well. She dropped the placenta into a snowdrift and hauled herself to the woodpile, where she filled up her arms with logs like lifeless babies. Beside the stove she drew off her sodden socks and her bloody skirt. Firelight danced over her skin. She sat down with the mewling being and cracked her nipples beneath its lips, and with the pigeon corpse at her feet she waited the long day for her husband to come home.

He would not come home, for he was going to kill her.

Amos was afraid of himself, and the thought wouldn't let him alone. Though he'd never touched her except to love her, one day his axe was going to lop off her head. And so he wouldn't go home. He didn't decide it, but he knew it. He knew it when he sucked on a handful of blackened rosehips, knew it when the ice screeched beneath his skis. Knew it, without thinking it, the same way he knew the trees were calling, the same way he felt the world hitch and change the night of the railway accident, then hitch again the night the lady died, and again when the car pulled out of the driveway and the boy's sad face peered through the back window, telling him that he'd never return. Then Donna declared she was pregnant, and the trees began to haunt him, and the anticipation of a baby made their haunting louder. Amos drove spikes into tree trunks and let Donna think he was felling them. But he was doing the opposite, the only thing he could do. Now the world hitched and changed again, because he couldn't go home.

He was skiing past the old Cobb homestead, where snow hummocks of rusted sap buckets and bedsprings like a pit of red adders were the remnants of his forebears who'd left long ago. Ever since Runaway Pond, one impoverished generation after another had hauled themselves out of the Bend. Now Amos was leaving too. Abandoning his doves and his child made him sad, but sadness didn't change reality; some things weren't chosen, they were given. He bent down and petted his dog in the snow, for he liked its stubborn muscles. "Go home to Donna," he said, but the dog too was afraid of itself, and it wouldn't go.

Amos was skiing north, with his axe looped through his belt and his backpack sagging with nails. The wind ate through his gloves, and he blew on his hands to warm them up. Though he could hardly bend his fingers, he pulled out his axe and, turning it backwards to use like a hammer, pounded a nail into the trunk of a maple. The tree was no older than he was, the bark no thicker than his skin, and showed a ragged wound from a lightning strike. But Amos didn't choose one tree over another; he let them do the choosing, and obeyed. The spikes wouldn't harm the trees; the bark would grow around them like a man grows round his sorrows. And when the logging companies came to cut them down, one nail after another would break the saws. He'd never been an obedient type, but now he obeyed the trees.

Up a logging road, he followed the ice-brittle path of Runaway Pond leading out of the Bend. He cut across a frozen brook towards the higher grounds beyond Barr Hill, where he pounded nails into Delia's cliffs of conifers. He skied dairy fields black and white with Holstein cows, crows and snow, the massive barns set red against the dearth of colour, their weathercocks stilled to the north. He crossed fields reverting to forests where quick-sprouting pines triumphed over slow-growth oaks, and folk would say time had turned back to the days of primordial woods, but having no memory of the majestic diversity of primordial woods, they'd be wrong. Except in the joists of farmhouses, he himself had never seen the trees of antiquity that had built New England's cities. But somewhere inside his scarred head, Amos saw his fatherless child grown into an old woman: she was walking through a great centurial forest.

A black-capped chickadee made its coy appearance in a poplar, and when its song filled the day and the world entire, Amos stopped to listen. He was grateful that the tits wintered over in the silence left by the Canada geese. He was grateful too for the male cardinal brazen in the dead-white snow, and the woodpecker exposed in the naked oak. The world was uncovered above and covered below, such is the endless contradiction of the place of our births. He smiled as faintly as the dog. The two had been spiking trees all morning, and both of them were hungry. Amos whistled the tit's workaday song, wooing the bird closer, then reached out his hard, massive hand, snatched the delicate bird off its branch and crushed it. Though there wasn't much meat on the tiny creature, he sucked what he could from the bones, and he wished it weren't always the small and powerless that in an instant he and the cold could kill.

He smelled the sweet snow coming down from the north, and the sour wounds from the high Quebec mines, and he heard the thunder of trees in faraway forests being sliced into matchsticks. He turned his skis towards Canada. On the northern edges of Greensboro, he joined up with the remnants of the Bailey-Hazen Road, an old Yankee military road dovetailing in and out of newer roads firmed smooth by the blades of horse sleighs. He flew through the drifts, his dog panting behind him. It was a strong man who could ski all day and be free of doubt, leaving the land the Indians had called Coos, after the pine trees, and that the settlers had called Coos County after the Indians, and that the French renamed *Verts-monts*. He stopped a moment, the way a man does at the altar or on his deathbed, to collect his thoughts. *Do not go beyond the mountains,* said the original people. *Your prayers live within their sight.* Those people were extinct.

"Coos," he said aloud, and the word, sounding like a bird call, made his dog cock its head. Then Amos heard a tree call.

The snow was beginning to fall again. He took off along the road. His clothes were wet with sweat, but he didn't dare slacken his pace and let the frost come in, and he didn't think of sleeping. Man and dog followed the diminishing military road as it turned up the mountain in the night. There was nothing to mark the juncture between Vermont and Canada, just one pine tree after another. The moon was high though the woods were dark. The pines were blackened with winter and twice blackened with night. Now the view from the notch favoured the north, and he could not see home again.

The dog asked, "Where are we going?"

Amos could not answer. His thoughts hadn't caught up with his deeper intentions. He was spiking trees and couldn't say why. Maybe for the past and maybe for the future, or maybe because men's lives were short, stunted things compared to those of white cedars and pines. Brevity should keep men humble, but it didn't. A man grabbed as much as he could in his time and dragged it with him down to hell. Amos couldn't put coal or quartzite back in the ground, he was powerless to undo what was done; but he could spike the trees.

As to Donna, with her black hydra hair and her baby born that day, he knew it somewhere in the tunnel between his scars. He saw something flash into life and fade away almost as quick as it had come. He felt something stir on the wind only to be stilled by that which stirred deeper. He was leaving his legacy in the trees. He was leaving. He was heading north, spiking trees as he went, and there was nothing to be said about it.

The new mother shivered by the cold stove, unwilling to lug more wood from the pile. The baby looked withered and was crying for food again, and Donna's nipples were angry. Her baby sucked as if expecting to be abandoned. Past midnight and her husband hadn't come home, and every minute that he didn't return, Donna grew more furious. She imagined leaving both father and child, pawning her wedding ring and buying a railway ticket to Hollywood – where an agent would pass her his card and say, "You're a dark Mae West. Come up and see me sometime."

She heard the dry moon mock her dreams, and she screamed at the light through the windows. When her shouting made the newborn cry, she said, "Good. If I ain't happy, you ain't." She wanted to run away; she wanted to be happy. But she refused to leave Amos the gift of a baby girl. Being the cause of her sorrows, he should pay for them. He'd never been willing to pay for anything else. How did he expect them to live? She'd exchanged one misery for another by marrying him. Had she risen out of her rotten home, crawled out of that bog, for this?

By morning, Donna was stale with hatred, but she knew what she would do. She threw on a coat and walked out the kitchen door to the dovecote, where she reached for a bird and wrung its neck. There was a flutter of panic amongst the pigeons. One after another, she wrung their necks. Then she gathered all of them up in her apron and brought them inside the house. Removing her coat, she wrapped the dead creatures inside it and went to the tool room and found the hammer. She mashed the doves into her coat like a lunatic magician determined to make them disappear, then strode out into the cold and dumped the coat's contents into the well. She raised the coat against the hard sky to inspect the bloodstains.

Back in the house, the baby, sleeping on the ground by the hearth, woke and screamed as Donna pulled dishes from the cupboard and, with unusual dispassion, threw them against the walls. She overturned a chair, yawned, and overturned another. She packed a sack with her best clothes, then a second with ratty clothes, and she dragged the second sack into the kitchen and spilled its load on the floor. It looked like all hell had broken loose in that kitchen. Pleased, she changed into a pristine white frock and lined her lips with red.

The child had been screaming for close on an hour, but its mother paid it no mind. She sat down to write a note to her husband for the police to find: "Amos, I am taking the baby to where it will be safe, before you hurt the child or me. I have been too afraid to tell you that the baby isn't yours. Forgive me." She imagined her moment of fame in tomorrow's *Bulletin*: "The repentant wife was caught by her husband in the act of writing her confession, whereupon he killed her and dragged her lovely body into the woods, never to be found. The village of Greensboro Bend has long known Amos Cobb as the brute who survived a spike through his skull. Many have suspected that he was not right in the head. Meanwhile, the squalling child was abandoned on the floorboards." The abandoned child squalling on the floorboards, that much at least was true. Still bleeding lightly from the birth, Donna dipped her hand into her crotch and streaked blood across the note.

Lifting a loose plank in the floor, she reached down to find the treasure: pearl earrings sent as a wedding present from Amos's late employer. She'd pawn them with her wedding ring to pay for the train fare west. She'd walk the seven miles to Hardwick station to avoid being spotted at the Bend. The door of the shack she left ajar, and the bloody coat she dropped in a heap on the porch. She offered her child to God's will. Someone would find the infant, alive or dead, the note bloodied, the coat bloodied, the mother removed from the face of the earth, and her husband, if he deigned to come home at all, would hang for murder.

As if nature attended to her will, the snow was falling heavy, and Donna would leave no tracks. Following the vanishing footprints of man and dog, she crossed the field towards the rosehip woods. She turned south where their steps went north, and disappeared.

J ack had business in Berlin and wished to make a holiday of it to escape the Mexican heat, so it was arranged that his nephew should finish the school year in Princeton and then, instead of travelling north to Vermont, join the Shaw family for a visit to the Teutonic lands before settling into his new life in their home in Mexico City.

"You have no grounds to object to a trip to Germany," said Old Mrs Shaw as she puffed out her formidable chest and awaited Everett's concession. Cocktail in hand, he had stammered something about war with Hitler and the Huns and failed to make his point. "I forbid the prejudices of history. Germany is the land of Rilke and Goethe! Heidegger and Nietzsche! And as to the Nazis – you know full well I am not a determinist. War is not inevitable. Furthermore, if it *is*, then German culture is about to vanish like one of Faust's spirits, and Aubrey should go there *now* before it does!"

She thought the sooner he left home, the better. His father's hands trembled, and he stilled them with drinking at any time of the day. Everett could weep suddenly and inexplicably, even in the lecture hall, and there was talk at the university of his taking a forced sabbatical. Old Mrs

Shaw did not have the stamina to raise her grandson single-handedly – over the winter, she'd fallen on an icy sidewalk, and the resulting fracture in her hip and the immobility in the joint made her feel old at last. Berlin or Mexico, anywhere was better than here. A boy, she thought, should never see his father fail.

Everett knocked over the crystal salt shaker; he could not control his hands. The chlorine gas that lingered in his lungs made him cough uncontrollably, as if coughing were a kind of crying. "Jack, damn it, has never been to war! I am the only man in this house who knows what it means to fight!" But that wasn't much of an argument, and history was already forbidden. Everett was weeping, and he could not speak. He wanted to say, as Faust did: *The spirits that I summoned up, I now cannot rid myself of.*

At Pier 88 on the Hudson River, Aubrey waved goodbye to his father. Grandmother had stayed at home, for the same doctor who had once advised her daughter never to marry advised her on account of her hip not to travel, and if she *must* drive to Vermont that summer, which of course she must, she certainly didn't need to drive to New York as well. This much she'd conceded.

Jack and Ethyl Shaw and their three young sons leaned in their whites over the guardrail and, alongside their new ward, waved at the solitary father. Having travelled up from the Gulf to New York City on the SS *Oriente*, they had rendezvoused with the pubescent addition to their family and boarded the SS *Normandie*. The Shaw family surrounded Aubrey. Jack threw a strong arm around his shoulder, mussed his hair and called to Everett – who, over the crowds and the honking car horns couldn't hear a word – "Don't worry, we'll take care of him!"

Father was sobbing. Humiliated, Aubrey squeezed deeper into his uncle's armpit, from which vantage point the view changed: on second inspection, Father was only coughing. Now Aubrey wanted it both ways and felt hurt. His father cried for almost anything, but not for him.

"Goodbye, Uncle Everett!" Aubrey's seven-year-old cousin yelled over the guardrail. "We won't sink and be eaten by sharks! I'll eat the shark before he eats me!" Aged five, six and seven, Jack's feral sons shoved at each other ceaselessly while their Mexican nanny pulled them down from the railing, over which the oldest threatened to topple the youngest into the murky Hudson. The seven-year-old squeezed the six-year-old's hand until the six-year-old screamed.

Aunt Ethyl – wearing long grey gloves in the heat that pointed to the moist stillness in the crook of her elbows – ignored the frenzy around her. But she wasn't an oblivious woman; rather, she was discriminating in her attentions, and with great deliberateness she ignored her children. As she leaned in to Aubrey, noticing his grandmother's mark on him, she took a handkerchief from her snakeskin purse and wiped the old woman's lipstick off his cheek.

The hanky scented with musk, diesel hanging in the salty air, and Uncle Jack's armpit blending men's cologne and dampness in the heat: these were the smells of Aubrey's departure. The ship's horn blasted and the SS *Normandie* pulled away from the dock. Short as he was, Uncle Jack was life-sized, while down on dry land Father had become a toy.

Father, it seemed, was moving farther and farther away. Aubrey reached for the camera that hung around his neck

– the Retina II was a parting gift – and instead of waving goodbye, snapped a picture of his fading parent, shrunken down to an indistinct blur in the mass. As the liner chugged out of the bay, the skyscrapers became a smudge on carbon paper. Like a man living backwards through his life, as if childhood were giving way to infancy and infancy to birth, Aubrey saw the shores of America vanish into nothing.

"I'm sick of ships," said the six-year-old.

"Rough luck," said Jack jovially. The crowds were moving towards deck chairs or shuffleboards, but the Shaw family lingered by the railing.

"One more week and you'll be on a train, *Señorito*," said the helpful nanny. "You like trains."

"I hate trains," said the oldest.

"I hate trains too," said the youngest.

"I hate trains more than you do," said the oldest.

Aubrey wondered if there were indeed sharks in these waters. Or dolphins, who were said to be not only more intelligent but more civilized than man. Or nothing except jellyfish, passive drifters who had no sense organs and no brain.

With a gesture of friendly ownership, his uncle mussed his hair again. With his mother's brother to protect him, Aubrey felt the world was solid, despite the water beneath. Uncle Jack was laughing at something, so Aubrey laughed too. His breath shortened and caught beneath his collarbone as the harbour opened onto the Atlantic and the sea wind flattened his ears.

Aunt Ethyl kissed him on the cheek to welcome him once more and plant her own red lipstick where his grandmother's had been. Finished with the cheery charade of the embarkation, she now turned a rigid back on her family. Her negligence of her children was benign, but the silence towards her husband was killing. Their problems were perennial: having long bouts of dormancy, which could be misread as forgiveness, they'd invariably reappear. And so they had, somewhere near the Gulf of Mexico on the SS *Oriente*. As his aunt walked away, Aubrey looked to his uncle for an explanation but saw none. Uncle Jack, like a mountaineer, was sucking in the fresh air.

"Is she all right? Is she seasick? Is she seasick so soon?" asked Aubrey, unaware he was, already, providing excuses for his aunt.

Jack laughed. "Maybe. You never know."

Which of the women on the *Oriente* had upset her, Jack didn't know. There were always other women, always had been. If Darwin was correct, a man was a disseminator of his seed, while a woman was a hoarder of her eggs, making the tension between the sexes inevitable. He hadn't seen his wife naked in over a week: she'd kept herself covered, and she'd insisted on separate rooms on the *Normandie*. Now, with a bang, a heavy door closed behind her, and Ethyl forsook her family on the deck.

Some days later, lolling by the *Normandie*'s indoor swimming pool, Jack told himself that his wife's unmarital behaviour was the reason he was more appreciative than usual of the Mexican nanny in her modest black bathing costume. Aubrey, who lolled beside him, followed his uncle's gaze to the mole on the nanny's plump left thigh. Her left leg was plumper than her right, but both thighs jiggled like pudding as she rushed around the edge of the pool, desperate to stop her wards from drowning each other. Aubrey looked from the nanny's thighs to his uncle's smile. In swimming shorts without a tank, his hairy legs dangling in the pool, Jack laid his back across the tiled floor. Anyone could tell he'd been lifting weights: the sweat remained, and his biceps glistened.

On the far side of the pool was the gymnasium. There a dark man in a turban conducted a group of pear-shaped women in the swinging of Indian clubs, and the wooden pins swirled haphazardly. An Englishman, with great aplomb, posted an electric riding horse. And when a French Olympic contender ascended the horizontal bars, even the swimmers in the pool stopped to admire his simian swinging, and someone hummed the *Marseillaise*.

Wherever first-class passengers wandered, waiters followed close behind. White tails and bow ties hurried through the doors to the adjacent smoking room, and the whiff of expensive cigars filled the sweaty gym. While smoke seeped from the inner chambers, sunlight poured through the outer: floor-to-ceiling windows graced the Turkish-tiled walls. Outside, a few intrepid shuffleboard players battled the cold wind, while the sun inside was warm and soporific.

Jack ordered a Bloody Mary for himself and a Black Cow for Aubrey. Then he leaned on his elbows, dropped back his head and spoke to the man behind him: the millionaire Irénée du Pont, a man who hated his womanly name and liked to sunbathe in any available rays. In the light of the long windows, he'd slathered coconut oil on his hot hairless chest. His overtanned skin resembled nitrocellulose-based artificial leather, one of the few non-explosive substances DuPont Chemical produced. Jack and he knew each other both personally and professionally, their companies having collaborated to form Ethyl Incorporated, developing tetraethyl lead additive for gasoline. "Funny, my wife's named Ethyl," Jack had said upon their first acquaintance.

Though it was only eleven in the morning, Irénée drank gin and tonic, making a habit of the English cocktail not for the medical benefit of avoiding malaria but to ease the nocturnal leg cramps that had begun on his sixtieth birthday. Between cramps and a failing bladder, he often rose at night. His age offended his own sensibilities – the skin on his neck had puckered like cellophane, and though his blonde hair refused to grey, like a tatty carpet it had faded and thinned around the edges. He took his distaste for his appearance out on others. He disliked aging in old men as much as he disliked weakness in young men. With close-set eyes, he observed the scrawny arms and shallow chest of the boy, who was sucking on a straw. (The root beer and ice cream concoction was one of many wonderful things that, in his previous life, Aubrey had never had the chance to try.)

"Twenty laps!" Jack cried, with an energetic burst that defied the languid atmosphere. Jumping to his feet and snatching the glass from his nephew's hand, he scooped Aubrey up and threw him into the pool. "Or no *crème brulée* tonight!" These last words were lost as Aubrey cannonballed down and sputtered up to the surface, pathetically stirring the water. "Not the breaststroke!" Jack called to him. "The crawl!"

"Keep coaching," droned Irénée. "He'll toughen up one day if his stock is good."

Jack looked across the pool at the three brutish children he himself had spawned and the fleshy Mexican nanny grappling with the brood.

"Is it?" asked Irénée impatiently, as if the question had been implied and only Jack's distracted interest in the nanny's thighs had made him spell it out.

"His stock? God, I don't know," said Jack. "It depends on how you look at it. My sister was a beautiful invalid who was the light of everyone's life and then died young. And Aubrey's father is a handsome professor who's killing himself and everyone around him with grief."

Irénée didn't like intellectuals, perhaps because in the business of chemistry and materials science he was beholden to them, or because he himself was too intelligent to enslave himself to his mind. "Is his father a Jew or a communist?"

Jack observed that his friend had had too many gin and tonics.

Irénée was aware of being irritable, but it was only, he believed, on account of being hot, not drunk. Prying an ice cube out of his glass, he ran it across his navel till it melted in the little wrinkled hole.

"That's one lap," called Jack as the boy swam by.

"It's two," Aubrey panted. His eyes stung, which was a new sensation, for his father had never allowed him to swim in chlorinated pools.

"Don't tread water," called Jack. "Keep swimming."

Irénée asked Jack, "What do you press?"

"One eighty."

"I pressed more when I was your age. That blonde by the window is looking at you as if she wanted to drink you with a cherry!"

Jack looked over to see a yellow-haired woman leaning against the blue-tiled walls. She had been reading in the brilliant light of the windows: *Ocean Records: A Pocket Handbook for Travelers.* She had been idly comparing the descriptions of cirrus, cirrostratus and cirrocumulus clouds to the milky sky outside, but now she was caught with her eyes above her book, staring at Jack in his swim trunks. Like the sun, he smiled directly upon her, and she reddened and returned to her reading.

"Who is she?" asked Irénée.

"No idea. Pretty, though."

Irénée was feeling testy. "Why the hell does a man who never needs to lift anything heavier than a phone to his ear lift weights to fill out his shirtsleeves?"

"Obviously, because women like it," laughed Jack, as he watched for the blonde to look up from her book again.

"And why the hell is a woman attracted to a trait which in the Stone Age might have implied prowess, but in the twentieth century is more likely to indicate brute delinquency?"

"I don't know," said Jack.

"Then think. Your nephew is practising swimming; his uncle can practise thinking."

Jack found the chemical man's saturnine disposition amusing, but it was unwise to cross Irénée by not taking him seriously. Rumour had it that, under the guise of the American Liberty League, nicknamed the Cellophane League – such were its suspected connections to DuPont Chemical – Irénée's lackeys were nightly exterminating those who did not take them seriously enough. In General Motors towns in Michigan and Ohio – Irénée being a controlling shareholder of GM – car caravans of hooded white men tore through Negro and Jewish neighbourhoods, bombing union halls, burning houses and torturing and killing difficult employees.

Aubrey swam by and called to his uncle, "That's three, not two."

"Two," called Jack. "Why aren't you a better swimmer?" He was further amused by his nephew's athletic incompetence, which the boy made up for with intelligence and which stood as a refreshing contrast to his own sons. "Didn't you swim in Vermont?"

"A bit," said Aubrey, "but the lake was cold."

His nephew having gone up the deep end, Jack flexed his arm and answered Irénée's question. "A girl likes a good bicep because it reminds her of her inherent vulnerability."

Now the door swung open to the cool outside, and a wind-blown woman with a tennis racquet tumbled in, her long red hair licking around her neck. The gust blew a doily off a drink stand, and a waiter raced along the tiles to catch it before it sailed into the pool.

Irénée turned his nose up and sniffed the saline air, which reminded him that a little Indian man in rags had marched on the salt mines of Gujarat. Suddenly he was more irritated than before. Turning over onto his leathery stomach, he breathed through the holes in the wicker chaise.

Jack, swirling his straw lightly in his drink, watched his nephew swimming painfully and dutifully up and down the pool. His own children were thuggish things, heaving and churning in the water. Though the voluptuous nanny wore a traumatized face, he enjoyed the way her thighs jiggled as she ran, their opulence like ripe plums swaying. Life, Jack thought, is a charm. But now his nephew was choking on a large mouthful of chlorinated water.

The incident at the pool brought Ethyl out of her room. Entering Aubrey's cabin just as Jack was leaving, she squeezed past him in the doorway, navigating the small entrance so that her flesh didn't touch his. Aubrey watched them mindlessly, for though he lay tucked up in bed, he remained in the pool. *Water is one moment something you swim in, the next something you drown in. Water holds you.* At swimming lessons at the public beach, on the windy side of Caspian Lake, he'd learned to let it hold him. *Then, once you trust it, the water pulls you down.* Aubrey was still in shock, which, being a place he'd been once before, was almost comforting. *You float away in it.*

"I wasn't drowning," he said.

Ethyl, knowing the difference between lying and self-deception, asked, "What did it feel like, not drowning?"

"I don't know. First it was fast, then it was slow. I remember thinking the swimming pool has no bottom and jellyfish have no brains. But I wasn't drowning."

Ethyl shrugged and sat on the end of the bed to pick over the room-service menu. She suspected that all her nephew actually remembered was fear and water. She let the subject drop.

His uncle had forbidden him to rise for the rest of the day, but having already been confined to bed for an hour, after a *crème brulée,* Aubrey was bored.

"Can I get up?"

"You have to stay warm," said Ethyl. "Are you wearing your pyjama trousers under those blankets?"

"Yes, of course. Can I get up?"

"No, it's cold. Whatever shall we do?"

There being nothing to do, he and his aunt thumbed through his photo album.

"So much for the Christmas tree," she said.

In the picture it was lying sadly on the side of the road, the tip cut off by the photograph's white border. The family had left it up till the needles dried, fell on the rug and became a fire hazard, well past Twelfth Night, which the maids said brought bad luck.

"Uncle Jack lugged it out to the street to get rid of it, remember?" Aubrey asked his aunt. He hoped that, reminded of her husband's strength, she'd forgive Uncle Jack for whatever there was to forgive. It was a childishly simplistic hope, but he wanted a happy family, and since Christmas he'd pretended that come summer he'd have one. Away from his father and the year's horrors, he felt, in the absence of pain, the need for something to replace it. He needed a happy family.

"My father said this picture is an example of perspective, because the tree looks smaller than the car going by, though in reality it wasn't. It was huge. Uncle Jack is the best, don't you think?"

"The best at what?" she asked.

She had a way of twisting words back on themselves and turning his thoughts into knots she loosened with her fingers. Instead of answering, he asked, "Does Uncle Jack work with Mr du Pont?"

"More or less," she said.

"What does Mr du Pont do?"

"Everything. He makes gunpowder, newspapers, cellophane, rayon. My dress is made of rayon, so I suppose you could say that Mr du Pont gets me dressed."

The thought of an old, wrinkly man, with hands like burnt plastic, easing his aunt's dress over her hips, the straps snagging on the hooks of her lacy brassiere, made Aubrey queasy. The sugar in his *crème brulée* had given him a headache. Feeling a wave of possessiveness, he touched her silk-like gown.

Ethyl smoothed the material over her lap and observed in a soft voice, "It doesn't wrinkle." Then her mouth hardened, and she added, "He also makes synthetic rubber for tires, and lead-tetraethyl fuel for planes, but *no one* could say that DuPont Chemical doesn't serve American interests."

"And what does Uncle Jack do?" he asked, unsettled by the ugly tone that had entered her pretty voice but still wanting to talk about his uncle. He said his uncle's name the way another boy might say a football star's, absorbing some of its prowess.

Ethyl tightened a bobby pin into her coronet bun. "You have the evidence there," she said, pulling the hairpin out again and pointing it at the photograph. "He lugs things out to the street to get rid of them." Then she said she should get going, "because there's so much to do on a boat." She touched his lips, which she claimed looked blue, and said, "I'll bring you the extra blanket from the closet."

When she opened the closet door, Ethyl gasped. She didn't scream; after all, she'd seen the skull at Christmas, having got down on her hands and knees to look at it under the bed. "Oh, Aubrey," she said, and almost laughed, "you brought Amos! You'll never get him past customs. You should throw him overboard."

"I can't do that."

"No, I suppose you can't."

Ethyl understood. She respected Amos – the concept of him, anyway, the man with a spike through his head who'd carried the dead mother down the stairs – and even though the skull wasn't actually his, she respected it as if it were.

Aubrey felt scared to tell her the news. He said, "Aunt Ethyl?"

"Yes?"

"Amos killed his wife and left his baby to die."

"Good God! Really?"

"The paper said he did, but I don't know how anyone can be so sure."

The thought of it upset him: the thought that a man who looked like a murderer maybe therefore was one, maybe wasn't; that maybe good and evil were separate and discernible, maybe not. Even Grandmother didn't know. Even Grandmother had said, after reading the *Hardwick Bulletin* (its circulation entirely local, except the family received it in Princeton), "I prefer to stick to the facts, yet there are always so few of them. I don't know what to believe, so I choose to believe nothing at all."

"There wasn't even a dead body except the baby's," Aubrey told his aunt, "and babies die sometimes just from being born."

"Everyone dies from being born," said Ethyl, taking the blanket from the shelf and closing the closet door.

"Just because he looks like a murderer doesn't mean –"

"No, it doesn't."

"Things look different than they are." He knew this from photography, from the tree seeming smaller than the car. Also from squinting into the sun until he saw suns everywhere. And he would have sworn, while he brushed his dead mother's hair that night, that he saw her breathing.

"Don't doubt it," Ethyl said firmly. "Murderers don't look like murderers." She tucked the blanket tightly under the mattress. Drawing from her purse a postcard of the SS *Normandie,* she laid it by the bedside table. "If you write to your grandmother," she said, appearing to change the subject, "just tell her you swam five laps today and met the richest man in the world."

"Is Mr du Pont really that rich?"

"Do you think your uncle is easily intimidated?"

"No, of course not."

"Even Jack stood dumbstruck in the halls of Xanadu."

She let the image of her cowed husband hover silently in the room, then leaned over her nephew, placed her cool hand on his clammy forehead and said, as if she were telling a ghost story, "Down the monumental hallway, mirrors reflected mirrors, creating an infinite nesting of enormous rooms. At the end of it all was a fireplace as massive as the mouth of the Mulu cave. Have you heard of the Mulu cave? In its darkness, a hundred thousand bats feed on a million cockroaches. So in the mirrored hall, the old, withered man, with Jack standing beside him, was replicated in superabundance. And in the southern breeze – Mr du Pont's estate is in Cuba – the flag on the ninth hole of the private golf course nodded like a head saying, 'Yes, yes, yes,' while a cockatoo shrieked in its golden cage and your uncle became friends with the richest man on earth." She kissed him goodbye near his lips, then asked ambiguously as she left the room, "Would you know it if you drowned?"

The sea air, the sun through the porthole, the exhausted descent from the heights of drowning, his confinement to bed, all this made Aubrey sleep through the rest of the afternoon. That night, he lay staring at the ceiling, thinking about his family. Children didn't have lives of their own, just family. He recalled the starchy smell of his grandmother. He imagined his father sailing away down a lake that seemed unending. He thought of his aunt's teasing breasts, her sentences like the hitch knots Amos had taught him to tie around his anchor. He threw the extra blanket off the bed; he was boiling up. His mother ... but when Aubrey attempted to conjure his mother, he couldn't. Though she appeared in dreams fully embodied, his awake mind punished him with her absence. To see her, he thought of his uncle, but though Jack had Mother's face, it was somehow nothing like it.

Aubrey's cabin was adjacent to his three cousins' on one side and his uncle's on the other, while his aunt slept far away down another passageway. It was past 2 a.m., and even Jack would be asleep. But Aubrey hadn't heard him snoring. There was only the noise of engines thrumming beneath the floor. Suddenly, the clatter of heels in the corridor, muffled by the runner underfoot. He heard the door to his uncle's cabin open, close and latch. And now the hum of voices. A man's voice: Jack's. And a woman's voice, which was not Aunt Ethyl's. Not the nanny's, either.

A Vermont accent? Don't be silly, he told himself as he leaned over and switched on the bedside lamp, as if the light would help him to hear better. He was thirteen years old, he reminded himself. How awful. He was thirteen years old. *You know where nature hides things.*

Aubrey shot up in bed. Yes, he thought, he did.

He could have stayed in bed and trusted what wasn't true, believed the voice was Aunt Ethyl's even when he knew it wasn't. That's what his grandmother would have advised: she'd have called that good behaviour. But he didn't feel good or well behaved. He put on his slippers, checked the film in his camera and stole from the cabin into the empty passageway. At his uncle's door, he got down on his knees like a boy at confession and looked through the keyhole.

A blonde woman dropped onto Jack's bed, shot glass in her hand. Aubrey studied her through the peephole as the woman had studied the clouds through the windows that morning. Her smoke and perfume siphoned themselves through the keyhole into his lungs. As he covered his mouth to stop from coughing, he heard his uncle's laugh and saw a strong hand seize the woman's wrist.

"Oh, God!" she cried.

Jack muzzled her with his other hand, and her mouth opened and kissed it. Jack's foot appeared. It was raised against the headboard. There was silence as Jack untied his shoes. He unbuttoned his fly and disappeared from view, probably to place his trousers on the trouser press. He reappeared, naked, on the bed, seated with his back to the board, his bent knees fringed by the hair on his chest, his full scrotum resting on the bedsheet. He was watching the woman casually, unceremoniously, expectantly, as he flipped his hardening penis from side to side and it smacked against his thighs. "I'm waiting," he said.

Aubrey heard, "Then take down my zipper."

The blonde woman moved into sight again. Jack helped her out of a black dress, which sank to the floor and lay like another porthole looking downward on a sunken night. When Jack pulled her slip over her head, Aubrey heard him say, "Skin the rabbit."

She stood, naked, at the head of the bed, a small gap between her inner thighs, just enough for Jack to slip his hand through. Moaning with what might have been seasickness had it not been pleasure, she swung her hips back and forth. The swinging became writhing. Her white buttocks descended like lazy moons over the horizon.

The view through the keyhole was narrow, and body parts passed in and out of view. Though Aubrey's own body didn't budge, like bore worms, the fingers on his left hand sought a way into the woodwork, as if they might suck out its marrow. Finally, he wrenched away his gaze, and blindly he lifted his camera to the keyhole. The index finger of his right hand twitched on the shutter button, his thumb scrolled over the lever to advance the film and he heard the hard cocking, again and again, of the shutter and the shallow abrasion of his own breath.

"Boy!" Aubrey was roused from his absorption by a voice shouting down the passageway. It was Irénée du Pont.

Aubrey hurried to his own cabin door but found it wouldn't open. In his panic, he did not remember what he had done with the key. He ran down the passageway, up another, through a corridor until it dead-ended, and heaved open an iron hatch. He stepped through, and the watertight entrance sealed behind him.

Aubrey stood at the top of a series of platforms that led to steel-grate catwalks that led to ladders, turning and diminishing into the substratum of the hull. Electric generators lit strings of caged lamps, and flies and midges, sucked off the Hudson River and carried out to sea, beat against the bulbs. The central turbine towered seventeen feet high, and reciprocating engines drove the propellers at a hundred and sixty-five revolutions a minute. Speed: twenty-nine knots. The air pulsed with thermal power, while massive ventilation fans ineffectively cut the overwhelming heat. Twenty-nine boilers towered identically three stories high. One hundred and fifty-nine furnaces stewed the waters, and in a single night six hundred and fifty tons of coal alchemized into fire and fire into steam and steam into maximum thrust. Under the light of exposed bulbs, night was minced into a fine dust, and sweat was the fixative that held it to men – hundreds of men, shirtless, soot-darkened workers, their wet backs glowing in the light of the furnaces like blackened mirrors in which to observe the sordid source of things. What were they under the coal dust? Had they been gleaned from the pits and adits that spewed forth lumpers in upper New York? Or incubated in the Brazilian diamond mines, where slavery had ended only in name? Many of them were as big as Amos.

Aubrey didn't have long to wonder, because the iron door behind him opened again, and now du Pont stepped through. The two were dressed similarly: for bed, in silk pyjamas. "Well, boy," du Pont said, as if he disdained to use Aubrey's name, "go down."

His heart pounding in his ears, he obeyed. They descended as if into the Escher print that hung over Father's desk.

At the bottom, in a filthy corner, du Pont found a metal chair. He pulled a handkerchief from his dressing-gown pocket and wiped away the soot, then sat and smoothed his pyjamas. From another pocket, he took a thin cigar and a silver lighter. When the lighter failed to ignite, a giant emerged from the shadows and lit the cigarillo with a match. Du Pont smoked, but not in silence, for the iron hull roared with the systematic conversion of coal into power.

"How old are you, boy?" His voice was wiry and sharp.

"Thirteen."

"Speak up."

Aubrey's voice had shrunken. His pyjamas stuck to his skin. He was damp throughout, but his mouth was dry.

"Thirteen," he said again, and wanted to disappear.

"The age the Buddhists consider perfect, and the avatars appear." Du Pont's tone lacked irony.

"I don't feel perfect," Aubrey muttered, and, fearing he'd be ordered to say it again, he said it again, loudly. It sounded like the truest thing he'd ever said. He had the impulse to chew on his pyjama sleeve, which he hadn't done since he was ten years old.

"So, how does your father compare to your Uncle Jack?"

It was a strange question, but everything down here was aberrant.

"He doesn't. They're too different."

"They're not apples and oranges; they are members of the same species and therefore can be compared. Tell me the difference between a lump of coal and a man."

Aubrey looked up from the iron bolt in the steel floor into whose denseness he was trying to disappear. His pink freckled skin had gone blotchy with heat, and a dusting of coal lined his eyes. He said, "Men are living."

"What does that mean, *living*?"

"They do things."

"So does coal. Coal is moving us across the sea."

"They do them by themselves."

"Over a million microbes live in your stomach, and without them you would do nothing! Men do not do things by themselves! The difference between coal and men is that coal's behaviour is consistent!"

Irénée detested wrong answers. His throat swelled and purpled, but with a great execution of will he brought himself under control. He observed his own breed of charity: that he bothered with the boy at all, that he took the time to care, that he'd followed him when he ran was more than most men would do. It was, in fact, fatherly. If children thought parents were there to protect them, they were wrong. Parents were there to initiate them.

"I have no qualms about disciplining another man's son," said du Pont. "Tonight I caught a boy taking filthy pictures through a keyhole. What do you think I should do?"

Aubrey stared at the bolt in the floor and whimpered, "Nothing."

"What?!"

His girlish voice cracked as he repeated, "Nothing."

"You defined a man as a thing that *does* something: you are therefore inconsistent. Do you believe in hell?"

Aubrey thought of his grandmother. He longed to lay his head in her atheistic lap. "I'm not a Christian," he said.

"Did I ask you if you believe in the Christian hell? The Christian hell is a fairy tale, but the Buddhist hells are real because people aren't sent there, they're born there. There are hot hells and there are cold hells. Do you know what my favourite hell is? It's called the Resurrection, where the ground is forged out of molten iron and a person arrives fully grown and sick with fear, his fear giving birth to demons the way filth is said to give birth to flies. His tormentors rush upon him with iron claws and tear him to pieces, but at the moment of death he is restored to health, and from his fear his tormentors rise again, attack him and tear him to pieces. At death again, he is restored to health, and racked with fear again. But it doesn't last forever. Life in the Resurrection is only one hundred and sixty-two times ten to the tenth years long." Du Pont drew sourly on his cigar and observed the vapours. "Answer me," he said.

Aubrey, confused as to what the question was, tried to perform the arithmetic and failed. Watching the firelight flash across the naked back of a monstrous man who stoked the coals, he blurted out, "There was a time before iron; then there must have been a time before hell."

It was just a hope.

Du Pont digested the answer: the boy was impressive in a weak sort of way. A skilful hand could drum out the weakness. Du Pont stretched out his arms with their slack, tan skin, and multiple shadows emerged like suckers across the walls. He said, "Unfortunately for you, those days are long gone. Give me your camera, boy."

Lifting it off of his neck, Aubrey felt completely exposed. His fear was in full view.

"Smile," du Pont said. There was only one shot left. As he took the picture, the shutter was hushed by the bull-roar of the dungeon. Du Pont laid the camera down in his lap. Answering his own original question, he said, "Your uncle knows how to be a man."

Aubrey's sopping pyjamas clung to his nipples and stomach and penis, but his mouth was dried closed. His eye twitched, and dirty sweat slipped down his nose. He looked towards the exit.

"Look at me!"

Aubrey obeyed.

"You think you're a man because you can take a picture of another man screwing a slut?" said du Pont. "A man is only as good as what he's fit for, and if he's fit only to be another man's dog, don't blame the man who puts the collar on him." He gave a proprietary wave over flesh and iron in the torrid hull. "You're not watching this world go by, boy, you're eating it and shitting it out every time you order your damn *crème brulée*. Do you know that?"

Aubrey was silent.

"Do you know that?!"

"Yes." It seemed to be the right answer.

Du Pont sucked on his cigar as if it were a snorkel; his crimson face faded to pink; his merciless lips grinned. "Your horny uncle thinks you're pretty smart. Are you?"

Aubrey tried again. "Yes."

"You are?"

"No."

"Yes or no?"

"I don't know."

It was the right answer at last, because it was a humiliating one.

"I hear your father is so smart he's killing himself. He thinks because your mother died, something awful happened and something is wrong with the world." Feeling parental, he rolled his cigar between his fingers, enjoying its perfect blend of moist and dry. "You can tell him for me: 'People die all the time. That's what people are.'"

Irénée was pleased with these last words. He'd given the boy something he wouldn't forget. Children were, as they said, the future, and for this, for a moment, he liked the boy, though his likes and dislikes were interchangeable and – he agreed with the Buddhists – the cause of all suffering. He rewound and extracted the film and put it in his pyjama pocket.

"Smarts won't get you laid, boy. And despite whatever intellectual crap your father told you, they won't make you rich or happy. Being you, not them," he waved at the coal-black men, "that's happiness. If you don't enjoy it, you don't deserve it. And if you have to kill for it, you'd better learn right now that everything here is designed to die for men – beasts, trees, other men, even the dead are dug up so we can kill them all over again." He paused, looking for understanding in the child's eyes, but it wasn't there. Children were smart one moment, stupid as cows the next. "You're not so smart," du Pont sneered. "I'm talking about coal and oil, which are the residue of dead things."

Against his will, Aubrey started to cry. He tried to tell himself it wasn't fear or hopelessness or the mention of his mother, just the sting of coal dust in his eyes.

"The innocence of children is a sham!" du Pont shouted, angry at the sight of tears, then angry at having been roused to anger. "You've been killing since the day your pretty mother shoved you out. Get used to it! Wipe your eyes, boy! Pay attention! You're afraid I'm going to punish you?" He laughed hoarsely and felt his age. "Look around you! You're not one of these poor brutes; you're one of us. You don't get punished. But you're always on the verge of pissing in your pants, aren't you?" The boy wasn't worth the effort. Irénée adjusted his dressing gown and said, "Dismissed."

Aubrey climbed the ladders alone. The sweat had cooked onto his face. He stumbled back along the velvet runner. His wet pyjamas clinging to him, he could feel his room key digging into his chest. Once inside his cabin, he locked the door again and leaned his forehead against the cold black porthole. Though he had been released, he waited all night for sleep. A slim sheen of light from drunken nocturnes in dining rooms and smoking rooms glanced off the waters. Light bled into the ocean and illuminated both its natural and unnatural waves.

The next day in the dining hall, to Aubrey's surprise, Aunt Ethyl reappeared at dinner on her husband's arm, her fingers lying slack on the white cuff that edged beneath his black tuxedo. Her neck looked longer than usual, her eyes tight and possessive. The handsome and seemingly happy couple passed last night's blonde sitting amongst a group of fair-haired passengers. Jack nodded to her, but she didn't look up.

When Mr du Pont joined the family for dinner, Aubrey nudged closer to his uncle, where he could smell Jack's cologne and hear the ticking of his silver wristwatch. In his uncle's proximity he felt his own right to exist. He followed Jack's eyes back to the blonde and then to Aunt Ethyl's breasts. He obeyed his uncle's wishes and ate oysters instead of lobster. He obeyed his aunt when she told him to try a bite of her beef tartare.

Their marriage was as changeable as mid-Atlantic weather. The wind had calmed in the last two days, and the liner ploughed through the doldrums. Then, suddenly, the wind returned.

Over just a few days, Aunt Ethyl had come to rely on Aubrey as her witness. He was breakfasting with them in his uncle's cabin while the younger boys ate somewhere else with their nanny, when his aunt let it be known she was irritated with her husband again.

"I don't actually want to go to Germany," she said as she cut her sausage. "I don't like Adolf Hitler. He became a vegetarian only after he killed his niece."

"You don't know that he killed his niece," said Jack, enjoying the sauerkraut, which acidified his eggs. "The newspapers said it was suicide."

"The last time we ate with him it was awful," she said. "He gave the most gruesome details about the meat he served us at dinner. Imagine, Aubrey! Hundreds of bulls emptying their bowels in terror while waiting in the *disassembly* line to have their throats cut, their guts pulled out and their carcasses inflated by a blowpipe. Pass the coffee. Did you know that the slaughterhouse gave Henry Ford the inspiration for the assembly line? I don't like him, either."

"Animals don't feel fear," said Jack.

"Who told you that? An animal?" She glared at him. "When I couldn't eat another bite, Mr Hitler actually said to me, 'That shows how cowardly people are. They can't face doing horrible things themselves, but they enjoy the benefits of them without a pang.'"

"And you don't think that's true?" asked Jack, winking at Aubrey.

He joined the conversation: "Animals can't imagine the future, so how could they feel fear?"

"Pass me my cigarette case, Aubrey." Ethyl did not want him to enter the argument, only to attend it. She withdrew from the case a lean cigarette with an already reddened tip, and her husband offered his lighter. When she bent over the table towards it, the opening in her kimono spread.

After a cigarette and coffee, Ethyl felt somewhat more friendly. She leaned back in her chair and blew three perfect smoke rings that drifted across the table towards her nephew.

"You know, Aubrey," she spoke through the last ring, "you don't look like your mother or your father. Some people might say you do, but I don't think so."

"Who do I look like?"

She shrugged. "Like no one."

"You look like Marlene Dietrich," Aubrey said.

"I look more like Loretta Young."

The two of them had been talking about film stars for days: in Berlin, they would be staying at the Hotel Bristol, where all the great stars had stayed. Aunt Ethyl had explained, however, that Aubrey shouldn't get his hopes up. "No stars will be there now," she'd said, "because most of them are Jewish. But you know, Germany's first car show was held in the lobby. Maybe Henry Ford's still wandering around."

"You look more like Jean Harlow," said Aubrey.

Jack, tackling his sausage, observed to his nephew, "You're in your aunt's thrall."

Ethyl opened her mouth as if to protest, but instead she blew a smoke ring.

Aubrey, embarrassed by the conversation, read aloud from his guidebook on Germany. "'*Ignis fatuus* once plagued the marshes of Berlin, and peasants mistook this natural phenomenon for ghosts, though in fact the bursts of fluorescent light are caused by the spontaneous combustion of gases from rotting matter.' Can we see Moses Mendelssohn's grave?"

"Why should we?" Aunt Ethyl asked. "His music is undanceable." Then, turning to her husband, she reminded him, "You promised to take me dancing tonight. Don't forget."

"Not the composer," said Aubrey. "Moses Mendelssohn was the composer's father. The Jews call him the second Moses because ..." but though he flipped through the guidebook, he was unable to find the reason.

"Your uncle's promised to take me dancing in the ballroom," Ethyl said, glancing doubtfully at Jack.

To prove to his uncle that he was in no one's thrall, Aubrey ignored his aunt. "We should also see the giant concrete mushroom. They've built it to test the earth's strength before they make the Volkshalle, which is nicknamed the Monster Building. It says here it will hold so many people that their breath will condense on the dome and fall as rain. Is that possible?"

"Anything's possible," Jack said. "Excited?"

Yes, Aubrey was excited. Germany had made the front page of *The New York Times* almost every day this year. Of course he was excited.

"And the eagle," said Aubrey. "I want to see the eagle." Now he turned to his aunt, unable to ignore her any longer. "Amos used to say that an eagle's eyes are almost as large as a human's, but four times as powerful. It can see a rabbit moving a mile away."

"You can't miss the eagle," his uncle said, enjoying his nephew's enthusiasm. "It's everywhere. It's as common as the eagle on the dollar bill. Who's Amos?"

"Just someone I used to know."

Aubrey read on through the guidebook. He read how the Jews in the graveyard in Weissensee were buried in identical shrouds, because death was meant to reveal the equality of men.

Jack smiled at his wife and said, "Of course we're going dancing."

That evening, when Aunt Ethyl knocked on his bathroom door, Aubrey was pointing his camera at the mirrors: there were three of them, one above and one on either side of the sink. He was attempting to photograph himself photographing himself in infinite regress. Before opening the door, he sat his camera on the edge of the bathtub behind the shower curtain and flushed the already empty toilet.

"Your uncle's disappeared again," she said, leaning against the threshold. She was palming an icy cocktail, her fingernails painted red. "You shouldn't leave your cabin door unlocked. Who knows who might wander in and steal *you* away?"

"Uncle Jack didn't say where he was going?"

She sipped her drink and shrugged. "It's a boat. Maybe the sirens got him."

Stepping into the bathroom beside him, she said, "You're a messy boy," and with the bell sleeve of her evening gown rubbed the smudges off the mirror. Sliding her fingers under his belt, she said to him, "Your uncle was supposed to dance with me. Won't you dance with me?"

Ethyl led him down to the ballroom and taught him to dance the Charleston. "Don't worry about getting me wet," she said when his hands began to sweat.

She led him in a merry dance – that's what Grandmother would have called it. They were whirling and stumbling about the room, the soles of his shoes scuffing along the floor. Her proximity swallowed him up. He could do little more than concentrate on putting one foot in front of or behind or next to the other.

"What does Uncle Jack *really* do?" he asked when he'd learned the steps well enough to attempt to do two things at once.

"I told you, whatever is needed. Pay attention."

"Why is he visiting Germany?"

"There's a reason they call it the Fatherland."

"Will he meet with Mr Hitler?"

"I won't eat another Bavarian soufflé!"

"Why is he taking us to Poland too?"

"Because Germans have methods of dealing with problems that Jack thinks …"

When her voice trailed off, Aubrey was reminded of his mother, who often hadn't finished her sentences. Without noticing it, he held his aunt's hands more tightly and gave up the space between them, as if he were afraid she might die.

"What kind of methods?" he persisted. He was whispering in her ear.

"I haven't the slightest idea."

"You don't?"

"Oh, Aubrey, you dear sweet boy, you know I can't bear too much reality!" She pulled her hands away from him and threw them up in apparent frustration, but she had only transitioned into demonstrating how to dance the jitterbug. "Put your hands behind your head and wave them about like this!"

As they disembarked from the ship, he noticed the cars: even the taxis were Mercedes-Benzes. Unaccustomed to cobbled roads, Aubrey tripped again and again as they walked from the dock to the taxi rank. The family – seven of them, and so much luggage – took two cabs to the train station, where they boarded a train to Berlin.

Berlin was a vibrant ruin of reconstruction. Wrecking balls left wallpaper hanging from the ribcages of middle-class living rooms, while new enclosures arose in the angular shapes of triumph – what the guidebook called "severe deco" and "decadent baroque." Forsaking degradable modern materials, Nazi architecture was an aesthetic of absolutism, constructed in marble and granite, designed for ruin value in a far-off mythical future. Hitler's scaffolded chancellery stood in the cityscape like a skeletal behemoth. The Brandenburg Gate, once a sign of eighteenth-century peace, was now the entrance to Hitler's new world.

The Hotel Bristol proved to be a stone's throw from everything. Wielding his camera, Aubrey took pleasure in being a tourist. Because everyone in uniform resembled each other, he appeared to shoot the same man again and again, or rather two men: Waffen SS, who were armed with pistols, allowing them to kill at an intimate range, and the standard military, who carried rifles.

He had hoped to see Adolf Hitler, but apparently Hitler didn't like children. Aunt Ethyl said he didn't like women either, and had invited her along to dinner for only one of two reasons: for the sake of protocol or to watch her squirm.

Jack, dressed in his white dinner jacket, wrapped his arms around his wife's waist, kissed her neck and whispered, "Definitely to watch you squirm."

A taut look of pleasure entered Aunt Ethyl's face, and Aubrey preoccupied himself with the view from their top-floor suite. Below in the street, the people resembled hollow-cast figures, and businessmen, workmen, shoppers, soldiers and secret service officials carried on their lives in what looked like complete conviction that the future belonged to them. Hitler had sent a car to fetch the Shaws, and the black Mercedes was waiting under the swastika-emblazoned flags that hung from the hotel entry.

"Escort us down," Aunt Ethyl said, plunking a hat on her head and tipping it fashionably over one eye, like Greta Garbo in *Romance*. She draped a light silk coat over her puff-sleeved gown and offered Aubrey her arm. Her vanilla perfume suffused the elevator, and as they descended she spoke of the inevitability of vegetarian lasagna "due to the Italian contingent tonight. I don't like lasagna."

Uncle Jack said to Aubrey, "Buck up! You're not missing much. You already know what he looks like anyway; his picture is everywhere."

Though the elevator was lined with mirrors, a photograph was affixed to the glass. In it, Hitler was wearing jackboots and petting a fawn. Behind him: deck chairs, a high, dark hedge and crisp California-style shadows. Jack translated the inscription: "The Fuehrer is an animal lover."

"I don't want to go," Ethyl moaned as she released Aubrey's arm and fixed her hair in the mirror. "Can't Aubrey be me tonight?"

Jack kissed her again on the neck and said in her ear, "No."

"*Scheisse,*" she said.

Jack laughed but didn't translate, and Aubrey didn't understand.

As the car rolled away, Aunt Ethyl shot her head out the window and cried, "Aubrey, I almost forgot. Zarah Leander is staying at the Bristol tonight. Take her picture for me when she comes, won't you?" The Swedish actress with the baritone voice was the highest-paid film star in Germany, darling of the Nazi regime, but Aubrey had never heard of her.

"Is it true Zarah Leander is coming tonight?" he asked the concierge.

Though staff at the Bristol spoke little English, the concierge appeared at first to understand. He said, "*Ja, ja,* Zarah Leander."

"Do you know what time she's coming?"

The concierge pulled up his white cuff so as to display the face on his watch.

"No," said Aubrey. "What time she's *coming*. What time she's coming *later*."

The man showed him his watch again.

Because Aubrey wished to please his aunt, he sat for hours in the lobby, his camera around his neck, waiting for the star. In the lobby hung a picture of the lobby, taken at the first automobile exhibition – eight shiny cars parked on the marble floors. The walls also retained the rectangular shadows of photographs that had been removed. One of the shadows was partially covered by yet another picture of Hitler. The shot didn't pretend to be candid: he held a whip and scowled at the camera as if it were his favourite enemy, and between it and its subject there was something perversely affectionate.

Near midnight, Aunt Ethyl and Uncle Jack returned. They found Aubrey sleeping upright on the couch. When he opened his eyes, he saw his aunt nestling under his uncle's arm. Uncle Jack's buff-coloured cummerbund had ridden up his waist. The two looked happy. Aubrey told them he'd sat in the lobby all night, but the movie star hadn't showed.

Aunt Ethyl's hand went to her mouth, lipstick smudging on her palm. "Oh, Aubrey," she cried, "I must have got it wrong!" Then, turning to Jack, she asked, "Did I? I could have sworn someone said she was coming."

Jack shrugged, which, because it was *her* gesture, implied an intimacy between them that made Aubrey look down at the floor. Jack said, "People change their plans."

As they entered the elevator, Aunt Ethyl stepped away from Uncle Jack and leaned against the mirrored wall. "I have to bathe before you touch me," she said, as if Aubrey weren't present in the small moving room. "I smell like Mr Hitler."

Jack grabbed her waist and said, "Don't be ridiculous. You smell like garlic and fennel and gin."

Germany proved uneventful. Aubrey didn't visit Mendelssohn's grave, and though he did make the trip to the suburbs to see to the giant mushroom, it wasn't really worth the effort. After Germany came Poland. Uncle Jack said the visit to Krakow was purely for pleasure, but he failed to explain why he'd booked a circuitous route, and why a German colleague, whom he never introduced by name, accompanied the family. Jack and the German pored over maps as their train steamed its way from the Nazi grandeur of Berlin towards the turnip fields of the Upper Silesian Coal Basin and the small town of Oświęcim, which the conductor pronounced as "Auschwitz."

In the glow of the lamps in the first-class dining car, a geologic survey lay on the table. The lights were lit unnecessarily: it was noon on a sunny day. Jack called Aubrey to the table and asked, "Can you spot the oil?" He'd already taught his nephew to identify the dome-like rocks that signify petroleum.

"That's easy," said Aubrey, who was a quick study. He liked appearing smart, sniffing out the right answer and winning Jack's approval. Aubrey held on to the rim of Jack's chair to steady himself against the rocking of the train and examined the map. He held his breath, let it out in a puff, put his free hand into his pocket, took it out again and returned it to his pocket. He couldn't make up his mind.

Laughing loudly, Jack said, "It's a trick question, Aubrey. There's no oil in Germany!" Then, laying out the blueprints of an industrial complex to be erected by IG Farben for the production of oil from coal, Jack explained to his nephew that the factory would use as much electricity as the entire city of Berlin and demand twenty-two thousand labourers to work it.

The German beside him said, "*Birkenau*. It is the word for birch tree."

Though the train roared east, they were still many hours away from the birch woods that appeared on the geologic survey as pale swaths of grey. They hadn't yet left Germany, weren't even as far as Frankfurt (Oder).

Aubrey asked the man, "Do Germans make syrup from birch trees? The American Indians did. Mostly, they made maple syrup from maples, but sometimes from birch trees too. I suppose that's not *maple* syrup."

The German told Jack his son was endearing and delightfully young for his age.

In the dining car, over dessert, Aubrey met a German boy who was also thirteen years old, but several inches taller. The boy had dark hair and dark, smart eyes and spoke a slow and clear English. He said his father had attended Oxford University before returning home to teach philosophy at Friedrich-Wilhelms-Universität. Aubrey learned that the boy's father was now unemployed and the boy was being sent to his grandmother in Poland to escape Berlin for the summer. Imagining his own father dismissed for drunkenness and his grandmother in her cottage by the lake, Aubrey didn't ask the right questions.

"Are you a Hitler Boy?" he asked, meaning Hitler Youth but unable to remember the name.

"No," said the boy.

Chatting over his rhubarb pudding, Aubrey felt he'd made a friend. After the bowl was empty, the boy invited him back to his coach to play a game of rummy.

He occupied a first-class compartment. As there were still two free seats adjacent to his friend's, Aubrey took the far one, and the boy laid the cards in the vacant seat between them. They had only begun to play when the train pulled into Frankfurt station. A fat woman in a felt hat who'd been seated across from them disembarked, and a man in a yellow shirt peered in but carried on down the corridor. Aubrey hoped to get lucky and keep the spare seat between them for their cards, and when an SS officer entered, Aubrey was relieved that he chose the seat left hot and damp by the fat lady.

The officer lit a cigarette. The skull on his cap nodded beneath the eagle. On his sleeve was the black swastika, which resembled the massive water spider that had lived beneath the dock on Caspian Lake. He smoked with a deep deliberation, and he stared at the German boy. When the train lurched forward, sending the queen of diamonds to the floor, the SS officer picked up the card for the boys and returned it to the deck.

He leaned across the empty space and whispered, "You're a Jew. Jews don't travel first class. If I want to, I can shoot you. I asked you," he said, though he hadn't asked, "you are a Jew?"

The train pulled out of the station. The boys were still holding their cards.

"Yes, sir," said the boy, and without looking up he retrieved his identity papers from his pocket.

"From Berlin?"

"Yes, sir."

The officer took the boy's papers as if he'd been dealt a card. "And where are you going?"

"Rybnik, sir."

"Where are your parents?"

"My parents sent me away for the summer to visit my grandmother."

"Why did your parents send you first class? Your parents don't know the laws?"

The boy hesitated. "My grandmother insisted, sir."

"Your grandmother only follows the Laws of Moses?"

Uncertain how to answer, the boy gave no answer at all. The window in the compartment was open, and the SS officer leaned his elbow against it so that the papers in his hands flapped like a sullied bird. The town had disappeared quickly, and out the window the Oder River turned uneasily towards Poland.

"Moses was found in a basket on a river. His mother hid him when all the other boys were killed by Pharaoh. Is that right, Jew?"

"Yes, sir."

The river twitched to the east, and in its shallows a heron caught a fish that continued to fight in the great bird's beak as the window left it behind.

"He was found by an Egyptian royal family and raised as one of their own. When he killed a slave master, he ran away and became a shepherd. Then he was commanded by God to deliver the Hebrews from slavery. Am I still right?"

"Yes, sir."

"He led the Hebrews out of Egypt and they wandered in the desert for forty years. Because his people were thirsty, he brought water out of a rock by hitting it with his staff. He saved the Jews, didn't he?"

"Yes, sir."

The officer paused and examined the tip of his cigarette: it blinked between grey and red with each burst of oxygen. "What is the difference between the past and the future?"

"I don't know, sir."

"What is the difference between the past and the future?" he asked again.

"I don't know, sir."

"What is the difference?" he shouted.

"I don't know," the boy whimpered.

The officer looked at the window, where he saw himself smoking, and beyond himself, the view. "I'll give you a clue. What river is that?" He asked this question with a serenity that terrified the boy.

"The Oder River, sir."

"Do you see Moses floating down *that* river?"

"No, sir."

Aubrey stared blankly at the king of hearts. It sat beside the jack of the same suit; he had only needed to draw the queen. He did not look up when the boy reached for his hat on the hook above and pulled his bags from the cubby. Aubrey shifted slightly: he was sitting on the boy's coattail. Only when the officer and the boy had left the cabin did he notice he was still holding the boy's playing cards. He did not speak German. He did not know where the boy had gone. He could not say for certain what had happened. He did not know why his hands were shaking.

He stared at the king of hearts, whose arm, strangely detached from the body, stabbed a sword through his own head: either the king was killing himself or someone else had reached into the frame to do it. Aubrey tucked the cards into his jacket pocket. As he stood, feeling suddenly ill, he wondered if eating pudding on a train had been a bad idea. He stumbled down the corridor, hoping to play "monster" with his cousins.

Soon he was chasing them up and down the carriage with his arms held out as stiff as train tracks and his teeth as wide as the grill of the firebox. Occasionally, the rocking of the train threw all four boys onto their knees as they ran up and down the corridors. And when one of them banged himself hard enough to pull a piece of flesh from his shin, they all looked down at the pulpy pit where the blood had begun to puddle. The wounded child shrugged like his mother and ran off squealing, Aubrey running monster-footed behind.

As the train slowed towards the station, Donna Cobb looked out through the crack in the freight-car doors and saw the Chicago River crusted in dirty ice. It was five days since she'd given birth and boarded her first train westward. She looked the worse for wear. Somewhere near Poughkeepsie, New York, the Yankee Line conductor had caught her huddled like a rat underneath her blanket. He had a beery, round belly that blunted his dick and, unable to make good contact, had slipped out of her again and again. But he let her ride for free on account of her thick hair and her big breasts still aching with milk. So, on the Twentieth Century Limited she hadn't even bothered to hide. Crossing the wheat stubble of snow-flattened Ohio, the machinery under her rump stained her panties with grease. Passing through the industrial city of Gary, Indiana, despite the great wind that roared off the lake, the freight car stank of rotten eggs, and when she accused the conductor of stinking he buttoned his fly and told her, "Next stop, Chicago."

She'd seen pictures of Chicago before – of the monolithic Board of Trade building, ornamented with bulls and hooded Indians stooping over the corn and topped by a masculine grain goddess cast from six thousand pounds of aluminium.

She'd thumbed through photo spreads in *Harper's Bazaar:* gangsters in pinstripes, Southside jazz clubs, dream cars, a zeppelin, a village of Lilliputians – not because all Chicagoans were small but because the Century of Progress world's fair had been held here. The next one was scheduled for spring in the Big Apple. Donna couldn't imagine spring ever coming to Chicago. This was flat, hard cereal land; it was a cold new world, square and straight, its skyscrapers more insistent than a horny man, though not the kind of man she was used to.

She strutted out of Union Station and followed her nose. She kept to the river, walking forty minutes down Wacker Drive till she came to the drawbridge on Michigan Avenue, where the gleaming terracotta Wrigley Building stared at the pseudo-church of the Tribune Tower. Gum and news meant money in Chicago, while Donna wore a blanket for a coat. When the leaves of the drawbridge lowered and she crossed the water, she walked past a street sign: The Magnificent Mile. Her mouth dropped open and her teeth burned with cold. She'd never seen anything like it except in the movies. Magnificent window after magnificent window, magnificent shop after magnificent shop, magnificent furriers, magnificent millineries, magnificent jewellers, magnificent perfumers and haute couture, whatever that meant.

A man was admiring a diamond necklace in the copper-trimmed window of Marshall Field's. Donna leaned her cheek against the glass, loosened the blanket around her chest, and asked him, "You think that's *real?*" But he barely seemed to notice her before he walked away. He might as well have slugged her. Exhausted from childbirth and travel and cold, she stood alone before the window, wondering if all this magnificence was smoke and mirrors, and asked again, "You think that's *real?*"

A poor woman talking to herself on the Magnificent Mile was invisible. Donna tried to catch a glimpse of her reflection in the glass, herself superimposed on the diamond necklace, but the stark morning light didn't let her. The pit in her stomach was only partly caused by hunger. She hadn't planned to stay in Chicago – just pawn her jewellery and travel on, because it was a straight, flat line to Hollywood. But looking down at her oil-stained blanket, Donna pulled herself tightly together and revamped her plans.

A bludgeoning wind rose off the lake. Waves froze as they crested the beaches. Under the tracks of the elevated railway, between a storefront church and a liquor store, Donna found a pawnbroker. With a dollar in her pocket, she'd feel lighter and freer; she'd feel like a lucky American. The commuter trains roared overhead. Forsaken Indian heirlooms rattled in the glass cases as she counted her cash. Her wedding band was phony, but the pearl earrings from Ruth Shaw Brown were natural and expensive.

Back out in the street, wind tangling her hair and searing her thighs, she slammed her foot down on a layer of ice on the sidewalk. It broke with a satisfying crack. Lowering her head against the wind, she walked back up the Magnificent Mile and swept through the revolving doors into Marshall Field's. There she applied scarlet lipstick from the cosmetic counter samples and, clutching the brass handrail, rode the escalator to Ladies' Fashions.

In the dressing-room mirror, her belly hung like an empty purse. "Old Indian trick," she joked to her wretched reflection, then yanked a girdle over her hips to bring back her girlish figure.

The saleslady opened the door and held out a red dress on a hanger cushioned with pink satin. "Your size," she said.

"Hang it there," said Donna, who didn't dare touch it. "I'm dying for a pee." She slipped her old soiled dress over the brand new girdle and rushed down the hall to the ladies' room to wash her filthy hands. Finding a bobby pin on the floor, she used it to clean her nails. In a stall, she washed her feet in the toilet basin.

The saleslady was loitering by the door, suspecting the tramp would flee with the girdle on. She'd have refused her entry to the dressing room if the so-called customer hadn't waved a handful of dollar bills about as if it were a fortune.

Donna knew the pawn money wasn't a fortune, just the means to get one. Back in the dressing room, she admired herself in the mirror: how the cut of the dress made her breasts into hills to be climbed. She examined the tags on the dress, the girdle, the pair of stockings and shoes, added up the numbers and counted out her money. She lifted her thick, matted hair and, making a claw of her fingers, combed it out. She'd go without the stockings and use what was left on a hairdo.

There'd be nothing with which to eat or lodge in a cheap hotel, let alone buy a ticket west. But between here and Hollywood there were hundreds of dumb, pretty girls dreaming of becoming stars. She knew people called her crazy, but except for having married Amos, nobody had ever had reason to call her stupid. When she drew the red dress over her head, Donna was transformed. She'd always been a beauty, but now she was something more useful: she was captivating. Her purchases were only partly to thank; more important was the look in her eyes: she was hungry. She had tamped down her dreams for too many years, and now she was stirring up the embers. She left her old clothes and the moth-eaten blanket hanging from a hook.

Up the Mile, in her slingback pumps and tight dress, with her large painted lips and her hair holding its bounce against the wind, the remade woman swung her hips like a baby in a cradle. She wouldn't fight the elements; she'd let the wind rock her. And though she was numb with the Chicago cold, it could only make her paler and prettier. Holding her hands out at her sides, she cocked her wrists and flaunted her naked ring finger.

Men's heads turned like hands on a clock. Donna appraised each one, while appearing not to see them. Bitter as it was, she'd take her time; she'd hold out for a manly man with enough cash and confidence to say to her, "You must have a steaming hot furnace under that dress to be out in this cold without a coat."

Her first night in the Windy City, Donna ate meat off a plate and bathed in a lion-footed tub. The man was jowly and ham-handed and probably a crook. But he was a beginning, and she believed it could only get better. Within a month, she had a mink. She'd seen minks before, slinking along the Lamoille River in and out of holes.

Lonely, Amos reached down to pet his dog, forgetting no dog was there. The dog had died almost a year ago on the outskirts of a Quebec town where Amos had worked long enough to earn a bag of nails and a tired rifle. The wooded edges of towns were dangerous: the dog got caught in a bear trap and its hind leg had blackened with gangrene. Amos would have shot it, but he couldn't spare the bullet. So he'd rubbed its ear a while, then lopped its head off with his axe. He'd skinned the dog he loved, so as not to waste it, and lining the inside of his lumberjack jacket with its fur, he'd travelled on.

How many miles he'd skied to get here, wherever here was, he couldn't guess. He might have counted the telephone poles, but they'd fallen away to the east and west as he skied alone into the fathomless north. He'd left no sign of himself; the snow had erased the trail behind him, snow upon snow, as seamless as life and death where each is the source of the other. Only a handful of nails remained in his sack, but no one wanted this scrag wood anyway – from here on, the trees were dwarfs. If there was gold or iron underground, the miners hadn't found it yet. Canada was cold and beautiful for its own sake.

He slid down over bedrock towards a frozen river. Over its ice, the crazy woman snow lifted its skirts and spun around, but under its ice a walleye meandered dumbfounded with cold-blooded sluggishness. After pounding a hole in the ice with his axe, he rolled up his sleeve and, dunking his hand in the steely river, waited for the fish. Staring at the pale, reflective water, he thought if he caught himself, he'd think himself too filthy to eat. His beard was knitted with drippings of fat, and the oils in his hair had frozen. The checks on his lumberjack jacket had dimmed with the unifying greyness of dirt. Fleas bred in the dog's fur. Earth had worked into him everywhere his surfaces were porous or rutted: it lay in the lines in his cheeks and stuck in the corners of his lips, left a chisel mark under his eye. He could wash in the freezing waters and grind sand into his skin every day, but there'd be no stopping these changes: the earth had worked into him deep enough to make a hybrid thing of his flesh. Now a thaw in the air sweetened the scent of conifer mulch and Amos's hand in the ice hole grabbed a fish through the gills. He scrambled back up the bank, walleye under his armpit. The jagged rocks bloodied his knees, and his fingers ballooned with cold till he was forced to hold the fish with the flat of his palms because his thumbs no longer worked. He saw, beyond the river, a black bear eating its catch.

Digging into a high drift, he built himself a cave from snow that was coarse as sand. He sealed the entrance with an ice block, which dripped in the heat of the fire when he cooked his fish. He lived on perch and caribou. It was late spring, the time of soft antlers, when the caribou, having finished their mating rituals, remade themselves in miniature. The cubs were easy, reckless targets, and the cold allowed time to butcher and smoke their meat before the maggots appeared. But summer was on its way. The ice on the river cracked and shouted, and the northern land moaned longingly towards the hope of warmer days.

The star-bright nights were brief. Daylight played on the edges of sleep, the birds barely dozing. Amos slept on a mattress he'd woven from scrub willow, but like the birds he didn't sleep much. At night, through the smoke hole, he watched the revolving sky. The northern lights were the night's compensation for the monotony of snow. No myrtle or trout lily blooming, but the frozen north had the lights, and stars so close he might have tried to pick them.

The stars revealed that time was passing: Orion was gone, just as somewhere in the woods of southern Quebec, when Amos's dog was still alive, it had vanished a whole year ago. The hunter was no longer in the heavens, nor was his good dog chasing a hare. But there was Boötes, the herdsman, with his seven oxen, and Hydra, the serpent, whose decapitated head re-emerged from its stump, and Ursa Major. The thin, clear air was unusually quiet; unthreatened, the trees didn't call. Exactly how long Amos had been here he didn't know – a month, two months, three? He might have believed the peaceful nights would stretch on forever, though he knew, like the weather, they wouldn't.

The night they ended, the ground shook. Amos shot up out of half-sleep and hit his head on the ice roof. He emerged from his cave to see a herd of caribou storm the horizon, immingle in the darkness and be gone. A brilliant green glow spanned as far as the dropped-off end of the world.

The northern lights were familiar, but tonight they were screaming.

Covering his ears didn't help. His scars ached, his head ached as if his brain had become a tuning fork humming with all the violence of the universe, yet nothing in the known universe compared to the noise in the sky. Not the screech of a hundred thousand saws, the scratching of every child down the blackboards of every school, the trill of a million women's tongues, or a hundred thousand newborns hurtling headfirst into life. As his dog once bayed at invisible things, a rare wolf howled from its lonely den. Amos swayed his head and growled and smiled with his dirt-yellow teeth. The voice of the sky was awful, in the godliest sense of awful. Amos sank to his knees in the snow and howled too.

When he crawled back to his snow cave, he lay as if dead on his willow twigs. When he awoke, the cuff of his sleeve was in a pool of water. The house was melting. He stomped down the embers in his fire pit, picked up his sack and his gun. At the door, he looked into the distance, then stepped out into the sunlight and the first real stirrings of heat. He knew the trees were waiting for him. He knew they were growing impatient. Amos glanced over his shoulder at his cave, into whose darkness time had faded. Beside it, a caribou calf suckled from its mother with such fierceness it could have pulled milk out of iron.

The snow was softening, and in the slush his skis were reluctant to slide. He slapped a blackfly against the festering scar on his cheek, then another against his chin. Though he wrapped his dirty long johns around his head to keep the flies from his hair, they swarmed around his mouth and he breathed them in. The season had changed overnight – in no time there'd be mosquitoes. He smelt the low-pressure front of an approaching storm and tasted the thaw in the back of his throat. Reaching a river he'd intended on crossing, he found the ice had broken. The water roared like a moose in estrus, and even the ducks were frightened of its shores. An eagle flew from north to south with a field mouse in its clutches. Until the cold returned, only birds would pass that way.

He followed the northern bank of the river westward, and soon he could hear the trees call in the closer distance. His last few nails jangled in his sack. When his skis sank in the soft snow, he hooked them to his pack, and they reached over his head as if the sun had sprouted antlers from his brow. His walk was splayfooted for many miles before it again became human. The pines had grown up tall. Deer replaced the caribou. They moved in single families through the woods, and they offered themselves up to his gun, and their blood in the woods mimicked the first red trillium of the year.

The first sign of humanity was a junked car. In a swamp still scummed with ice, its rusted-out body had crumbled away, leaching iron into the runoff. A blue-green sputum of fuel glamoured up the mud. Amos peered through the broken windows into the interior of an abandoned Studebaker. On the raccoon-tattered seat was a rayon scarf and a Bakelite cup from a picnic set – some fashionable couple had driven into the swamp and left the evidence to rot. A vodka bottle lay in the underwood, slowly turning to sand.

The second sign of humanity was the sound of the saws, followed by the cracking of a tree in two, followed by an earthquaking thud as it hit the ground and what lived in and under the tree were killed. Amos walked down a logging road, descending into a valley called Bitter Valley, though he didn't know its name. It wasn't named for the dandelion greens that grew there in the summer, but for the cold that inhabited the place even when the frost was off the hills.

The forest was budding out everywhere except in Bitter Valley. On the higher outcrops, mosses grew plush with emerald shoots and red stamens, but where the bedrock dropped towards a frozen lake, the rocks remained winter-black. As dusk came down, all the mosses blackened. If a village was nearby, it hunkered down like something hunted, and Amos wouldn't find it tonight. No lights or music or any man-made thing gave away its location, though an ice fishing shack sat precariously on the lake. He'd sleep there: it was better than anywhere he'd laid his head in months.

Amos took a long step over the water's edge where the ice had melted in the shallows, onto the deeper ice farther out, which was firm enough to bear his weight. Opening the door to the fishing hut, he found a tiny room with an ice floor, a tin bucket and the dead remnants of an open fire. He hit two flints together and rekindled the half-charred wood. Seated on the bucket, he leaned his chin in the glassless window frame like his dog used to do.

A warm front was moving under the cold, and both currents of air bathed his face while the fire at his back made him sweat. Amos gazed out the window across the frozen water, up the cliff and over the woods towards a lonely planet. Venus was in the sky.

Venus rising. Venus fixing her eye upon Amos and speaking to him. *Swish swish*, a solitary noise through the valley. When Venus descended, Amos saw her: a girl in ice skates marking up the lake.

Her dirty white skates flashed like dingy stars as the blades inscribed the ice. She appeared to be sixteen or seventeen years old, hovering on the edge between worlds, having not yet swelled into a woman. As she skated a one-footed figure eight, in a red bonnet with red feathers, she might have been a whooping crane on the verge of taking off. Reaching out her arms, she struck back her leg and pivoted on her smooth hips. Believing herself to be alone, she moved with the elemental abandon of an animal. But when she balanced on one leg, kicked her foot up behind her and threw back her head, Amos, seeing the blade flash towards her ear, jumped up, and the bucket beneath him tottered. The girl turned the side of her skate into the ice and stopped. She was skittish, like a deer about to bolt.

Amos stepped back from the window, his heart pounding. *Raccoons,* he prompted her, *I'm just raccoons.* But she wasn't so easily fooled. She'd seen the smoke rising from the hole in the roof, and now she disappeared from view and the door to the fishing shack opened. The girl frowned at the sight of the giant man in her hut.

What he'd thought she was – a bird, a planet, a deer – she wasn't. She was better. Though silent and lean – long, tawny legs and thin arms, straight black hair tucked into a weathered sheepskin coat that broadened her slim figure – she was not a deer. She was beautiful. Amos felt the fire at his feet grow hotter and the ice around it melt. Overcome by the heat, he tugged at the fur of his lumberjack jacket. The girl didn't say a word. She took the bucket he'd been seated on and sat on it herself, then leaned her elbows on her knees, her chin in her hands, and stared up at him.

It seemed an eternity before she spoke. She didn't speak in words. By curling her fingers towards the floor, she told him to sit. Amos sank against the wall and squatted on the ice.

She picked an ashy twig from the fire, and in the loose frost of the floor between her skates, wrote her name: Kona. She prodded the flames, coated the stick with ash again and handed it to Amos. He began to write, which was hard for him, so he brushed away the A and said, "Amos."

"Shh." The first sound of her voice was the sound of the wind.

Sweeping up a handful of snow, she placed it by her name, because Kona meant "snow" in Cree. The little pile quickly melted. With her stick, she drew the stars in the sky and the world beneath: below the outline of a bear, she drew a shack, in the shack an old bent man, around the old man a village, a few of its people standing up, most of them laid out on the ground.

When she gave the ashy stylus to Amos, he drew a mountain, a valley and a lake. Then a train on fire, a man with an axe, a tree with a nail in it, a dog without a head, caribou in the boreal forest, river ice cracking.

The cry of the ice broke the silence. Amos jumped to his feet as the floor split in two, one ice sheet slipping beneath another. In an instant, the fire dropped into the lake and was gone. The bucket sank. The girl stumbled on the picks of her skates and, before she could reach for Amos's hand, fell into the water. She didn't even scream. As she descended, the sheets continued to slide, and the ice closed above her.

Amos dropped to his knees and with his axe beat a hole in the ice. Reaching down his arm, he pulled up the bucket, but reaching again found nothing. He stripped off his clothes, tied jacket to shirt and shirt to overalls and overalls to long johns and, knotting the long johns around the handle of the axe, slammed the blade into the ice to hold it firm. He lowered himself on the rope of clothes into the bitter lake. The merciless cold engulfed him as he groped for the touch of the girl. At last, in his red and swollen hands, he brought up her sputtering body. He heaved her onto the ice and climbed up beside her, scooped her up in his arms and rose, naked and red.

He walked towards the bear in the sky, as Kona's drawing had told him to do, the beautiful girl in his massive arms. Hives swelled up on his back and thighs. His thumbs couldn't move; the nub of his foreshortened finger throbbed. Cold painted his face mulberry and blotchy. Frost sticking to his lashes made his eyes tear up, and the salt ran into his beard. But he didn't see himself from the outside; he didn't think how he looked with the girl in his arms. He saw a hut in the woods and was running towards it. He threw open the door as an old bent man by the stove reached for a rifle.

Amos walked in, unblinking, his eye fixed open with ice. Though the old man cocked his gun and shouted something, Amos, his ears dead with cold, didn't hear a word. With the barrel of a rifle under his cheek where his scar burned, he placed the girl by the stove. He saw only her: the Indian girl, her brown skin so pale with hypothermia, it seemed she might fade into a white girl on the spot. His organs groaned towards the heat of the fire; his huge body shuddered involuntarily.

"Don't move," the old man said as he nudged the mouth of the gun into Amos's stitched-over eye socket. Amos tried not to move. The two of them stood so still that, in the time of myths, the gods might have plucked them out of their mortal setting and placed them in the starry sky.

What the old man read in the stranger's face made him lower his gun. "Hell," he said, "bring me the blankets off the bed in the room over there. Only one of them is for you." From a cupboard he took a stash of herbs and ground them in a mortar, then added hot water from the kettle that sat steaming on the wood stove. "Gotta warm the core, or the cold blood will go to the heart and kill her." He muttered instructions to himself, then, bending down to pull off his granddaughter's frozen clothes, he painted red paste from her breasts to her crotch.

When Amos returned with the blankets and deposited them by the fire, the old man said, "Are you gonna stand there naked all night? I said take a blanket for yourself. Or don't you heed your elders?"

Eighty years old, slump-shouldered, bowlegged, short of breath and nearsighted, he tended gravely to his granddaughter. Amos watched the red paste dry to a deep maroon. Then the old man piled the blankets over the girl until all but her long black hair had disappeared beneath them. As the tin roof leaked heat to the stars, and the foreshortened chimney caught the downdraft and choked the room with smoke, Amos pulled the last blanket over himself and crouched down in a corner, stunned to his soul with cold.

He was woken by a poker in his side. "Your ribs bump up like a logging road," the man said, turning away to stoke the coals. "There's food on the table."

Amos couldn't have counted how long it had been since he'd dined at a table or used a fork. Wearing only a blanket, he gazed over his breakfast as if over a promised land: black tea, black beans and pork and molasses in stewed dough, what the old fellow called bangbellies.

"Take more," said his host, passing the last one.

"You ain't hungry?"

"I'm not growing."

"She's the only one still growing, I guess," said Amos, turning in his seat to look at the girl, who slept by the stove.

"She's not growing, either. She's older than she looks. Eat your breakfast."

"Yes, sir."

Amos chewed on the last bangbelly and stared at the old man's eyes. Blue, like two deep waterholes.

"Stop staring, you damn giant! Can't you let a person eat?"

"I didn't know Indians had blue eyes," said Amos.

"Daddy was as English as Wellington boots." The old man swallowed a poorly chewed piece of pork and dough and choked on a vision of his daddy. "Always more folk in a room than take up the space," he muttered. "Of course, I've been under the impression," he continued, "that a white man with blue eyes and a brown woman with brown eyes give birth to brown-eyed children. So it's a mystery, ain't it?" His accent as well as his sentence structure lurched back and forth between two irreconcilable poles of education. Half raised by his father, half by his tribe, he'd begin a sentence like a college graduate and finish it with the flattened-out tone of an Indian forced to speak English. Now he was mopping up his beans with his leftover dough.

"I guess some things can't be explained," said Amos.

"My eyes are like the water you both almost drowned in last night, and that's all the explanation anyone needs. Though people say water is blue, separate it from the sunny sky and it's black as tea. Same goes for my eyes." Having poured out the dregs of the teapot, he walked to the tin kettle on the stove to fill it for a second sitting. "One pinch of tea a day, these days, with rationing, just in case we forget in the woods that somewhere else the world's at war. And so the pot gets weaker as the day progresses, like the rest of us old men."

Amos was again looking at the girl, entombed in her blankets – he had a hard time not looking. "Her parents both Indians?" he asked.

"Both Iyiniwok and both dead. We don't talk about the dead."

"She's lucky to be alive after that dunk."

"Only fools believe in luck, son."

When the girl wrestled in her sleep, her hair trapped in the roll of blankets, Amos instinctively stood up to help her, but the grandfather waved him back.

"Go on and avert your eyes." With his deep-ploughed hands, he applied more herbs to his granddaughter's body. A fixative to hold her to this world like an ambrotype to glass.

As her breath came and went indecisively and her small bosom rose and fell, Amos remembered Mrs Brown, who sat as still as a statue erected to something perfect until, through a simple movement like shifting her hair from her eyes, she came alive. If it moved, it was alive, Amos thought. Then again, there were chickens that ran around with their heads cut off. So Amos revised his thinking: life moved with some kind of intention.

"I got a daughter too," he said into the crumbs of his breakfast. "Never seen her, though, or heard nothing about her. I left before she was born."

"How come you know you have a daughter, then?"

The old man was dipping his hand into the warming tin on the pot-bellied stove and smearing more paste across the girl's chest. When she twisted in her sleep and her hair dirtied in the muck, he cleaned it off with two pinched fingers, and she fell so deeply into sleep her breath appeared to leave her.

"Same way you know you're alive," answered Amos. "A person just knows some things."

"There's things that are true, and then there are things that people believe 'cause it suits them. My daddy once sat me on his knee and told me I might be dead and gone to hell, 'cause without a thing to compare it to, I could never know for sure. 'You can't know what a thing is,' Daddy said, 'unless you know what it's not. The devil gives you a taste of heaven so you can know hell all the better.' Daddy was a philosophical type, but he didn't like us Indians."

Amos stood up, jostling the table. "How far's the village? I gotta find some nails."

"You going to town in my blanket? Or going fishing first?"

Amos hadn't considered his clothes at the bottom of the thawed-out lake. Being single-minded, he said, "Sixtypenny nails will do, if they don't got nothing bigger."

"You name it, we don't got it. There's a war on, don't you know."

Amos hadn't known.

The old man, finished with his granddaughter's poultice, stirred up more herbs in a dish. "Come over here," he said.

"I don't like those scars of yours." But considering Amos's size, he added, "And get down on your knees."

Kneeling so close to the girl, he couldn't help but look at her. "She sleeping?" Amos asked.

"She look like she's sleeping?"

"Yup."

"You asking if she's dead, then?"

"No, sir. Just making talk."

In the silence of her sleeping, Amos heard his own desire and it scared him.

"White folks make a lot of talk," said the old man. He smeared a gritty yellow substance on the ragged entry and exit points of the railway spike and asked, "You gonna tell me about it?"

Amos told his story badly. For the part about the spikes and the trees, he couldn't find sensible words. He couldn't explain why he did what he did, not because there wasn't a reason, but because words hadn't made him do it. He felt exposed and awkward, knowing he was talking only to fill up the space between himself and the sleeping girl. Outside, storm clouds threatened, rain beat on the roof and the low-pressure air put a smothering hand on the chimney so that the fire sputtered in the stove.

The old man hadn't nodded once to show he understood. Done with his medicines, he didn't speak, just opened the cabin door. He looked over the earth where Amos had walked with Kona in his arms last night. It was raining hard. What was left of the snow was melting, and if there were footprints, now they were washing away. Hanging in the threshold, he stared up at the pregnant burden of the sky, and then he fixed his blue eyes on Amos.

"There's a beat-up car about five miles from here," he said.

"I saw it," answered Amos.

"It's got rivets just rusting away in the swamp. They'd work as good as penny nails if you can get them out."

"Can't pound rivets out of a car," said Amos.

"Fire might do the trick."

Amos thought about it. Yes, a fire might get them out.

"But the car is cursed," the old man said. "It'll give you ghost sickness."

"What kind of sickness can you catch from a car?"

"Ghost sickness, like I said. Still, we're gonna do some surgery on that car when Kona's on her feet." Then he said, as if Amos should understand him, "She's a beautiful girl, and I'm an old man."

Kona wore the red cap that had been a gift from her grandfather's English father to her grandfather's Iyiniwok mother. This and the skates had come down to her, but today her feet were bare. She was a sight beyond words, a sight Amos had watched speechless through her recovery. As soon as she was well enough to lift her head and sip broth from a chipped mug with a broken handle, Amos lost his tongue. He hardly said a word to her, and she said nothing to him, though she sometimes smiled.

Love rose in silence. And yet there was no such thing in the woods, where hundreds of birds sang the first five notes of a refrain they never finished. The dark bullfrog croaked for a mate. The shrill treble of bees resounded in the sunlight. Even in the stagnant acres where the loggers had replaced the trees with trash, there was the song of the inanimate and the wind. The valley was in bloom as Amos, Kona and the old man passed the logging spurs, down which they could hear the saws unthwarted by the rain. Today there were no bees humming, for it was raining hard.

Amongst the desolate punk wood of clear cuts, the old man lifted his rifle to take aim at an empty bean can on a stump. "I'm gonna open a can of beans!" He laughed dryly at his own joke. Then he dropped his gun to his side and said, "Ain't no point in wasting a bullet. Such a one can't be killed."

He ordered Amos to give him the box of matches and insisted on lighting the fire himself. The body of the car was made of steel, while the rivets were made of iron, which meant a fire could crack the steel and loosen its grip. Only then could a man pound the rivets out. The old man added the match to the fuel tank, and they waited as the swamp burnt.

He said, "Story goes that long ago, before our people had axes or saws or any iron weapon, when we needed to bring down a tree, a shaman would visit it every night. The first night, he'd climb up to the treetop and let out a shout, then clamber back down again. The next night, he'd climb up the tree, shout, and come back down. A third night, he'd do it again. Night after night, he woke the tree up from its sleep. In the end, the tree weakened, and when he was done, it was dead." The old man sat down to wait on a stump in a sea of stumps. He was wet all over.

Kona gathered cattails from the ditch for tomorrow's dinner, expertly picking through the poisonous lookalikes. The wild iris, which grew side by side with the cattails, could kill a person in a single bite, but Kona could tell which was which.

Amos saw how her bronze face had recovered its dark colour, like a river stone thrown back into the water. He saw how, like a stone, she stood with a steady fixity, knowing that the current would move her on again: her village had been uprooted nine times in the nineteen years since her birth, pressed on by land claims and mineral prospects from one smallpox-sickened barrenment to the next.

"Can I see where the train nail came out your head?" she asked. It was the first English he'd heard her speak, and the first words she'd said to him.

He knelt down in the storm and parted his hair to show her. When she bent her head towards his, her hair fell like a blackout curtain around their two close faces. He burned with the heat from her eyes. Coming closer, there was thunder. She touched her finger to the scar. Its texture was like skin on boiled milk.

She said, "You got powerful gods as friends."

"I don't know about that," whispered Amos. "But out here," he said, as he gestured to the clear cuts, "I can hear the trees that are gone and the birds that are gone with them."

"It's ugly," said Kona.

"Yup," he said, uncertain whether she was talking about the clear-cuts or the scar on his head but happy she was talking to him.

The dark came down as they waited on the fire. The car burned, and what was left of the forest strobed with lightning. Amos and Kona stood side by side. He fixed his eye on her face as it appeared briefly out of the blackness and just as quickly was gone. Further off on the lake, lightning struck the water and one pebble-black trout eye, rising to the surface, stared sightless at the sky. The ground shook as a tree snapped, its unfurling leaves too heavy for the wind. A roar of thunder answered another, the echo roiling through the valley.

When the car stopped burning, Amos beat the loosened rivets out of it with his axe and stuffed his pack full. The old man said, "Well, that's that, and no ghosts yet, so to hell with the curse," which was itself a sort of curse.

Amos planned on leaving in the morning. That night, he lay by the smoking wood stove, next to the snoring old man. Beyond the closed door to the other room, he could hear Kona moving, and though he tried to pull his mind away from her private undressing, he couldn't. He envisioned the flash of her breasts and the swell of her buttocks. He saw her beauty, and between her beauty and the old man's rasping, he thought he'd never sleep. He wanted to knock at her door, and he knew if he did that she'd open it. But then he'd have to leave in the morning – he had no excuse to stay – and that he couldn't do. So he laid his head on the rough floor and listened to the wind rattle in the chimney pipe. He told himself he'd never sleep, and then somehow he did.

In the morning, in the sunlight, he woke and found Kona seated perfectly still beside what had been her grandfather. The old man was dead; anyone could feel that. He was just a bundle of sticks by the fire.

Kona said to Amos, "He said he wouldn't make it through the night."

It was uneventful for a death and as private as the dead man's dreams. Kona rose and walked into the woods and returned some hours later with the people from her village. For four days the drums beat like the echo of a heart, and Amos waited through the rituals of grieving, his sack of

Studebaker rivets in the corner. An old man, as old as the dead man, smudged Amos's forehead with blue paste. Amos was rinsed in the smell of sage burning. He ate venison and pinyon nuts, fried nettles and plantain, and drank from a communal cup. And though not much was said to him, everyone stared at him. Then, when the village departed back to wherever it hid in the woods, Amos was left alone with Kona.

Aubrey shot up in bed. The moonlight hacked by the shutters lay over him in stuttering shadows. He peeled off his sweaty sheet and switched on the bedside lamp, the Tiffany shade casting a crimson glow that coloured his glass of water. Sleep gummed up his eyes, and the light made him squint. The worse he slept, the more residue stuck to his lashes. He slept particularly poorly when holidaying at Xanadu, Mr du Pont's estate in Cuba.

Fumbling for the pencil and photo album on the bedside table, he recorded the nightmare that woke him. Car accident ... fire ... a woman strangled like Isadora Duncan by her own fashionable scarf. His photo album was part journal and scrapbook; he filled it with anything that caught his eye and revealed itself. He himself revealed little – he was seventeen, not a kid anymore, and he knew how to control himself – but he'd written his name on the cover as if *he* were the album. Taking pictures had become as necessary to him as opening his eyes in the morning. He kept his camera always near him, spent hours printing negatives, but a snapshot was too small a window for truth and what was outside the frame remained uncertain.

There was a shot of Uncle Jack and Mr du Pont, seated by Xanadu's massive hearth, leaning towards each other like two men sharing a hookah. On the table between them was a radio: they were listening to President Roosevelt deliver his fireside chat. But according to Aunt Ethyl, the picture gave little away. It didn't show that Nazi planes flew on lead-tetraethyl fuel and Nazi tanks rode on synthetic rubber tires manufactured by Standard Oil of New Jersey and DuPont Chemical. It didn't show that Ethyl Inc. was a collaborative venture with IG Farben of the Third Reich, or that synthetic oil ran every machine on the Axis side of the war. It didn't show the American workers in the New Jersey plant going mad and dying from lead poisoning, or the lawyers convincing the Attorney General that "lead is a gift from God." It didn't show Aunt Ethyl telling Aubrey one barbed night that a subsidiary of DuPont Chemical offered to supply the gunpowder for a *coup d'état* against Roosevelt, or Uncle Jack telling Ethyl to shut her mouth, or Ethyl saying, "Forget about it, Aubrey, that's what I try to do. I can't stand too much reality in my own life, let alone in everyone else's." It didn't show any of this. Photographs, like words, were pale secrets. And in black and white, everything was a shade of grey.

His aunt called his name from the hallway, so he quickly finished writing down his nightmare. Having spotted the light under his door, Aunt Ethyl entered without knocking. She wove between the dresser and the armchair and arrived, languid and hot, at the foot of the bed. Around her blanched face, strands of hair had pulled from their bun. She slouched beside him against the headboard and attempted to light the wrong end of her cigarette. Aubrey reversed its position in her mouth.

"Everything goes in the wrong way these days! Even your uncle!" she laughed, having recently taken to laughing, though her eyes almost never smiled. She slipped down onto his pillow and waved to the taxidermied boar's head that nodded from the wall. "How do you sleep with that fellow leering down over you? Irénée is bad enough. Doesn't he give you bad dreams?"

"Yes," said Aubrey, knowing neither yes nor no would satisfy Aunt Ethyl.

"Yes," she mocked him, "yes, yes, yes, yes, yes! That's what we always say, isn't it, Aubrey?" She lifted herself precariously off of the bed, yanking her silk-like dress out from between her thighs. "And the moon," she said, as she opened the shutters, "what does the moon say? Same as Irénée? 'Roosevelt is a cripple and a pinko!'" As she screamed across the ocean that separated her from America, a midnight gardener – Irénée worked his staff around the clock – looked up from the irrigated lawn. "It's nothing," she called to the bewildered Cuban. "We weren't talking to you."

"*No es nada*," called Aubrey, rising from the bed and leaning out the window. He was embarrassed for his aunt, but nights like this were customary: Aunt Ethyl saying nonsensical things, and the possibility of truth in the nonsense nagging him for months.

Ethyl stared blackly at her nephew, standing there in his pyjama trousers, his hairless chest toned by swimming. Outside, a cockatoo screeched in a golden cage. The boar's head seemed to smirk from above the bed, and in the mirror across the moon-flooded room Aubrey saw his own dumb smile. He had learned to smile when he didn't know what to do.

"What were you writing?" Ethyl asked.

"Nothing."

"What are you hiding? Everyone's hiding something!"

As she snatched up the album off the bedside table, she tottered on her heels. Aubrey reached out to catch her, his hand on her breast beneath her diamond choker. She was dressed finely for the night's entertainment, her sleeveless gown cinching her armpits, in which were flecks of lint from a discarded sweater.

"What are you doing?" She laughed and did not remove his hand.

"You were falling," he said. He didn't remove his hand, either. He could feel the slick texture of her dress and the hard edge of her bra's underwire.

She laughed again, then sidled away with the album. "I'm going to read it!" she declared. "That is an elder's prerogative. Do you think I look elderly?" Drawing her smooth legs up onto his bed, she sank deeply into his dank sheets and smoked her Julep cigarette – its chemical mint designed to soothe the throats of people who smoked sixty a day.

Aubrey surrendered and sat beside his aunt while she read his nightmare. No matter how high she was or how mortifying, he was glad she invaded his room; he'd come to rely on her presence.

She read in silence, but her lips twitched, because words were forming in her pretty mouth and her tongue was moving. He sat near enough to smell her lipstick. The smell reminded him of the Bolivian dictator's daughter, the girl to whom he'd lost his virginity when travelling with his uncle, while the oil tankers filled in Puerto Quijarro. The memory made him feel unfaithful because Aunt Ethyl hated Bolivia, which supplied oil to both sides and was clearly waiting to see which was winning before joining the war.

"Whose oil made that possible?!" she'd screamed at Jack when her brother died in the bombing of the USS *Sentinel*. After the news, she'd taken to bed for a week of pills and mourning, and Aubrey sat like a ghost beside her. He'd hated to see her so upset, but these days she was always upset. She said to him once, "Isn't it amazing, Aubrey, what a person can get used to?"

Aunt Ethyl read his nightmare without the slightest expression. But when her name was called down the hallway, she jumped to her feet and whispered hurriedly, "Well, I suppose you're free to dream what you like. *My* nightmares are written by others."

"There you are!" said Jack, standing in the doorway, looking stressed but dapper in a double-breasted cream tuxedo. "Ethyl, darling, you know you can't speak to Irénée like *that*."

Aubrey disliked his tone. He stood up from the bed and positioned himself beside his aunt as if to defend her, though he knew – and already blamed himself for it – he wouldn't. He could easily imagine the nature of *that*: inebriated most nights, Aunt Ethyl had become a hazard. She'd announced to the servants that her husband was a spy. She'd *sieg-heiled* Irénée. She'd French-kissed a Parisian chef, declaring, "At least this much I can do for your country!"

"We are guests in Irénée's house," Jack continued, insisting upon a stiff politeness he'd reluctantly cultivated in the face of his wife's decline.

"The whole world is a guest in Irénée's house," shrugged Ethyl. Leaning against a bookcase, she pulled out a dog-eared copy of Henry Ford's *The International Jew, The World's Foremost Problem*. "Have you read this, Aubrey?" she asked, and dropped it on the parquet floor.

"For God's sake, Ethyl!" Jack said.

"Oh, I know, Henry Ford is a great man. Everyone thinks Henry's a great man. *The New York Times* named him the third-greatest man in history, after Napoleon and Jesus Christ, and in Hitler's *Mein Kampf* he receives an honourable mention. *That's* saying something, isn't it, Jack?" Then, turning again to Aubrey, "You know, there's a life-sized painting of Henry over Hitler's desk. Henry Ford is a great man," she repeated herself, as if it were a new discovery. "And Irénée du Pont is a great man, too, though he doesn't like it when I call him my shrivelled, insipid, demonic Merchant of Death."

Jack laid a strong hand on Ethyl's shoulder. Beyond them, filling up the doorway, stood Irénée, his lips on his cigar as tight as the button on his collar.

"Jack," du Pont said, "I believe your wife is tired."

Aunt Ethyl actually smiled, though unpleasantly. "Merchant of Death is a *compliment,* Irénée." She tossed her cigarette through the open window, and it gleamed in the bushes below. Aubrey feared – or hoped – it would ignite the grasses and burn down Xanadu.

"I suspect," Jack said, with a laugh that could slice meat, "my wife's not tired at all. Ethyl, you are drunk and high. You can apologize in the morning. I'm taking you to bed."

"I'm not tired."

"Of course you're not." He offered his wife his arm, for he would punish her only in private places.

Ethyl shrugged, and a strand of hair fell from her bun and stuck to her lipstick. Aubrey suppressed the urge to reach out his hand and remove it. She parted her pretty lips and extracted the golden hair herself.

"Isn't it a shame," she said to Aubrey, as she swayed across the floor, "that Hitler has banned the jitterbug?" She did not refuse her husband's muscular arm as he escorted her out of the room.

As Irénée walked to the bookcase to put Henry Ford back in his place, he glanced at the open album on the bed. "What's in it?" he pried.

"Just photos and dreams and stuff," Aubrey said. He closed the album and hid it away in a drawer. Aunt Ethyl was right: he was hiding something, though it felt more like he was hiding everything. He sat up on the bed, throwing a pillow against the headboard, and crossed his arms over his chest.

On the bookcase was a polished box made of petrified wood, and from it Irénée took a cigar and passed it to him. "The Indians say that smoke dispels the demons, but I've never found it works," he said, holding out a match to light the thick tube, which sat there like a plug between Aubrey's lips. Perched on the side of the bed, Irénée ran his fingers down the crease of his pinstriped trousers. His nose flared with the scent of perspiration in the linen sheets. He said, "You can't dream yourself into a person, boy."

Aubrey puffed heavily at the cigar and tried to ignore the millionaire's intoxicated wisdom. All adults drank too much. Almost an adult himself, he drank sometimes in the back alleys of Mexico City with the displaced Indians. When he travelled with his uncle, he helped himself to brandy nightcaps while listening to lovers fighting and the arguments of important men, some with German accents, through the thin walls of South American hotels. But Xanadu's walls were thick. With du Pont seated on the dank sheets perfumed by Aunt Ethyl, Aubrey watched the smoke rising into the rafters and imagined going up with it.

Irénée followed his eyes and said, "Those beams came from a seventeenth-century ship in which every passenger drowned. The gold bullion it was carrying sank, but the wood floated to shore. The impressive thing about wood is that it burns when you want it to, but it also floats."

Jack shot his head through the door. "Still wide awake, Aubrey? All's clear, Irénée. I'm sorry about my wife."

"She's a plague!"

"A little monster, but a pretty one."

Aubrey felt sick, but maybe it was just the cigar. Reaching for the tumbler of water by his bed, he spilled it on the floor. Du Pont called down the hall to a maid, who, arranging late-night flowers, immediately rushed into the room with a cloth and a handful of peonies. As the crouching woman mopped up the water, du Pont said to Aubrey, "In Japanese, the word for peony is a euphemism for wild boar's meat. Buddhists disapprove of meat, so they don't like to call it what it is, and peonies look like thinly sliced flesh."

Despite the nausea, Aubrey continued to smoke. He blew rings, which held their shape until they met a draft and distorted.

Jack said to Aubrey, "I'm flying to Canada next month. Want to get away from your crazy aunt for a couple of days? Someone's making trouble in Alberta."

"No, thanks," said Aubrey, not wanting to go to cold Alberta, and also wanting to say no to his uncle.

"Suit yourself," said Jack.

Du Pont stood to leave, leaving behind a hot indentation in the mattress. "Your wife's making trouble in Xanadu, Jack."

"God, yes. I'm all apologies."

Aubrey was borrowing a book from Jack's study. Jack, seated at his desk, the Mexican sun splashed across his papers, was examining the roster of workers from the oilfields of Turner Valley, Alberta, where he was scheduled to visit the following week.

"What kind of name is Dick Palmer?" Jack laughed.

Jack's sharp laughter made Aubrey laugh too.

"I knew a girl back in Princeton named Holly Wood," said Aubrey. "Now she's in the Red Cross, stationed somewhere in Africa, but Grandmother can't remember where. Grandmother forgets things now, and her handwriting's hard to read."

Closing a leather portfolio over his papers, Jack said, "To hell with this! It's too hot to work. Eighty-five degrees in February! What's wrong with the weather this winter? How about a swim?"

The sun was not only hot, but unyielding; there hadn't been a single overcast day in a month. Outside, the dark porcelain tiles were warm underfoot. The air and the water being close to the same temperature, Aubrey slipped into the pool without flinching.

"Beats Caspian, huh?" said Jack.

That night, it was not much cooler. If he'd been a deep sleeper, Aubrey might have believed the sun never set at all. But like his aunt, he was up most nights. Aunt Ethyl kept nocturnal hours, for although no Spitfires flew over Mexico City, she'd hung blackout curtains on her bedroom windows, enabling her to sleep late into the day.

It was past midnight when she came to his bedroom and sat at the end of his bed. She was clutching something. "Are you awake, Aubrey?" she asked.

"No," he said. "You?"

She laughed, which was what he wanted. He liked to make her laugh.

He propped himself up against the headboard, his right arm cushioning the back of his head. A sheet covered his lower body, but under it he was naked. He leaned back as she bent across him to switch on the bedside lamp. He could smell gin.

In the lamp light, a scar in his armpit was clearly visible because he didn't have much body hair, just a small cluster of armpit strands like a thin patch of weeds. Ethyl touched it and asked, "Where did you get that?"

"I've had it since I was a kid. A light bulb exploded above me in the trainyard. I never got stitches for that one because no one even noticed it."

"You didn't cry?"

"No."

"That was a waste. You should get your crying in when you're young."

He could see now that she was holding Jack's portfolio. She opened it, turned it towards him and laid it on his lap.

"I was in Jack's office, looking for something," she said.

"For what?"

"God knows. Anyhow, I didn't find it. But I found something else instead." She pointed to a name in the Turner Valley roster. "It might not be your Amos Cobb, or it might be. You never know."

Ethyl stretched across the single bed, across the bump that was Aubrey's legs, her head dropping back over the side of the mattress. She stared at the ceiling. Her vocal cords pinched by the weight of her head, her voice sounded slimmer than usual. "My stockings ran when I crawled on my knees to look at that skull under your bed in Princeton. They were my favourite stockings. You were so young back then. You thought the skull would cheer me up, and it did, but you didn't know it. Shame you had to throw Amos overboard in the end. You almost cried then. But you didn't. No, you didn't. So many didn'ts." She sat up and added, "I'm hungry."

Aubrey was glad to move. His heart was racing. After he slipped his pyjama trousers on under the sheet, the two of them went down to the moonlit kitchen, where the cooks left crates of oranges on the long marble counters to be squeezed into juice in the morning. They ate oranges in the dark.

The next day, Aubrey asked his uncle, "Is it too late to change my mind? Can I come to Alberta with you?"

Amos was happy. When he slammed his axe into a spike, Kona took the axe in her earthen hands and taught him how to swing it like a tomahawk. After that, he never left her side. Together they followed the rail tracks west. From sea to shining sea, like the song except truncated, because they didn't start at the Atlantic and they didn't arrive at the Pacific. They never made it past Alberta.

In cargo cars they lay side by side, listening to the rhythmic thud of gargantuan tonnage propelled by coal and engine over the jointed tracks, and sound repeated became like another silence. They listened for the voice of the trees and spoke little as they crossed the country. They spent months in the dark, sappy pinewoods of northern Ontario, and walked slowly by the great unsheltered lakes and stood sadly by the slag hills of Sudbury. Further west, they reached the prairies, where there had never been trees, and where now, since the farms had stolen across them, there weren't even prairies. But nothing could devour the Manitoba sky except tornadoes. The wind coiled and uncoiled like a tortured snake, and Amos and Kona, caught out on the road, huddled in an irrigation ditch as the sky ripped in two. Then, when the sun shone in

Saskatchewan, they thought the lid had been taken off the world.

When they finally passed the last oil rig in Alberta's dried-out basin, the Rockies reared up, untameable, and a hundred million trees called out at once. Over the forest's shouting came the thunder of a train and the whooping and yelling of new recruits, who leaned out the windows of passenger cars and the open doors of freight cars and cattle cars. While the world fought its war, Amos and Kona were spiking trees, leaving a trail across Canada that the newspapers called Nazi sabotage.

In the highest valleys of the Rockies, the couple lived on fish and deer, ate the warm organs raw, cut the flesh thin as stockings, hung them on wet birch sticks to smoke over cool fires. When the jerky snapped like a dead twig, they stowed the meat in their sacks and carried on. Most nights by the campfire, they were silent, but often they took a stick and drew pictures in the snow. She smiled at him in the woods as she had in her grandfather's shack. But whenever they ran out of spikes and were forced into town to steal some, walking down a street full of white men she took off her red cap and hid it, and her face disappeared in stone.

When Kona became pregnant, Amos propped his skis against a cedar that twisted its shallow roots into the mountain scree. Down on his knees in the snow, he held her belly. Then he pounded two iron nails into bands and called them pledge rings. They stepped into the trees like clouds colliding, and their skins burned in the shadows. They did not speak, but Kona ran her hand over Amos's flesh – the scar on his head, the scar on his cheek, the slim, unmoving eyelid – as if injury were the heart of identity.

Some nights, when they tussled in bed, the rings drew blood.

He went to the nearby town alone. Men emerged dirty and bedraggled from the mountains all the time, but no one looked as bad as Amos. His scarred, one-eyed face seemed a signature of guilt, and shoplifting was a risk that Kona didn't need to share in. There was a cop leaning on a black-and-white car in front of the hardware store, so Amos slipped into the nearest shop, waited for the officer to move on, and thumbed through a magazine. He didn't expect to find Donna in a Pears soap advertisement. About to drop her bathrobe, she was peering over her shoulder at him. Even all cleaned up, there was no mistaking her, and yet what was in her eyes was something foreign. She'd never looked at any man in the Bend the way she looked at the camera. She both was and wasn't Donna. He tore the page out of the magazine, coughing to cover the sound like he'd seen someone do in the movies. He shoved it into his overalls pocket and walked out of the shop, right past the hardware store and the police car. The picture gave him a terrible craving: in almost five years, he hadn't heard a word about his firstborn.

He turned down a residential street where an old man sat rocking on a porch in a cold patch of sun while a small girl broke icicles off of the eaves and sucked on the tips. It was a perfect blue winter day in a mountain town – picturesque except for the smell. The wind pushed hard from the southeast, and in the air you could catch the rotten-egg stench from the gas flares in Turner Valley, though it was miles away.

He was walking up and down the roads where people lived. He was looking for an opportunity, and eventually he found one. Through the window of a corner house, its front door open to one road and its side door open to the other, he could see a woman baking. He saw her wipe her hands on her apron, exit the kitchen and leave the house by the front. Needing to borrow lard or sugar or some other ingredient rationed by the war, she ran across the street to a neighbour's. Amos entered through her side door, found the telephone in the back hall and asked the operator to put him through to Delia MacAllister in Greensboro, Vermont.

"Jessum Crow, Amos, where in hell are you?"

"Canada. I was thinking. I was wondering how's my baby."

He heard her suck in her breath and hold it.

"Delia, You still there?"

She didn't have to tell him. He'd known it, somewhere in his wounded head, the moment the girl had died, and because he'd known it, he'd told himself, vigorously, the opposite. He'd buried her deeper than she was actually buried. All these years, not wanting the news, not wanting to blame himself, just wanting to be happy doing what he had to do. But now he'd seen Donna's picture, and Kona was pregnant.

Delia didn't spare him any details. She described how the infant had been found a week later, how the coroner had concluded she'd been dead six days, how she hadn't lived long enough to starve to death but had died of hypothermia because the hearth was cold and the door was open and both of her parents were gone.

"Amos, what in hell were you doing? What in hell were you thinking?"

Amos couldn't answer, because he heard the door open at the front of the house. But he couldn't have answered anyway. Without speaking, he hung up and slipped out the back. He returned to the mountains empty-handed, and there wasn't any food that night, either.

"No nails?" asked Kona.

"Policeman," said Amos. "Hungry?" he asked.

"Yup."

They were lying in a snow house in the foothills.

"I'm gonna get work tomorrow," he said.

Kona looked up over her belly, which in the thick of winter was as large as a haymow in summer. There wasn't any work in the mountains. "What kinda work?"

"Oil work. In Turner Valley."

She fixed her eyes on the snow above her. A single drip fell onto her forehead, then a second, in the exact same place. She said, "No you ain't."

With her protruding navel staring up from her belly as if it were a third eye, it was hard for Amos to know where to look. So, like her, he stared at the ice roof.

Kona held a black silence between her teeth and said nothing for a long while. She took his equal silence as determination, and so when she finally spoke, she asked, "Why?"

He said, "'Cause I gotta get you a house that don't melt." That he'd killed his own child weren't words that would come out of his mouth.

She rolled over onto her side. The weight of the baby was pressing on her blood and putting her legs to sleep. Her long black hair catching under her hips, she arched her back and shifted her bottom to free it. She screwed her gaze into the wall; a drip fell beside her ear and slid down her cheek.

Hoping his mass could replace his words, Amos spooned his big naked body around her. But Kona crossed her arms over her chest so he couldn't hold her breasts.

"You're not gonna tend the trees no more," she said. "You don't even know why you're spiking trees no more."

"I do."

"Why?"

He hesitated. "So our baby can see old forests."

"That ain't all of it, Amos, it ain't all of it. Forests ain't all of it by a far shot." If Kona said it three times, she meant it. "It never mattered to my people whether it was loggers, gold diggers, coal men or oilmen that moved our village on. Sometimes you really only got one eye. Oil work! How can a man like you do oil work?"

"'Cause I got only one eye, but I can see two sides of things. I ain't gonna watch with this one good eye while another baby freezes in a bad winter 'cause its daddy don't got work. Oil work's what there is."

The sadness in his voice was bigger than he was, so Kona loosened her closed arms and let Amos's hands slip around her. He held her breasts like unbaked loaves.

"Promise," she said, "if we go to the oilfields, you still gonna stay with the trees."

"You want me to?"

She nodded. Then whispered, as if she were afraid she might wake the baby, "But I don't want all those oilmen snooping in a tree spiker's business."

Tree spikers were what they were called when the news-papermen were feeling merciful. More often, they were branded as traitors and Nazis. Spotting a headline about their doings in the *Calgary Times*, Amos had said, "I ain't German, and Christly, you're a Indian." Kona had laughed, and because she was pregnant, peed a little into her skirt. But now she was afraid. Amos saw her perfect skin shudder as if a fly had landed on it.

"I promise," he said.

"What you promise?"

"I promise everything."

He slid one hand down to her belly while the hand on her breast melted fully into its softness. He felt the baby kicking. Seen like that by no one, the three of them fell asleep.

Men called the oilfields Hell's Half Acre. An oilcan clanked against a chain and a belated dried-out Christmas wreath hung from the wooden archway at the entrance. Since the first blowout back in 1914, Hell had expanded. It was Canada's largest field, employing hundreds of men and supplying oil to peashooters and thunderbolts flying over Italy and M4 Shermans rolling through the Marshall Islands. New massive steel derrick towers stood by old wooden ones. Ninety-foot flare stacks burnt sour gases day and night; their relentless light, like the spawn of the star of Bethlehem, might, on a moonless night, be visible from as far as Calgary. Squatters' slums were everywhere: Mortgage Heights, Poverty Flats, Cufflink Flats, Old Naphtha, Boiler Camp, Mill City, Little Gap, Little Chicago. Dogtown was closest, a cluster of tarpaper shanties plunked randomly down beside Sheep Creek on the field's southern haunches. Though there were dogs there – and chickens and pigs in the street – it took its name from the quality of life. It was a place where husbands and wives argued for the sake of warming up. Babies mewled and shat where they stood with bare bottoms, and shit froze in the gassy earth. A roughed-up whore slouched in an alley in a state of half-undress.

Between the butcher's and the grocer's shacks were a bar, a brothel and a pool hall. Oilmen who worked twelve hours a day, seven days a week, with only Christmas off, got as skunk-drunk as they could when they got paid. Every man knew every other man's business and broadcast it with boozy authority. So Amos and Kona looked outside Hell's boundaries for a room in a boarding house.

"Christians?" the landlady asked them. She turned hard eyes on their makeshift rings and spoke with the flatness of the fields.

Kona lied with an equal flatness, "Church of England."

"Well, I don't know," hawed the landlady, and didn't step aside from the door. "You Indian? You a squaw?"

Kona set her teeth so as not to answer. Amos said, "My wife." He put his hand on her belly. "It's gonna be a boy," he said.

Though she looked at the two of them as if they had broken and entered, the landlady drew open the door. She led them down a mean hallway and up the stairs to a dingy chamber. When they closed the bedroom door, they could feel how she listened behind it, and they waited silently until her steps retreated down the stairway.

Kona sat cross-legged on the bed, holding the room key on her belly, her gaze on the sharp-pointed crucifix hanging above the headboard. She said to Amos, "It could fall off the wall and take out your other eye. You think we're safe here?"

"Yup."

"Yup," she repeated, so as to make it true.

Amos looked out the window at the dog-pissy snow covering the winter dross. The squalid little oil outpost – it couldn't be called a town or even a village – consisted of the boarding house, a store that sold dusty tins of food, a bar and a single gravel road leading one way to the rigs and the other to the railway station. Yet to the north Amos could still see the mountains, and to the south the invisible border that was the United States. According to the two-cent postcards for sale on the hallway sideboard, somewhere out there was the world's largest rock to be flung miles from its place of origin by the power of moving ice. Clear-cuts blighted the view to the west, and the emptiness reeked of sulphur from the methane fires dotting the naked distance. The loggers had left only nurse trees, miserable totems shivering in a graveyard of stumps. The few listless branches zagged about like roads that forgot where they were going.

"It's ugly," he said. "And it stinks."

Kona pressed her hands into the stained bedspread on the mattress and lifted herself belly-first to her feet. She walked to the window and leaned her forehead on the icy glass. "*Pishna-kona-kaw*," she said.

"What's that mean?"

"The snow is hard. It'll ski noisy. Got your sack of nails?" she asked.

"Yup."

Over the next several months, every day on his way to work, Amos spiked the trees. The best Canadian oilers had gone to war and Turner Valley had lost its derrickman, and although Amos lacked experience, being strong with steady hands and no fear of heights, he got the job. His aluminium hardhat would, when the summer arrived, call the lightning down on him, but that risk was far away. In winter, the danger was his hands. Though he'd known extreme cold before, he'd never met it so close to the sky as in a steel tower overlooking a barren lowland. While Canada geese, drawn by the artificial dog days of the flare stacks, didn't bother to travel south, Amos up in his tower stood frigid and alone and exposed to the northern winds. Winter turned his hands into two thick slabs of cold. Ice lined the footholds of every rung up the derrick, and when the pipes came up for tripping – when the bit wore down or the mud motors broke, or for half a dozen other reasons the pipes were pulled – numb hands could be lethal.

Even back in her room, Kona wore gloves as she whittled and strung a cradleboard of aspen and buckskin. Onto the buckskin she fixed the buttons off Amos's shirt, which in his first week had got caught in the oil rig elevator and ripped to shreds.

At the boarding house, mornings began with prayers. Roughnecks and roustabouts – oilers who, for their own reasons, had taken refuge outside of Dogtown – sat at the landlady's table preparing to scoff down coffee and bacon and bullet-hard brown bread – no one could conjure up white flour during a war. When the landlady banged her breakfast gong, the grimy-fingered men folded their hands perfunctorily, the yellow wallpaper yellowed some more with their smoky intonations, and the baby kicked at Kona's belly as the old woman led them in grace.

This February morning began like every bitter and frozen morning. The pinched creature lifted up her eyes, but not to God: she peered over her fingertips at Kona. Kona, who didn't bend her head and mumble along with the rest of them, was watching the hands of the wall clock. It clanged out its chimes on the hour, then again at two minutes past, in case a person lost count the first time.

"Damn Nazis! Fucking Nazis!" the landlady shouted, prayers now over, her mouth full of pork. "Fucking Nazis stopped logging over in the foothills!" She fingered the morning paper.

Amos said, "Pass the bacon, please, ma'am."

"Certainly, dear." She smiled at him with cracked lips, for though the man spoke as little as a beast, unlike anyone else at her table, when he did he spoke politely. "The lumberyard's wide-toothed saw got busted up by a nail," she crooned to Amos. "The whole valley will be upping security." She tugged at the bacon gristle in her teeth, then shouted at the lot of them, "Your foreman's going to have a derrick pipe up his ass!" She sat back in her Victorian dining chair and observed the unbridled snickering of her boarders.

"You got any more of that pig grease, please, ma'am?" Amos rose and waited to be dismissed to the kitchen, where the landlady saved him grease drippings in a coffee can, though even with the insulating stuff smeared all over his hands, up in the derrick tower, in the deep degrees below zero, he struggled to bend his fingers.

"That's what you fucking stink of!" came a voice further down the table, as a tattooed roughneck crammed more meat into his mouth. Oil filled the furrow in his brow, and dark lines of ink from the tattooist's needle scrawled up his wiry arms. He was one of the many convicts who – due to the shortage of men and the necessity of oil in the war – was set loose to work the fields.

Kona was seated beside him, and when she crossed her hands on her belly and prepared to leave the table, he slid his elbows down the tablecloth. Onto her plate, he spat out the cud of mint he'd been storing in one cheek – the troops were hoarding tobacco – while champing on bacon in the other. His breath was both fresh and rancid. "You know, little girl," he said, leaning in to her close, "your fellow could hang hisself from his derrick if he wanted."

Kona stared at the clock.

"Don't know why I'd want to," said Amos, as he stepped behind Kona's chair to help her up.

"Every ape's got a reason to die, Kong," the tattooed roughneck said.

Delighted by the dovetailing of conversation and the trivia in this morning's paper, the landlady declared, "It says here, Mr Derrick was a famous executioner in England who had a gallows named after him. The oil tower was named for a fucking gallows! I think we should hang some fucking Nazis from the derrick, don't you think? Or Jews maybe! Or a fucking redskin!"

Expressionless, Amos and Kona left the room.

Up in the bedroom, Amos threw his sack on his shoulder.

"You got your hammer and nails?" asked Kona, as if she were already a mother sending her child off to school.

"Yup," he said.

"You got your grease tin?"

"I got everything."

As one limousine escorted another through the gates of Hell, from the open window Aubrey saw workmen in filthy coveralls suctioning up the black skirt of oil that had leaked around Tankard Three. The holding tank had been sabotaged, and Nazis were hammering nails into forestry trees. That was the verdict. Now the Canadian Pacific Railway wished to discover whether these things were linked.

"What does it have to do with you?" Aubrey asked his uncle, but he learned only that the CPR had leased Turner Valley to Canadian Imperial, a subsidiary of Standard Oil of New Jersey.

Oil sprayed from beneath the limousine wheels.

Aubrey said, "What a mess."

"A man can clean anything up," said Jack. "I'm freezing. Close the window."

"It's too iced up to see out," said Aubrey, who was looking for Amos. He hoped that, even from a distance, he'd know him by his size, but worried that, having been so small himself, Amos wasn't as huge as he remembered.

"It's not much of a view," said Jack.

That wasn't entirely true. The gas flares were almost beautiful. Methane fires dotted the flatness, and even in the daylight they shone like stars shot down in a dogfight. Seventy-two flare stacks, seventy-two fallen suns. They looked like what they were: millions of years of sunlight had produced oil.

When Aubrey didn't close the window, Jack said, "I should have ridden with Joe."

The man in the other limousine, who wore a railway lapel pin, was billeting them for the night. It was clear he held sway in the field; when both cars pulled to a stop, a foreman rushed to greet him. Joe levered his fat asthmatic body into the frozen day, gasped for breath and shouted, "Bloody hell! I saw the spill driving up – what the hell's going on here?"

Jack, however, didn't hurry into the cold. He enjoyed the relative comfort of the warm back seat. Slowly, he fastened up the neck of his thick mink coat and turned the earflaps down on his grey fedora. Then he lit a Cuban cigar. Jack never smoked except to cover the stench of the oilfields.

"Wait in the boiler room," he said to Aubrey.

"I'm going to take pictures of the field."

"You'll freeze your balls off."

Jack spoke more freely when he wasn't at home. He left the car and strolled through the yard as if he owned it. When he glanced about for somewhere to flick his cigar ash, the foreman offered the palm of his hand and he accepted the fleshy ashtray. Then the foreman directed him under a derrick, where the crew was tripping pipes.

It was noisy work. Each thirty-foot, quarter-ton length of iron piping was being pulled from the earth and hooked to an elevator and sent up a hundred-and-fifty foot tower, where the derrickman would lasso it, unlock it and, lunging out into empty space, swing it into its rack. The winds made the derrick hum, and the Geronimo line – a cable to the ground, escape route in a blowout – trembled. There was no danger of a blowout today, because at thirty-nine hundred feet the crew had found only a trickle. Unaware that the valley had once been a lake – prime breeding ground for hydrocarbons at the depth of the Devonian reefs – and that at eighty nine hundred feet lay a massive reservoir of oil, Imperial was aborting the well.

Aubrey squinted in the glare off the snow. The sun on the steel tower was blinding. The winds were so cold they should have frozen themselves and immobilized, but instead they sliced through his cashmere coat and shocked his lungs, and the stench of sour gas was asphyxiating. Not just to stay warm, he wrapped his scarf tight around his mouth and nose. He followed his uncle under the derrick, but none of the men he saw there was Amos. "I'm going to take pictures," he shouted over the roar of the engines and walked off across the fields.

Though he found the snow too deep to walk in, the roads and the pipelines were clear. A snowplough driver swept mounds into the roadside ditches, and a team of men with shovels stood clearing the drifts, which had buried a pipe. Another team bent over a steamer thawing an auxiliary line. Big men were everywhere – roustabouts, drillers, welders, gas fitters, rotary engineers and cable engineers, roughnecks – seated in machines or standing beside them, dwarfed or aggrandized by them. But none of them were big enough. Amos might work in any corner of the field or live in any one of the squatter towns.

Aubrey walked an hour up the pipeline that joined Hell's Half Acre to the city of Calgary, then branched off and followed the smaller tendrils that linked processor plants and compression plants. Finally, he retraced his steps to the south towards Dogtown.

The shantytown was the oilfield in miniature. The inhabitants tapped into pipeline leaks and siphoned off unlimited gas; a hundred minor fires burnt day and night. Using three hundred pounds of pressure per square inch, women cooked turkeys at Christmas in almost the time it took to set the table. Their wood stoves glowed red, fed by tubes through the fireboxes and fitted with homemade valve caps. Children burnt the family trash in oil-drum incinerators in back alleys. Men played blackjack by gaslight at the twenty-four-hour pool hall; the establishment never closed to save on the cost of fuel. Cars never died because of the cold: a flame burning under the hood meant an engine turned over at forty degrees below zero. Flies that shouldn't have survived the winter flourished in the outhouses, where gas heaters warmed the top layer of shit. But this wasn't the same fuel that poured north to Calgary: it was unscrubbed gas, straight from the source and laced with hydrogen sulphide. It peeled the lead paint off the druggist's sign and blackened the silver reflectors on the car lamps. If it pooled in a ditch or a basement or latrine pit, condensed enough, it could kill you just to breathe it.

A hatchet-faced woman emerged from her shack in a furious attempt to houseclean. She dumped food scrapings into the snow. A dozen chickens ran up the road to see what they'd find, but a mangy dog chased them away and devoured the guts of something. When a man came outside to piss, the stream drilled down to the dormant grass beneath.

Outside a tarpaper saloon, Aubrey saw an upturned burnt-out car. He figured a gas explosion had thrown it on its haunches and buried the rear in the earth. Erect like that, it was hardly a car anymore; it was a monument to something awful.

Dogtown sapped his hope. He'd walked all morning. He would never find Amos. He turned back across the field towards the boiler room, thinking if he'd come all this way for nothing, he might as well get warm.

Amos was tripping pipes. He threw his rope hard to oppose the strong wind, and caught one. It hung heavy in the sharp air. He pulled the rope in with his left hand and unlatched the elevator with his right. As the pipe slid off to the side, he leaned his thick chest into its force, riding its momentum and guiding the five hundred pounds of iron into its holding rack. It was slow, hard, frozen work at the top of the derrick, and he'd been doing it for hours. Under his hardhat, sweat iced up his hair, and under his hide gloves his fingers swelled despite their coating of lard. Though his aim was still good, he couldn't feel his hands anymore.

He'd seen the two black limousines roar through the gate that morning, and like everyone else in Hell's Half Acre he'd heard Jack Shaw was coming. Shaw was known as the man who'd erected a monument to himself in Dogtown years ago, an incinerated car that had curbed any talk of unionizing. Everyone knew if Shaw was coming, his spies were already here.

Amos had seen the little man in a mink coat and the fat man and the teenager walk under the derrick. Figuring the man in the mink was Shaw, he'd watched him walk away towards the leaky holding tank. After that, he hadn't seen him for most of the morning, but when Shaw returned, the roughneck who lodged at the boarding house was with him. The two of them looked up at Amos on his platform. The tattooed man even pointed, before walking off towards the boiler room, where Amos's backpack was hidden. Amos didn't have time to think about that, because, harnessed to the rig, he was swinging out into the open air and throwing his rope again.

Maybe he was distracted, or his hands were to blame – whichever it was, he missed. He hovered in the empty air. Though he should have kept his eye on the job, he looked beneath him again. There he was still – Shaw – staring up through the derrick. Amos threw his rope and sideswiped the pipe. Now he looked towards the boiler room and saw the roughneck about to enter. He threw again; his rope caught. He reached to unlatch the pipe from its binding and guide it home as usual. But hearing the geese above him call, he looked up at them. Enough of them to darken the sky. His fingers were insensible, and in that instant his mind was up there in the sky with the birds, and his body was flying in the harness. So maybe the birds were to blame, not Shaw or the cold. It didn't matter. Whatever the reason, the pipe, released from its binding, was dropping. It was spearing down through the tower, and almost exactly beneath was Mr Shaw.

Amos unfastened his harness and threw himself down the Geronimo line. When his feet touched the ground, he found himself running. He ran without stopping or thinking, but above him, the geese followed.

When Aubrey walked through the boiler room door, he saw Uncle Jack warming his hands, and a dozen roughnecks and Joe.

A tattooed man shouted, "Where the hell have you been! Goddamn derrickman almost killed your uncle!" The man spat a wad of mint and added, "Ever been out in the cold five minutes without a hundred-dollar coat on?"

"Leave him alone," said Jack. He was calm but unusually pale, and by the pulsing heat of the boiler, he turned his palms up like a ghost giving benediction. "It's cold out there."

"Are you hurt?" Aubrey asked. "You don't look hurt. Are you?"

But Jack had returned to the conversation Aubrey's arrival had interrupted, and the tattooed man had his full attention.

"Fucking Nazi. Fucking American," the man said.

Jack reminded him that he, too, was American.

The roughneck wiped the juice from the corner of his mouth. "You can count on that pipe not being a accident, Mr Shaw."

"Show me," said Jack.

The man got down on his hands and knees and groped beneath the benches where the workmen stashed their bags and lunch pails. He pulled out a basket of dirty laundry and shoved it to the side. Above him, half-clean clothes hung on a line that was hooked from one wall to the other – the shantytowns having no running water, men washed their clothes in the boiler steam before they went to work. He pulled out a canvas backpack, tipped it upside down, and an axe, a clutch of nails and a coffee tin fell out. "These are Amos Cobb's," he said.

Aubrey stopped taking off his coat, one sleeve dangling like an amputee's. He watched his uncle run a finger along his lower lip. Jack was thinking, or was impressed by how his skin blazed with the heat of the boiler while inside he was cold. But it was Aubrey who was both burning up and frozen.

"You say he didn't talk much," said Jack.

"Kept himself to himself," said the man.

"Did he tell you anything about himself?"

"He's from Vermont."

Jack looked over at Aubrey. "Know him?"

It was only a joke.

The room, though brightened by the glare off the boiler, was darkened by heavy grime on the windows. Aubrey rubbed the glass clean with his hand, his palm blackening as it let in the sun. Through the window he could see the derrick. He'd walked right under it; he'd walked right under Amos.

From their talk, he pieced together the story: an ugly Vermonter with one eye, who shacked up in a boarding house with an Indian woman, had been sabotaging the war effort, and having tried unsuccessfully to kill Jack Shaw, had bolted. Slipping his blackened hand back into his sleeve, Aubrey might have bolted too. It would have been stupid and meaningless, but he was overcome by conflicting urges, to run after Amos, run with him, to warn him, or stop him, or help him, or ask him, "Why did you want to kill Uncle Jack? Who is he?" He didn't know which or what.

Joe was blocking the exit now, and Jack whispered in his ear. A drip of perspiration dropped from Joe's fat earlobe onto his Canadian Pacific Railway lapel pin. Suddenly, Jack turned to Aubrey and said, "I have to go. Wait here."

"Where?"

"In the boiler room."

"I mean where are you going?"

When Jack smiled, Aubrey knew his smiles meant nothing.

"Hunting," said Jack.

"I'm coming."

"No."

"I'm coming."

Jack raised his eyebrows, a gesture he might have stolen from Aunt Ethyl.

"You'll have to stay in the car," said Jack. "You'd be happier here."

"No. I'm coming."

"Really?" Jack actually looked confused. "Why?"

Aubrey said, "I like cars. There'll be something to drink. It smells like shit in here."

Outside, the limousines waited. After the boss climbed into one and drove away, Aubrey, Jack, the tattooed man and two other roughnecks climbed into the other.

Jack clinked about in the liquor cabinet as the car jostled over the frozen road. He poured himself a large French brandy and a small one for Aubrey. But he offered nothing to the roughnecks, nor did they look expectant.

The leather seats reeked of grease and oil from the men's overalls. Aubrey could hardly breathe. He pulled a handkerchief from his pocket and masked his face.

"Smell better in here?" laughed Jack.

"You crying?" asked the roughneck. He twisted his head around to grin at Aubrey, and the tattoo on his neck balled into a solid blackness.

Aubrey didn't answer either question. He swirled the brandy, watching the oily liquid rise and retreat on the side of the etched glass. It reminded him of the picture window that streamed with water as Amos carried his dead mother down the stairs. Amos wasn't a Nazi or a murderer.

"How do you know it wasn't just an accident, Uncle Jack? How do you know he wasn't just chopping wood with that axe and building a fence with the nails or something? Don't you need to be certain before you go after him? Why would a guy from Vermont want to kill you?"

Jack laughed at him. "Probably because I never liked Vermont. Too many cows, nothing but granite. And the women have thick waists. When I was a boy, your grandmother used to drag me there, kicking and screaming. You like the brandy?"

"I don't know what brandy's made from," said Aubrey, staring at his glass. "Grapes?"

"I thought you didn't know," said Jack.

Amos mounted his rifle on his shoulder and stared into the vanity mirror in his room at the boarding house. He could kill his reflection. Why had he run? Why hadn't he stayed in the mountains like Kona wanted?

Kona was out. Even at eight months pregnant, she couldn't be persuaded to stay inside. Amos scraped the ice-brittle from the window, hoping to catch sight of her coming out of the woods. His scars, which hadn't troubled him in over two years, were pounding. He leaned his cheek against the glass to cool down. His scars were burning up. In the mirror, they resembled mouths about to open.

He threw his belongings into a bag and Kona's into another. He tied the beaded cradleboard onto Kona's rucksack. He paced from one wall to the other, slumped onto the bed like a cliff giving way, and then jumped up suddenly, the bedclothes sliding to the floor.

At the sound of footsteps, he threw open the bedroom door. The landlady, kneeling by the keyhole, dropped a tin of cleanser from her hand and the white powder snowed over the floorboards. He dragged her by the arm into the room, fumbled in his pockets for some oily dollars and shoved them into her palm to settle the bill.

"Squaw sluts can't be trusted," she said, seeing Kona wasn't there.

More hotness poured into Amos's temples. He grabbed her by her stringy arms, wanting to squeeze the tick till she burst, but instead he flung her out of the bedroom door. Just then, Kona walked up the stairs and stepped over the cussing landlady.

Amos blurted, "I'm sorry."

The story came out nonsensically. Then, Amos could say nothing but "I'm sorry," again and again. As they skied through the woods to the train station, the hard snow screeched beneath them. Kona skied in silence, but Amos said, "I'm sorry," repetitive as birdsong.

The woods carried them secretly to the railway station, bringing them up the back side, where they took cover in the rear behind a tank car and a locomotive. Kona unfastened her skis and leaned them against a whistle board. On top of her sheepskin coat, around her ripe belly, she wore one of her grandfather's tatty blankets to keep the enormous baby inside her warm. To become invisible, she took off her thick red cap. Amos, who did not take off his skis, unbuttoned his fly and pissed into the snow.

"Amos?" asked Kona.

He was standing with his penis in his hand, looking at the yellow hole in the snow as if it were a means of escape. A giant man, with a rifle on his back and a small axe – it was Kona's axe – slung through his belt loop, his belt slack, fly open, looking down past his penis in his hand. Kona felt how his thoughts rushed through him poisoned. As if he were a child, she guided his penis back into his trousers. She placed her hands on his cheeks, where, even through her gloves, she could feel his stubble.

"It ain't your fault," she whispered.

As he opened his mouth to answer, a freight train hooted in the distance, and the tank train in front of them rolled away into a siding to allow it through. The earth trembled beneath the weight of the shifting trains, the one pulling away and the other slowing to pass without stopping at the station. The brakes screeched, and the smell of asbestos overwhelmed the smell of white pine and coal dust. Between the slow moving of one train and the slow passing of the other was a gap: in it, the station platform, where Mr Shaw and the roughnecks were waiting.

Seeing Amos and the Indian, Shaw touched his fedora and smiled, and the roughnecks lifted their guns.

Out of sight down a logging lane in the woods, not far from the railway station, Aubrey sat in the back of the limousine. Somewhat drunk already, he took another swig of brandy. He was angry and tired, and sick and tired, and scared. There was nothing to do, nothing to be done. Sitting there, stupidly shivering, was worse than not having come at all.

"What?" said the chauffeur from the front seat.

"I didn't say anything."

He never said anything. He asked a bunch of questions, then dropped it. He should have said to his uncle, "He's my friend. Leave him alone." That it was futile didn't make it worthless. The same was true of Aunt Ethyl: horrors occurred behind her closed doors and he never said a word.

He played roughly with his camera, randomly changing the aperture. Feeling guilty was irrational and unwarranted and made him angry: Amos wasn't his fault; Jack wasn't his fault. The guilt felt like some violence inflicted upon him.

"Nothing," he said.

"You're drunk," said the chauffeur and turned the radio up. Arthur Tracy was singing "East of the Sun."

Aubrey polished off the brandy. Jack had insisted he wait in the limousine when the men filed into the boarding house, and then wait again here near the railway station, and so the sun had set while he drank his uncle's brandy. Though he tried to convince himself he was bored, actually he was frightened. The roughnecks and his uncle were hunting Amos. He'd seen them leaving with guns.

"I'm going for a walk," he said to the chauffeur.

"Mr Shaw says you're not to go anywhere."

"He's not my goddamn father!"

Aubrey slammed the car door behind him. He ran through the woods in the direction he thought he'd seen his uncle disappear, but he found himself lost in a field of stumps and rubble. As he turned round in circles, he heard the sound of gunshots and a train pulling off.

In the brief gap, the view was unobstructed. A bullet aimed at Amos shattered Kona's skis leaning against the whistle board behind her. Through the blanket that hung from her belly, there was a clean hole no bigger than a cigarette burn. The baby inside was kicking.

Like a mountain awaking, Amos tore the rifle off his back. The tattooed man jumped down to the tracks before the incoming freight blocked his passage. Amos shot only once. The butt recoiled against his chin and his scars spasmed with the thrust. The roughneck stumbled, his fingers exploring the blood on his inky chest.

Amos swept his hands around Kona's waist and lifted her up into his arms. He was skiing, but not towards the woods. He was chasing the freight train as it pulled away down the tracks. With one hand, he caught the iron railing around the rear of the caboose, and Kona's small brown fingers curled around an upright. With the other hand, he heaved her up onto the train and let go. *They're gonna hunt me till they catch me, with or without you, but without me they're not gonna hunt you and the baby no more.* The sadness on her face blurred into a colourless vision receding. But Amos told himself Kona was safe. To the sound of gunfire, he skied alone into the woods.

Jack radioed the freight train and had it stopped. His men found the pregnant Indian crouching in a boxcar filled with tractors. The tattooed man, who had only suffered a flesh wound, entered first. Having stripped off his fouled shirt and used it under his coat as a bandage, his chest was red and naked.

When they sat her down, the Indian girl covered her belly. But when Jack said, "Put up your hands," and she complied, her hidden child rode defiantly in front of her. She never opened her mouth when Jack hit her.

There was a knock on the door, and Jack opened it a crack so the conductor could explain the importance of keeping the trains running on time. Jack smiled and said, "We're done here anyway." Then he smiled again, this time at the bloodied-up roughneck. "The girl's no use to me, but you look like you want her." So they dragged her off the train and back towards the empty station.

There, standing in the snow, was Aubrey, calling "Amos!"

"What's up?" Jack asked casually. "Going to catch the bad guy all by yourself?"

Aubrey stared at the pregnant girl, at the tattooed man's arm, crawling with ink, oil, blood and hair, around her neck. The man's other hand clutched at her breast. Aubrey couldn't see her clearly, but the girl's face looked made of stone.

"Did you shoot him?"

"No luck," said Jack.

"Did he get away?"

"For the moment," said Jack.

"Are you done then? Can we go?"

"Bored?"

"Cold. I'm cold. I want to go now."

Jack looked at the face of his wristwatch: it was smooth, moonlike and calm. He said, "Give me five minutes. I'll meet you back at the car."

It was dark now. In February in the north, the sun dropped early. Aubrey told himself he couldn't see, and that at least was true. He couldn't see clearly at all. He told himself there were things in the world he couldn't understand and didn't need to – he didn't need to know who the girl was, where Amos was, who his uncle was. Jack was his mother's brother; Jack wanted to protect him. That was all he needed to know. But not actually believing a word he told himself, he lifted his camera and, without adjusting the aperture, shot. He wanted proof.

"Get in the car," ordered Jack, visibly angry.

Aubrey obeyed, trudging through the snow back to the limousine. The moon hadn't risen, and in the woods it was even darker. Fearing he'd wandered off the logging road again, he stopped and stood and listened and feared what he was listening for. He tried not to think, his thoughts being terrible. He held his camera tightly, and his feet grew numb in the snow. He would have seen his breath if he'd been able to see anything at all. Five minutes later, his uncle returned as promised and led him to the car.

Jack wiped his hands on a handkerchief. "Now give me the camera," he said, his voice firm but calm. Yet before Aubrey could decide whether or not to obey, Jack changed his mind. "Forget it," he said, smiling. He knew the shot would never come out. Inside the car, the ceiling light lit up his lips and the crease in his forehead. Aubrey hated Jack's smile.

Two of the three roughnecks climbed into the limousine.

Aubrey asked his uncle, "Where's the other guy? The one with the tattoos."

Jack hesitated only briefly.

"He's getting paid."

Kona backed up against the waiting room wall, jostling a painting mounted on plywood. It was a cheap watercolour of the Rocky Mountains, with a rushing stream and an eagle in the sky circling a deer below, badly framed in rough cedar knocked together with a couple of nails.

"Passenger train only comes through on Monday," the tattooed man said. "We got the whole weekend, girl."

When she said nothing, but just looked straight past him as if her gaze on the exit could draw it to her, he stuck his face in hers. She could smell blood and his mint-meat breath. "That's right," he said. "Keep your mouth shut. I don't wanna hear a word out of you."

He touched her belly, almost tenderly, then slid his hand to her crotch and bruised her in an instant. "Room for me in there, you think? Think you'll stretch that far? Or burst?"

She raised her arms over her head, and as he dropped his hands to open his fly, he said, "I thought Indians were stupid, but you know when to lay back and take it."

She took hold of the painting above her head. She had no trouble smashing it against the wall and breaking it quickly. She shoved a sharp edge of the frame, its nail protruding, into the tattooed man's eye. She did not flinch or withdraw her hand. Blood rushed down her arm and over her breasts as the man staggered back, and she pursued him till he fell on the floor with his knees flopping open.

Kona ran out of the railway station and into the woods, calling, "Amos!"

D onna Cobb had become accustomed to luxury. Even
on the fringes of her mind, Amos no longer existed.
The only sign of him was his surname, and she planned to
leave that behind in Chicago. She was ascending a human
stairway, holding onto one man just long enough to be
introduced to a richer man. In exchange for four-star hotels
and haute couture, she put up with men's porkpie hands or
angry fists, their limp dicks or perpetually hard ones, their
droning conversations about their businesses or their wives.
She not only took a tour of a Southside slaughterhouse,
owned by a man who bought her a mink, she enthused over
the efficient manner of killing cows. She even took elocution
lessons so as not to embarrass the Wrigley Spearmint Gum
tycoon, though not without a tantrum. Men indulged her
moods, and if they sometimes punished her, forgiving them
paid off.

She slapped one fellow while he was driving his Caddy
down Lake Shore Drive and enjoying the power behind his
own wheel, the chauffeur seated in the back. She didn't know
why she did it; probably, she was drunk. He pulled onto the
shoulder, drew off his leather driving gloves, grabbed her
wrists with one hand and, with the other, belted her several

times. Time slowed while he hit her. Past his fedora, she could see the waves on Lake Michigan frozen in mid-crest. *I don't want to be like those waves,* she thought, *stuck halfway between one thing and another.* She saw everything through. She knew that in the end, after she'd locked herself in his bathroom and let him hear her weep, he'd buy her a pair of diamond earrings and a matching necklace.

She was unstoppable, her ambition impossible to deflect. Riding the escalator in Marshall Field's up to Luggage, she purchased a brass-edged trunk that quickly filled with clothes and jewels, everything she'd need for Hollywood, where she imagined she'd meet Orson Welles or become lovers with Charlie Chaplin or one of the other actors who hadn't gone to war.

The man who bought her a first-class ticket to the City of Angels would have kept her longer, long enough to buy her a golden wristwatch, if it weren't for Amos. That was ironic. She hadn't thought about him once since selling his shoddy ring. So why the memory of Runaway Pond overcame her that too-hot day, she'd never know. "It was voodoo," she said afterwards, in an attempt to smooth things over. Though she had a crisp new way of talking, she still quoted songs and picture shows. She ran her red lacquered nails down the man's starched white shirt. "Forget about him. You do voodoo to me," she said, swearing to herself that she'd never again utter the name Amos Cobb. She'd invent a new history, a birthplace, a spanking new name.

In their underwear, she and the man had been smoking cigarettes, one after another, their sweaty heads thrown back against the mahogany headboard. The pillows monogrammed D for the Drake had fallen off the bed and the blankets kicked down into a dank mess at the foot. Chicago summers being steam baths in eggy water, and the stink from Gary, Indiana, creeping like a tramp into the city, the dry cigarette smoke was the only relief from the humidity.

"There weren't days like this in Vermont," she said. Sick of the sunlight, she spoke with her eyes closed. Not really talking to the man beside her, Donna was just talking. "Except one weird summer when mosquitoes breeding in the Bend swamp wouldn't let me sleep. Amos got me to screw him by breeding mosquitoes. That's exactly what he did. Sucked me in with the story of Runaway Pond, made me feel like the world was coming undone, made me feel I should catch hold of the biggest thing around."

The man rolled over on her and placed her hand on his dick. But it was unpleasantly sweaty, so she pushed him off, dropped back against the headboard, and, closing her mascaraed eyes again, said, "It's too damn hot."

"What's Runaway Pond?" he asked, bored with her, lighting another cigarette.

"It happened in Greensboro Bend, even before the train came through and they called it the Bend – even before the train was invented, I suppose. But even back then, Amos's great-great-grandfather thought he knew what caused what, which Amos always said is something nobody knows for sure. His great-great-grandfather had two ponds – a big one uphill and a little one downhill. Though the little pond wasn't much of a pond, he was stupid enough to build a grist mill on it. Of course, when a summer drought came, the little pond dried up and the mill went dead. So he decided to dig a trench from the full pond uphill to the empty one under it, and let the law of nature do the rest. Amos always said his great-great-grandfather should have just done a rain dance.

"Everyone thought the trench was a good idea, and the whole village came with shovels and picks to help. They started at the bottom and worked to the top. When they got there, they were hot and sweaty and dirty, but happy enough for a moment. They didn't know their shovels had taken the hardpan off and it was the only thing fixing the pond to the earth. They didn't know that under the hardpan there was nothing but sand, till the water pouring downhill started taking the sand with it. And suddenly the earth split wide open, and the big pond – all of it – dumped out.

"Amos said the first tree to be torn from its roots was a two-hundred-year-old maple. Rocks got dragged from their lifelong homes. Rabbits and squirrels in their holes, groundhogs and foxes got drowned. The farmers were yelling and screaming and clutching each other, but they couldn't stop what they'd started. Nothing could stop the giant wave, not even the Cobbs' big red barn or white house, where the farmer's wife and children were about to get smashed instead of the corn in their mill. He leapt on his horse and chased the water, calling out his children's names. He saw the end of his world like some feversome dream: water, everywhere from nowhere, escorted northward by his home, barn, cattle and his giant trees in full leaf. Everything heading north and swept away.

"His children had been playing outside. They had run for the hills and were dotted about like stones. Amos's great-great-grandfather thought he was lucky, until he asked his son, 'Where's your mother? Where's your mother?! Wife!' he called, but no woman answered.

"The water didn't stop till it got to the Canadian border and met a huge lake called Memphremagog. Folks say a monster named Memphre lives in its depths. They say that day he opened his mouth and sucked down all the cow pails and cooking pots carried by the waves. But really it was just the Indians camped in their teepees on the shore who gathered up all that useful stuff. Two men paddled their canoe into the rising waters. They caught hold of Amos's great-great-grandmother's corpse and dragged it in to shore, put sweetgrass over her eyelids, said a prayer and buried Mrs Cobb as if she were one of theirs.

"That's the story of Runaway Pond," said Donna. "Amos liked to tell that story, because he said, while everything else got swept away, the story got passed down."

The Chicagoan didn't even feel jealous as he laid his sweaty thigh over hers and asked, "Who's Amos, honey?"

It was the way she shouted, "My blasted husband!" and broke the Chinese vase on the sideboard and smashed the champagne bottle on the room-service trolley that made him think, even when she ran her fingernails down his chest, that it was time to put her on a train.

N o one would find the roughneck's body in the station until Monday. The limousine dropped the other men outside a bar in Black Diamond and carried on to the big brick house on the town's periphery. There being no good hotels south of Calgary, Jack and Aubrey were Joe's guests for the night. He lived at the edge of the clear cuts, but even this far from the methane fires, the barrenment stank of sulphur. His walls, lit with oil sconces, were decorated with photographs of the famous blowout: Royalite No. 4, a derrick evaporated, the fire raging for three weeks before it was killed by dynamite.

Though Aubrey claimed he was going to bed, after putting on his pyjamas and turning down the blankets, he listened at the parlour door. The hallway was drafty and the liquor that remained in his body did nothing to warm his blood. But he stood there all the same for several hours. Jack and Joe were making phone calls, and Aubrey wanted to hear. Holding a glass of water in his hand, he could claim, if he were caught, to have come from the kitchen. The operator put Jack through to Cuba, Chicago, Dallas, Los Angeles, Calgary, Okotoks, Bragg Creek and Longview. Through the door, Aubrey learned that Amos had been tracked to the foothills. He pieced together what he could and imagined the rest.

The woods into which Amos had disappeared were shallow, and once he'd skied through them there'd be nowhere to hide till he entered the Rockies. In the west were unassailable peaks; in the east, the naked prairies. The foothills, though near, were too steep to ski, so he'd ascend at the pass many miles to the south. To get there, he'd follow the Cowboy Trail, a road used by ranchers and packed down by horse hooves. Though not fool enough to ski the road itself, he'd have no choice but to travel parallel to it over the open range. Somebody on the phone in Okotoks assured Uncle Jack it was certain: Amos would follow the Cowboy Trail.

Jack made a call to Calgary, where somebody said, "No roughnecks, get yourself expert skiers." Some years back, the dust bowl had blinded the Alberta plains, but now it was only snow that was blowing hard. Excellent skiers and decent gunmen could be found in Bragg Creek and Longview.

Wind drifted the snow against a split-log fence and lay bare the black earth on the low-level rises. Where the snow thinned, Amos's skis scraped over frozen needle-and-thread grass and spear grass. Though the northern wind pushed him along, he needed a storm to hide in. He didn't get one: the moon came on like a spotlight. Herds of cold white cattle standing shank to shank – facing north–south because their inner compasses align to the magnetic poles – raised their silent heads at the sight of the big man skiing. Everything was silent, not just the owl that swooped down on a rabbit. The only sound came from a truck with its lights off following the Cowboy Trail.

The truck kept pace with Amos. It stopped and started, and each time it stopped a man climbed out of the hooded bed and took off across the snow. Then the truck passed Amos and stopped again and dropped more skiers on the plain. He was hemmed between the road and the mountain. From the east, northeast and southeast, Amos saw them coming: a dozen expert skiers come to gun him flat like a buffalo, counting on him to dash for the Rockies and pen himself in against the bluffs in the steep western hills.

He did as they expected, except that an animal adapted to the mountains knows how to climb. He wrenched his feet from the bear-trap bindings of his skis and his leather belt from its loops. With the belt, he fastened his skis to his back. The moon blotted by pines, it was dark against the bluff. Even the ice didn't glisten. Amos slammed Kona's axe into the flow of a stream that had frozen as it fell down the cliff. He pulled himself up with one hand. The other scrambled for a notch in the stone. His boots found a foothold in the mouth of a rattlesnake nest – the cold-blooded creature too stupefied to care. He yanked the axe from the ice, reached higher and hoisted himself up again. If the skiers arrived before he made the top, he'd fall like a boulder on them. But if he cleared the bluff, he'd gun down every one of them and be done with it.

His luck was bad, as it had been all day. He did clear the bluff, but before the moon set only six men lay dead in the snow; the others had taken off.

Jack cursed. Hung up. Phoned Calgary again. Phoned Dallas, Chicago, Los Angeles, people who needed to know.

Six men were dead and the Nazi had disappeared into the mountains. Then Jack discovered Aubrey in the hall with a glass of water.

"Thirsty," said Aubrey. "It's dry here."

"We're heading home first thing in the morning," said Jack. "Try to get some sleep."

Aubrey took a sip of water, which might as well have been whisky, he felt so intoxicated with the news. Amos was safe in the mountains. "Can I ask you something?" he asked.

"Is it short?"

"Do you think one man can change world history? I know tyrants do. But what about heroes?"

"Heroes are cogs in a wheel. Go to sleep."

"I mean, do you ever think you should have killed Hitler when you had the chance? You *did* have the chance, didn't you?"

"Just because you have dinner with someone, Aubrey, doesn't mean you have the opportunity to kill him." Jack, in no mood for a grilling, struggled to remain polite. "Also, I don't know why I would have wanted to kill him at the time. What you're talking about is prescience, which isn't much of a motivation for murder."

"But a lot of people said that Hitler was going to do what he's done."

"I guess one of *them* should have killed him."

"You're awfully lucky that pipe didn't hit you today."

"It wasn't going to hit me."

"How do you know?"

"Because it didn't. It's time you went to bed. It's late."

"It's an hour later in Mexico. Did you phone Aunt Ethyl like she asked?"

Though Jack displayed his perfect teeth, it couldn't be called a smile. His open lips were a crack in his self-control. "No. I think you can imagine, Aubrey, it's been a busy night. Go to bed."

Joe came out of the parlour. "What the hell is *he* doing up?"

"Thirsty," said Jack.

On the drive home from the Mexico City airport, Aubrey sank back into the leather seat. He usually felt safe in a car – it was the smell of leather or gas, or the way the whole world was framed by a window. Protected from the sun by tinted glass, he tried to recapture that safe feeling. He pulled a magazine from the pocket on the door and thumbed through the pictures. He stopped at a cigarette ad: American ski troopers were smoking and admiring a view of the Alps. He knew better than to believe it. Having learned to develop his own photographs, he knew what it was to play God in the darkroom. He'd made blue skies stormy and turned day into night, changing his small world the only way he could. The ski troopers' uniforms, their skis and the snow were all a perfect white, but he knew the ugliness of war had been scrubbed from the frame.

The car stopped behind a mule and cart blocking the road, the mule driver beating his animal, who wouldn't budge. The chauffeur honked his horn furiously, rolled down his window and yelled. The mule braying, the *campesino* tied a rope to its nose and dragged it.

The car sped on past festive and decrepit haciendas, and the hot dirt rose around their wheels while the smog hung so low over the city that superstitious old ladies spoke of ghosts even in the middle of the day. "The lines in your hands are weak," a wrinkled *abuela* had once told Aubrey, for every Mexican grandmother could read a palm, "but sometimes hands can change."

The mansion gates opened automatically. Aubrey's sunburnt cousins were racing pink and bare-chested through a sprinkler on the lawn. The indigenous gardeners were bent double at their work like stunted shadows. Aunt Ethyl hung in the doorway of the mansion. Through the car's tinted glass she looked swarthy. She waved and stumbled, and shrugged her shoulders as if to say, "Sorry about being drunk."

Jack glanced at his watch and frowned at the early hour, then, turning to Aubrey, said with unexpected sincerity, "I'm sorry about this trip."

Aubrey didn't answer.

"What are you thinking?" asked Jack. "You've been awfully quiet."

"On my birthday," said Aubrey, "I'm going to join the Marines."

Jack's solemnity fell away. He was amused to imagine Aubrey huffing through the Solomon Islands. "You'd better stick to what you're good at," he laughed, as he opened the car door so that suddenly the sun broke in.

"What's that?"

"Watching."

I n the silence of the mountains, Amos thought he heard Kona call him, but it was only a bird. "I'm sorry," he said, not having tired of saying it, though his jaw shot through with pain whenever he spoke aloud. In the silence, there was space for grief. Overwhelmed with guilt and loss, Amos skied down slopes that were an invitation to die, but he couldn't die. When he raised his rifle to shoot a bighorn sheep and the gunshot caused the snow to avalanche, the sheep was sucked beneath the wave, but he skied to safety. The perpetual sorrow that robbed his spirit couldn't drain his strength. Amos had become a storm front, full of sour wind and force. The scavengers, who watched and waited, said to each other, "Amos is an undying thing."

It took a hard month on skis to cross into America. All month he'd seen no one, if bears and birds are no one. Now, below him, he could see the Montana foothills, where in the radiant heat of the rocks, snowdrops bloomed in March like perfect white teeth scattered across the land. Red roofs in a valley. Wood smoke covering the lower sky. But though he believed Canadian law couldn't pursue him over the border, he didn't wish to descend. He didn't desire human contact. Amos squatted in his skis in the snow, looking down. Loss was easier when there was wind and cold. An immovable Amos was himself a mountain, silent, grand and awful.

When he realized he was being followed, he didn't know by what. He spotted the thing in the lee of the cliff, but it didn't appear to be a man. A hundred yards away, almost invisible in the glare off the snow, was a blurred whiteness that seemed to have no eyes. Amos hesitated to shoot it. That was yet another mistake – his life had become full of them – for the white thing fired once, then merged back into the snow and vanished. Two more shots echoed against the peaks as Amos took off across the mountain. Behind him, he saw only snow on the move: it side-stepped, side-slipped, snowploughed and stem-turned, while Amos just skied to stay alive.

The gunman did have eyes, after all. Amos saw that now. They'd been hidden behind white binoculars. White snowsuit, white poles, white skis, white gun, and goggles beneath a white hood protecting his eyes from the weather. Better equipped, the man gained on him, but only briefly, because Amos was the better skier. If he could have kept skiing, he'd have lost him, but he hit the sheer face of the glaciers and there was nothing to do but descend.

The low sun was behind him as he sped down the slope and onto the Going-to-the-Sun Road, which he skied to the shaded valley. When the road ended at Main Street, where white peaks subsided into white picket fences, Amos yanked his boots from their bindings and ran through the slush, skis over one shoulder, rifle over the other, into the red-roofed town. He passed a hardware store with saws and axes and buckets of nails in the window, and a department store displaying life-sized man dolls trussed up in white rabbit-fur snowsuits, carrying white rifles and skis and an American flag. He aimed his gun at the glass and then down the empty street, but other than the mannequins in the window, no one was there.

He heard a female voice around the corner. An enthusiastic girl was rallying the last stragglers into a cinema where the marquee advertised "Ski Patrol, Free."

"Mountaineers, loggers, prospectors," the girl read aloud from a pamphlet, "cowboys and rugged outdoorsmen who want to learn to ski for their country …" Her voice blended with the oval tones of the narrator coming through the open doors: "Here they come, shooting down the slope like a string of comets!"

Amos went inside. He thought he could disappear amongst the crowd in the darkness. Taking a seat in the theatre, he saw men dressed like snow flying down the mountains. If the Nazis took Canada and skied over the border, or if the Italian front moved into the Alps, with the US Army ski troops of the 10th Mountain Division, the narrator told him, America would be prepared.

"You ski like a bird flies," said a man sitting down behind him and placing a white-gloved hand on his shoulder. As Amos stood and reached for his rifle, the man said quickly, "Three shots in the air means stop, you know. But I guess you didn't know that."

A surge of patriotic music came from the movie as Amos stood there, blocking the view, one hand on his rifle, the other on Kona's axe.

"How old are you?" the man asked.

"Older than them," said Amos, referring to the eager young men telling him to sit the hell down. He wasn't keeping count of his age anymore.

"Who cares, if you can ski like that?" the recruiter said. Sizing him up, he added, "The army can erase a man's history, you know. And when the war's over, there'll be a train ticket home, wherever that is. Watch the film. Then we'll talk."

Outside the movie hall, the sun was off the foothills and the snow was turning blue. Amos followed the man in white to a room with a desk, two chairs and a filing cabinet, where a man in khaki, holding a clipboard and pen, took one look at Amos's eye and scars and said, "He'd better be God on a ski." Then he asked, "Full name?"

By now the moon was shining on the snow, and the snow was shining back at it. Looking out of the window, Amos longed to see Kona cresting the peaks. He thought of her giving birth alone. He thought of her pulling away in the train, safe from Mr Shaw. Six dead men in the snow. He was sorry, but not for the dead men. He was sorry he couldn't go home to Kona, not without erasing the past.

The moon outside was casting shadows. He would step into shadows and disappear, and when he re-emerged – *if* he re-emerged – he would go home to Kona. The horrors of the winter made him bow his head, but the name Shaw stood up and struck him. He wouldn't make any mistakes anymore. He wouldn't say his own name again. His voice cracking from a month of disuse, he answered, "Everett Brown."

The darkroom was in the safe room. The mansion had been built in the 1920s in the middle of American Prohibition, and though alcohol was never banned in Mexico, expatriates felt more at ease drinking behind false walls. Ladies in loose, beaded dresses and men with waists bound by cummerbunds squeezed into fortified closet-sized rooms to sip *mojitos*, *cachuchas*, fizzes and absinthe. Because Americans feared revolution in Mexico and the seizing of foreign assets, safe rooms were both armouries and gin mills. In the Shaws' room, above the copper bar tinted green and black by photochemicals, was a gun rack: a dozen flintlock rifles with swamped barrels and sterling-silver inlays, and one large pistol with a bird-headed grip. The room, not wired with electricity, was equipped with candelabras and hurricane lamps. On the copper bar sat developer trays. Black-and-white photographs were pinned to a dartboard to dry.

When Aubrey entered the darkness and reached for a lamp, a hand caught his wrist.

Aunt Ethyl said, "Did I scare you? I didn't mean to. I'm not the one who should scare you. Don't light it. I don't want any light."

"You didn't scare me," he lied, wondering if she could hear his heart pound, or whether the beating in his chest wasn't actually a sound.

She'd scared him, but he was used to her tricks. He was always somewhat scared of her, or for her. Sometimes, when he came home from school, he'd find her lying on the living-room chaise with her knees curled up to her chest. She'd ask him to bring her a drink, but when he returned with the liquor, she'd be gone. Then he'd find her curled up on a different sofa in another room, propelled about the house by some horrible drive that moved her between volition and collapse. But now, in the darkness, he couldn't see his aunt at all.

"Smell this," said Ethyl, "and tell me if it's liquor or developer solution."

"Developer solution."

"I thought it tasted funny."

"Did you drink it?"

"Can't you tell I'm kidding?" She shook his wrist about in the air as if the trapped laughter needed shaking out. "Laugh, Aubrey," she said. Throwing back her head, she laughed as an example.

"Can't I light the lamp?" he asked.

Ethyl was suddenly sombre. "Don't you think the dark feels like arms around you? I don't know why people are scared of not being able to see. I'd like to go blind."

"No, you wouldn't," he said, hating when she talked like this, but not because he didn't understand it. Sometimes it seemed he understood her so well that when she opened her mouth it was him talking.

"How do you know?" she asked.

"You just wouldn't," he told her.

"But how *exactly* do you know?"

"I don't," he conceded. He knew so little. Everything was conjecture, assumption or intuition. "There's a blind Indian who begs in the Plaza Santo Domingo," he said. "Boys spit out their gum in his cup. You wouldn't want to be him."

"You saw them?"

"Yes."

"That's the problem," she said. "You *saw* them." She let go of his wrist. "Can you see me?"

"No. No, I can't."

He didn't dare ask her what was wrong for fear of making her cry. Her tears used to come as tight little drops that clogged in her powdered face, but now, if she cried, she sobbed. Sobbed and laughed and sometimes said, "I'm like Morton salt!" She no longer cried over Jack's other women, but that wasn't progress. Something worse had lodged inside her since the war began. She was, it seemed, in perfect health, but when she cried, she might as well have been coughing up blood.

In the blackness, he sat down on a couch. "Sit with me," he said.

She declined and asked, "Why do people make guns pretty?"

He stood up again. "You shouldn't –"

"Am I? How do you know? You can't see me."

He reached for her. His hand touched her back, ran round the silky drop of her dress, then up past her damp armpit and down her arm to her hard smooth fingernails and finally the shaft of the rifle.

"Put it back," he said.

"It's so stupid being pretty."

The two of them held the gun together.

"Killers aren't supposed to be pretty," she said. "You're pretty, Aubrey, but I don't mean you're girly. Those are biceps, aren't they?" With her free hand, she stroked his upper arm. "My boys aren't even good-looking. At least I don't think so. They used to torture the lizards they caught in the garden whenever their nanny turned her back. God knows what they're up to these days. God knows, so I don't need to."

"Put it back, please, Aunt Ethyl." He was stronger than her and could have forced her, but the size of his body and being in command of it were entirely different things. He felt powerless beside her.

"Even your grandmother is a killer," she said. "Did you know that?"

"Aunt Ethyl –"

"It's a good story to tell in the dark. How your grandmother cast aside her eternal soul on account of Jack's and my marriage. Her eternal soul," she lingered over the words. "If you believe in that nonsense. You don't believe that nonsense, do you?"

"I don't know what I believe," he said.

"Well, we'll all find out one day. Or we won't. One or the other."

Her grip had slackened on the gun, and Aubrey tried to ease it away from her. He'd lay it aside, then guide her upstairs to her bedroom and put her to sleep with a pill. But her hand snapped hard around the barrel.

"Jack had returned from the oil rigs," she continued. "He was determined to be married in Princeton over Easter. It was the early days of his career, and he only had one week off. But the Episcopal priest at your grandmother's church said a wedding over Easter was *verboten*." Pausing over visions Aubrey couldn't see, she tasted the word in her mouth. "The priest wasn't German," she said, "but I like that word, don't you?"

"Yes," he said obligingly, "I like it."

"Anyhow, your grandmother was furious. All of you, your mother and father and you, too, though you were only a baby – I met you as a baby, you know; you had dark red hair, which fell out and grew in dirty blonde – stopped going to church. That's when she became an atheist. And that's where the story gets good. Good or bad, depending on how you look at it, *if* you look at it. It was a few years later that your grandmother and your mother, who must have been feeling well at the time, were doing some shopping together in Princeton. When they spotted the priest stepping out of the church, your grandmother said to your mother, 'There's that dreadful man. I wish to God he would drop dead.' Astonishingly, he did, right then and there, on the steps of the First Episcopal Church in downtown Princeton. Right then and there, the priest dropped dead."

"That can't be true," said Aubrey.

"Every word of it is true. It appears your grandmother has God on her side. I don't. I've tried killing someone in the same way, but it's never worked."

There was a rapping on the wall. Uncle Jack's voice: "Aubrey? Is it safe to open up?"

Aubrey felt his aunt's hand stiffen around the barrel again.

"No," Aubrey called back. "Sorry. I'm just developing something."

He could feel Ethyl's pleasure at his lying.

"Never mind," called Jack. "I just wanted you to know the good news. I've arranged to get you a military post in a

South American port when you turn eighteen next month. You won't have to fight at all. You'll be able to ride out the war drinking sangria and coffee!"

Aunt Ethyl released the gun and turned towards Aubrey. Her chest against his, he could feel her blood flowing into her skin. She was suddenly hot, as women sometimes were at her age, but that wasn't the reason: she was ecstatic. She whispered in his ear, "Happy Early Birthday, Aubrey."

"Can you hear me?" said Jack.

"Yes," called Aubrey, heavy with the smell of sodium sulphite and hydroquinone and Aunt Ethyl's perfume. "Good news," he said blankly.

Aunt Ethyl was pleased with Jack's manipulations – so pleased, she shared her husband's bed that night. Aubrey would compare her one day to the orange tree that had grown in the orchard, its trunk whitewashed to protect it from the sun. The tree had suddenly died: putting out its buds defiantly, but not having the strength to open them, it succumbed within days to blight.

Happy to have slept with his wife, Jack presented her with a bouquet of roses the next morning at the breakfast table. "For the only Mrs Jack Shaw," he said.

But the weather had already changed. Aunt Ethyl smiled with the lower half of her face, while above her nose nothing moved. She turned to Aubrey, who was seated beside her, and, waving the bouquet above his egg tortilla, said, "These just go to show, you never know another person."

A maid waited in a shadow, expecting to trim the stems and arrange the bouquet in a vase. There were already flowers everywhere, for tonight was the annual costume party in honour of the Mexican holiday, El Día de Muertos.

"Don't hover like that," Ethyl snapped at the maid. "I'll take care of them myself."

Wishing to resuscitate his wife's goodwill, Jack said loudly to Aubrey, "Desk job in Bolivia. What do you think of that?"

But Ethyl spoke before Aubrey could answer. "You'll be late picking up the Merchant of Death. I don't suppose he bothered to bring a costume."

As Jack took off to the airport to meet Irénée du Pont, who was jetting in especially for the party, Aubrey smothered his eggs in salsa, which only made his breakfast less appealing. No matter how he chewed, nothing would go down his throat. The thought of a desk job in Bolivia sickened him, and he felt powerless against his uncle, because everyone was powerless against his uncle. Except maybe du Pont. And Amos, who had gotten away.

"What are you thinking, Old Shoe?" Aunt Ethyl asked.

It was an epithet from the game of Monopoly, and she used it when she wanted to remind him whose side he should be on. When the family played Monopoly, Aubrey always chose the tramp's shoe, even though Uncle Jack warned him that he'd never win with "that attitude." And when Aubrey purchased the slummish properties of the purple Baltic and Mediterranean Avenues, which would never amount to anything no matter how many hotels he built, or with greater recklessness bought Vermont Avenue simply because of its name, his uncle threatened to fire him from the oil job he was not yet old enough to have. A desk job was just the beginning: Jack believed in Aubrey's future.

Aunt Ethyl leaned over his eggs and took a bite. "You know what I'm thinking?" she said. "I'm thinking don't take the post."

For once, she'd said exactly what he wanted to hear. He wanted – he needed – to go to war, and hearing that it would please his aunt, he could actually imagine finding the strength to stand up to his uncle. He looked at her admiringly. She'd become thinner and paler despite the sun, but all the same was beautiful. He'd always thought she was pretty, but over the years had slipped into thinking she was beautiful. He'd fantasized the scene a thousand times: before leaving for the front, he'd ask her to sit on the couch in the safe room with a black curtain draped behind her, and he'd light her with candles and hurricane lamps and shoot her picture. He'd carry her photograph with him in his breast pocket and he'd write to her, taking comfort from the letters she returned: her strange, ridiculous, mysterious letters, always hinting, though never stating outright, that she knew everything about the horrible world out there and understood everything about the terrible world inside of him. With her help, he'd survive the war and return home a man. He'd be central to his own life, not creeping around the edges.

"Don't take any post," she said. "Sit tight. The war will be over before you're even drafted. You don't have to go at all."

Disappointed beyond imagination, Aubrey fixed his eyes on his eggs.

His aunt walked to the sideboard and dropped the roses in a vase without water. By the afternoon they'd wilted.

Uncle Jack was Henry VIII, who broke with the Church to marry Anne Boleyn and shortly afterward beheaded her. Aunt Ethyl was Cleopatra. Jack needed Ethyl's wig head, for he intended to call it Anne and carry it around all night, but Ethyl said he'd have to wait until after she'd donned the wig, otherwise the curls would tangle. He paced up and down the hall. Not only did Ethyl try his patience, but the maids were useless: they were supposed to have laid out his king costume on the trouser rack in his bedroom. Any moment now, diplomats dressed as sheikhs would be pulling up the drive in chauffeured cars. Their wives would be belly dancers. Everyone – businessmen, military men, Mexican congressmen, communist artists who wanted to sell their work – would come costumed as someone else. And though the staff was in position, the host and hostess still weren't dressed.

Grabbing a glass of champagne from a passing waiter whose flat nose betrayed his indigenous origins, Jack returned to his wife's boudoir.

Ethyl was purposefully taking her time. She sat on a swivel chair, smoking, staring at herself in the mirror.

"How much longer?" Jack asked.

"I love the naivety of Mexican art, but Frida Kahlo depresses me."

She was, in fact, not looking at herself but at the painting that hung beside her mirror: a portrait of a lightly moustached woman. On her shoulders were a monkey and a cat; butterflies adorned her topknot; a dead bird hung from a thorn necklace that pierced her skin so she bled.

"You're already drunk," said Jack.

Taking her hair in her hands, Ethyl twisted it tightly and skewered it with bobby pins in preparation for the Cleopatra wig. Then she removed the pins as if dissatisfied.

"You're doing this on purpose," said Jack.

"Transformation can't be rushed," Ethyl said, and shrugged.

"That's enough," Jack ordered. He lifted the head and, flipping it upside down, let the hair drop to the floor.

Ethyl jumped to her feet, screaming, "Murder!"

Someone cried out beyond the window: she'd frightened the chief gardener's son. The child, costumed for the holiday in a skull mask and black tunic, had come to the garden to collect flowers for the festival at the graveyard. El Día de Muertos was not, amongst the Mexicans, a night for fancy dress. Though they costumed themselves as skeletons, they were the skeletons of the actual dead, those they'd lost. Now the dead boy ran away across the lawn. Jack pulled the blackout curtains closed and commanded his wife to stop scaring the help.

Twenty minutes later, after taking the head into his bedroom and finding his king clothes were waiting, he was at last dressed and ready to take his place in the living room.

"Who are you?" Aubrey asked him.

"Henry VIII. Who are you?"

"Frankenstein," lied Aubrey, who had dressed as Amos Cobb. He wore workman's boots and tatty overalls cut into zigzags at the cuffs, and had dirtied the knees with shoe polish. A hammer hung from the loop on his hip. While football shoulder pads under a ratty shirt beefed up his torso, there was nothing he could do to increase his height. He'd painted a scar under his cheekbone with Aunt Ethyl's eye makeup. As for his blind eye, he could find no means of keeping just one of them closed, so he'd covered it with a patch, though Amos never wore one. A camera hung from his neck, because he was leaving the party before it had even begun, to take pictures.

"You look more like a cross between a hillbilly and a pirate," said Jack. "Your cousins are all devils. You could have gone as one too."

He walked down the drive past the manicured lawn, down the dirt road flanked by dusty yards. Cars steering towards the mansion honked at the hundreds of skeletons walking to the graveyard. It was harvest season, November 1, the day the dead were heard to speak. The night was noisy with the high-pitched excitement of barefoot children, the laughter of drunks and revellers muffled by skeleton masks, sombreroed men serenading corpses.

Families picnicked in folding chairs around the tombs of loved ones, their graves smothered in marigolds, "the flower of four hundred lives." The darkness of the night had paled in the light of ten thousand candles. Crêpe paper cutouts – corpses waving their hats, skeletons on skeleton horses, dead brides dancing with emaciated grooms – threatened to catch fire. This was not a funeral or even a wake, it was a homecoming: tonight the dead were welcomed back to earth.

Mariachi bands with guitars and trumpets and seashells rattling on the hems of dresses and the sleeves of shirts awoke the dead. Sweet smells lifted them out of their tombs: incense, beeswax, paraffin and copal resin burning, fresh-baked *chipatas*. There was coffee and agave liquor, stews in blackened terracotta pots, *mole*, sugared pumpkins, oranges, *tejocotes*, *jicama* and Dead Bread twisted into the shape of skulls or rabbits who hopped between the worlds. Tiny papier-mâché skeletons pictured the dead at leisure: there were gardeners, fishermen and prostitutes. New spinning tops and model trains, presents for dead children, were wrapped with bows and laid out on their graves. As above, so below: the desires of the breathless accorded with those of the breathing. Some of the skeleton dolls were transmigrating out of their human form: dead women becoming the trunks of *saguaros*, the stalks of *chollas* or the fruiting citrus trees; dead ladies with lilies growing up their thighs or snakes twisting out of their bellies.

Though the Mexicans entered the graveyard without fear, Aubrey hung at the gate. Yellow headlights continued to ease down the road and climb up the hill towards the mansion. The beams kicked against the granite graves and glanced over the marigolds. Crows, displaced by the celebrations, flapped into the trees and elided in the darkness.

Aubrey shot two rolls of film before returning to his uncle's party.

The night was in full swing. The partiers had strewn their props through the hallway; a pair of devil's horns rested on the hatrack. As a maid closed the door behind him, Aubrey was accosted by a middle-aged woman in a hyena mask. She reached for his arm and asked loudly, "Who are you? Who in hell are you?"

"No one," said Aubrey.

She was so drunk his answer made her laugh uncontrollably, and she fell backwards into a businessman dressed as an Indian. "No, really," she cried. "Who are you?" She recruited the Indian by the arm and asked him, "Who do *you* think he is?"

"I'm not anyone," said Aubrey. "I dress this way all the time." Not hanging around for a drink, he took advantage of her laughter to leave.

But as he slipped up the stairs, his uncle, who was radiant with wine and had lost Anne Boleyn's head, called, "Aubrey! Not going to bed are you?"

"I have a headache," said Aubrey.

"Check in on your aunt if you're going up. Convince her to come down. Tell her she at least has to make an appearance."

He didn't find her in her bedroom, but the door to the ensuite bathroom was cracked open and he saw candlelight flickering around the tub.

Standing off to the side of the door, he called, "Aunt Ethyl, are you decent? Are there bubbles? Can I come in?"

Often, when she ran a bubble bath, she let him perch beside her on the closed toilet seat and chat. They'd talk nonsense for hours until she said, "I used to be a plum, now I'm prune. Close your eyes, I'm getting out."

He asked again, "Can I come in?"

But Aunt Ethyl didn't answer.

Suddenly horribly cold, though the night was warm, he asked more loudly, "Aunt Ethyl, can't I come in?"

He turned his cheek to the wall. He looked at the painting beside him: a dead bird dangling from the woman's neck, the cat on her shoulder having killed it; a monkey taunting the cat. He remembered Aunt Ethyl telling him how the Japanese ate monkey brains, which were said to be delicious. Staring at Frida Kahlo, who was in the flesh downstairs, held the moment at bay.

He stepped back, lowered his eyepatch and took a picture of the picture, though his hands were shaking so badly it would come out a blur. His belly had started shaking first, then the shaking extended to his throat, then into his legs and arms. He dropped the camera to his chest and took his head in his palms as if he could lift it off. The makeup from his scar smeared across his hands. His heart was beating so violently he couldn't tell noise from deafening silence. His ears stuffed with blood, he couldn't hear the din of the partiers in the hallway.

He called out, "Aunt Ethyl!" and pushed through the bathroom door.

She was a picture in perfect focus. There were no bubbles in the tub. Ethyl's breasts floated with their own fatty lightness. In the clear water, her blonde pubic hair rested like seaweed, while the hair on her head remained winched in a bun. And her pretty face half submerged.

His heart wasn't racing anymore; it was static.

Aubrey sat down on the bathroom toilet, reached over and took his aunt's hand. So much colder than his, not pliant anymore, but there was no resistance in it.

"I don't believe you're dead, you know," he said, when he finally spoke. "It's just one of your little lies." He was silent again – how much time passed? – until he burst out angrily, "You didn't want me to leave you alone, but you left me instead!"

He felt guilty for scolding her, and he told her to ignore what he'd said. "Do you know what a man in the graveyard told me tonight?" He wanted to give her comfort. "That the dead aren't dead. They live in a place without the sun. They can come back one day every year. It never rains that day. It's always perfect."

Somehow that made him cry. Somehow that made him remember how much Aunt Ethyl had liked the sun, how she'd followed it around the house. His mouth was full of snot and salt. He asked her about her childhood, about her brother, about her father and mother, and whether she saw them now. Her eyes were open and looking sideways. He leaned over the bath to try to catch her gaze. Hours had passed. Many of the candles had drowned in their wax. Her pale body was blue.

"I want to see," he said. "I want to see what's real."

She farted and moved sharply as if she'd shrugged.

Aubrey took her picture as evidence of something he might never understand, but he wanted to, he desperately wanted to. Then he left her room and walked down the stairs to tell his uncle.

Two days later, in black trousers and jacket, his black camera at his chest, Aubrey sat on the scarlet chaise longue while the maids held platters of quesadillas and spicy meatballs on toothpicks under his nose. Aubrey waved them away. Like ants at a picnic, the mourners filled the room and ate. The padre, who drank copiously, declared Señora Shaw gone to a better world. Ethyl's sons by the buffet, who were three black lumps of basalt and didn't believe in better worlds, nodded, but Aubrey did not. He hated the pretense of a heaven and a padre who pretended to be father to them all but whose generalized love was a sham. The only person who loved him – even if you couldn't call such confused and desperate need real love – was buried.

He peered at the newspaper lying beside him on the chaise, his aunt's favourite place in the formal living room. The cushions still smelled of her. The notice declared the death an accident, regretted the dangers and complications of prescription drugs and reported more on her husband's impressive career than on Ethyl herself. Nowhere did it mention she had overdosed in the bathtub, and nothing about the violent row with Jack, or the fact that Mr du Pont was visiting when she died. The photograph that accompanied the obituary was ridiculously out of date: a young, hopeful bride, reprinted from the files. Aubrey placed the paper on the coffee table, put his sweating tumbler on it and watched the newsprint dissolve in a wet, expanding ring. Then he lifted his camera and shot his uncle.

Uncle Jack was leaning against the fireplace, Mr du Pont to his left in an upright chair. Aubrey shot again and again, and sometimes both of them appeared in the frame, sometimes only the open mouth of the empty hearth.

Jack went on talking to his friend. Aubrey had taken inappropriate pictures of the open casket, the hearse pulling off and the coffin lowered into the ground today, and Jack had forborne it all.

But the priest was less tolerant. "My boy, you forget yourself!"

"Forgive and forget, Father?" Aubrey said and shot him too. "Did you know that's backwards? Shakespeare wrote, 'Forget and forgive.' But how can you forgive what you already forgot? Aunt Ethyl used to say, 'Forget about it. That's what I try to do.' And then, if I asked, 'About what?' she'd say, 'Exactly.'"

Though the padre didn't laugh, Aubrey did. Hating his own laughter made him laugh even harder. He told himself he'd never forget how her eyes were a fine, cold blue.

"Aunt Ethyl never talked about forgiveness, Padre. But my grandmother used to say forgiveness is a Christian trap in which, if you can't rise to the ideal, you're the one who's guilty. Maybe that's because she murdered a priest. But I haven't killed anybody, and I feel guilty most of the time. Worse than that, Father, I don't know for certain exactly what there is to forgive."

"My glass is empty," the priest said, leaving to refill it.

Aubrey stood up, and with every step towards his uncle took a picture. The camera was a probe, searching him out, but when it pushed in for a close-up, Jack shielded his face with his hand. "Don't do that, Uncle," Aubrey said. "You look like a criminal."

"You are behaving no better than your aunt did!" du Pont shouted before Jack could speak. "Put the camera down!"

"I did my best to be like her, Mr du Pont, but I'm no better at being Aunt Ethyl than she was." Aubrey turned the camera on him. "Smile. No, don't smile. I want a candid shot."

Jack laid his hand on his nephew and said, "We all loved Ethyl."

The last thing she had said to Aubrey: "Don't look so glum. There's a reason we have skin. Your face is for hiding what is in your mind, not giving it away." She'd taken his chin in her soft hands and kissed him on the lips.

Now Aubrey tried to obey her advice and didn't cry. He stepped out from beneath his uncle's grip and said, "You know my father always hated you?"

Aubrey had spoken to his father earlier that day – for the first time in years – because death has certain rules. "I'm sorry about your aunt," Father had said when Uncle Jack handed Aubrey the phone.

"Thanks," Aubrey answered.

"I hear the funeral's today," his father said.

"Yes."

"What's the weather like there?"

"It's usually nice."

"That's good. Like Egypt."

"I guess. Yes."

"Do you swim a lot?"

"Yes, in a pool."

"I suppose it's warm."

"Usually. Do you want to speak to Uncle Jack again?"

"No, I don't think so."

"Well, then."

"Well, then."

"Yes."

"I always liked your Aunt Ethyl, though. I always liked her."

There was a long pause. Aubrey said, "I learned something you might like."

"What is it?"

"An image gets stuck in your eye for one-twenty-fourth of a second, even if the object is taken away. Filmmakers move stills at one-twenty-fourth of a second so that the eye, retaining the previous moment, creates continuity where there is none."

There was another long pause. In it, both of them could feel Ruth's funeral five years before.

At last, Father said, "That's only partly true. Professor Wertheimer debunked that theory of vision some time ago. Anyway, I won't keep you. I'm sure you need to get back to your duties."

"Good God!" said Jack, as if the accusation was funny. "Your father doesn't hate me. He hardly knows me. You might as well say he loves me. Pour yourself a drink, Aubrey. You're empty-handed."

But he didn't pour himself a drink. He left his uncle and du Pont by the unlit fire. He strode out the French doors and onto the verandah, down through the desert garden, with its agave plants and plump yuccas tipped with spikes, past the temperate zone, the irrigated lawn, the liquidambar trees already turning red because they were unhappy in the heat, and the pond where carob grew along the banks. Aunt Ethyl used to suck on carob to soothe her dry throat.

Beyond the pond in the gardener's shack, Aubrey found a hammer hung on the wall and a box of nails. He chose the thickest nail and the biggest tree, a large pine bearing heavy cones and so sappy the ants devoured it. He lay his camera safely on the dry grass. He swung the hammer the way Amos had shown him, swung it from the elbow for power. He pounded the nail into the trunk, but it didn't go very far. When he hit the edge of the head, the nail bent and refused to enter.

Aubrey was going to the front with the 5th Reconnaissance Unit, US Air Force. He was to take a limousine to the airport, then a private plane to Florida, then a military plane to South Carolina. After basic training he would be on a troop train to New York City and finally a luxury liner – refitted for service with five hundred bunks in the ballroom and a drained swimming pool – to war in Italy. In the driveway, he waved a perfunctory farewell as his cousins raised their square hands, and their redundant nanny, carrying shears and a trowel, waved her tools back and forth like a tired machine. As the mansion retreated in the dust, Aubrey shared a final cognac with his uncle, who smiled his prize-winning smile and said, "Reconnaissance – I always said you were observant." If Jack was disappointed his nephew had refused a South American desk job, Aubrey didn't care and Jack didn't show it. Since the funeral, conversation between them had been bitterly polite.

Aubrey tossed back his cognac.

"Drink up," said Jack, refilling his glass. "It's rotgut from now on."

I t wasn't the destiny she'd expected. Though she'd made it happen, it wasn't what she'd thought would happen. She had what a thousand women wanted, but not what Donna Cobb wanted. Or Lorna Bell, which was the only name by which anyone knew her. She raced back and forth between New York theatres and Hollywood studios by passenger train and kept a trunk permanently packed. Despite several national advertisements and a speaking role in an MGM musical, she'd been pigeonholed as a stage actress, which wasn't what she'd wanted.

That's what she told her Hollywood psychoanalyst while lying on his couch. The hard California sun sliced through his drawn blinds. As bars of black shadows combed her face, her hair shone like coal transforming into diamonds. She was better-looking than many stars. He advised her not to give up hope.

"Obviously," she said, wondering what she paid him for.

He was supposed to be the best, yet they hadn't even touched on the fact that she'd become neurotically private. Because she feared being spied on by tradesmen, she had a weekly supply of absolutely everything delivered to the top of her gated drive, and her overworked maid in a pinafore and ribbon streamers lugged the provisions to the house, which was not quite a mansion. Though big enough to throw extravagant parties, which she'd ceased to give, the house felt small. If she ever achieved the status of Dietrich or Garbo, she'd demolish it and erect a bigger one, if only to feel it was possible to vanish in her own home.

Donna said, "I need hypnosis. I'm gaining weight."

He suggested instead she needed exercise and fresh air. He had a cottage on a lake up north – wasn't her next play set on a lake? – and gave her the keys with the understanding that he'd join her. "I'll bring a case of Napa wine," he said.

But Lorna Bell, being a professional, told him she'd receive him only after she'd learned her lines.

She had the double bed to herself for three days, but after that she had to share.

"I'm awake," she yelled, loud enough to be heard by the help, because it was only a cottage. Just like a cockerel, Donna had, after three days in the countryside, grown accustomed to announcing her awakening each morning.

But her analyst said, "Shut up. I'm still sleeping."

She scowled at the pasty man in the bed beside her. Then she stretched and twisted and successfully cracked her back, slipped a silky robe over her nearly perfect skin, opened the bedroom door and whispered loudly, "I'm thirsty!"

Ten minutes later, when a knock on the door brought the coffee tray, Donna drank down two tall mugs like medicine. Then, in the dressing-table mirror, she inspected a blemish before carefully covering it over with powder. Her eyes grew when she lined the upper and lower lids in charcoal black.

Suddenly lunging deep into her own reflection, she declared, "I am a seagull!"

Following the stage directions, she practised rubbing her forehead – first with her fingers, then her palm, then settling on the back of her hand. She was working her most difficult moments.

"Men, women, lions, eagles, geese and fish, all life, all creatures invisible to the eye, all having gone through their tragic life cycles, are extinct. A thousand centuries have lapsed on this planet without a single living thing –"

"Shut up, Lorna! I'm sleeping!"

She shot her analyst a haughty look, but he'd thrown his shapeless forearm over his eyes. The look was wasted. With great discipline, she wept and smeared the tears across the mirror.

"Never mind, it's nothing," she said tenderly to her own reflection. "Crying gives me some relief. You realize I've gone two years without crying. No, no, I am a dove! No, blast it, that's not right! Where am I? You're throwing me off!"

Turning back to the mirror, she continued with unbroken concentration, "I thought you hated me. If you only knew me! We're caught in the whirlpool, you and I. When I was young, I was happy. Every morning, I woke up singing. I loved you and I dreamed of fame. Tomorrow I'm taking the train third class to Yelets, with the peasants. And when I get there, the businessmen will give me no peace. Ah, life is sad."

She tried it again: "Life is sad." She struck alternative moods: self-pitying, bitter, resigned, ironic, vengeful, hopeful, wise. "Life is sad. Life is sad. Life is sad. Life is sad."

"Which is it?" demanded her analyst.

"I don't know," she said. "I'll know when I get to the end. It's only a rehearsal."

Abandoning the mirror, she threw open the bedroom door and the morning light from the big-eyed windows facing the sun splashed against her face. She called to a maid, "Where's my rubber boots? The script says I walk by the lake."

Her performance in the end would be almost perfect. The New York critics would love her. But it was her analyst who would say, though they were no longer sleeping together, "You are the crafted replication of sorrow and nostalgia, its substrata of truth and lies become the ground itself. Crazy, murderous Lorna Bell is a perfect Chekhovian actress. Donna Cobb" – for he alone knew her name – "between tirades, has captured the passage of time."

Photography couldn't capture scent, thank God. Cypress buds and rosemary bushes could not shield the permanent stink of grease, fuel, sweat and fear. Except for the cameras in the aft bay and nose dome, the recon plane was identical to a bomber; the fore bay still dropped bombs. But photography was deceptive; it made the war scentless and silent. The camera created space between the eye and the observed, the cities burning on the ground or the chitchat of men on furlough to Florence who were likely, in the next few weeks, to die.

Even at war, Italy was photogenic. Even the degradation was. Aubrey shot two old men fighting in the dust for a cigarette butt as the orange sun rose gloriously over tracts of lavender. Photography eased the homesickness, though he couldn't imagine what home he was sick for, or who lived in that home anymore. Photography shut up his mind and his memories and reconnected him guiltlessly to the view. In rare, coveted moments, he could even imagine himself a tourist.

Now he was en route to Florence, in a Jeep full of soldiers bumping over the potholes. He shot a picture of a guy in the back seat who was hanging onto the roll bar and hollering obscenities at a girl in a lavender field. The guy was all teeth and jaundice and had a big loud mouth; said he'd paid for a virgin with a tin of Spam, he'd sell his mother's soul for a bottle of scotch, his dick looked like a cauliflower. The girl, having lost her black scarf in a gust of wind, was scrambling through the purple blooms as ashamed as if she were naked. Aubrey shot her too.

All he did was take pictures. The only thing he liked about war was the simplicity, not needing to know the meaning of men's actions, because knowing things wasn't his job. There were whole divisions assigned to deciphering the pictures he took.

It was a long trip to Florence, and they stopped for the night at a brothel. As the Jeep arrived, it honked loudly and a frightened chicken flapped up onto an outhouse roof and triggered a mine. American sappers, who made it a priority to clear the brothels, had overlooked the privy. At the sound of the explosion, whores rushed from the house: ladies in black slips and big brassieres flapping their arms and crossing themselves, as a furious rooster pecked at their hairy shins. Aubrey tried not to feel guilty as he took pictures – it was the Germans, not he, who had mined the shitholes and lemon groves of Italy – but the truth was he sometimes felt the whole war was his fault. He focused the camera on a weepy whore who was hanging like ammo on a soldier's arm and wondered if the whores were better off unhappy. Their sad faces showed an honesty their profession had erased.

Inside, he shot a close-up of a lock of hair between a sad girl's lips. A few years younger than him, tears on her cheeks and seated in front of a Virgin Mary tucked into a rut in the wall, she looked like an icon of honesty. When he asked her,

"What will you do when the war's over?" she quietly slipped her hair between her lips. He leaned across the table as if to kiss her and smelt the olive oil in her hair, leaned away and shot her picture.

He didn't really have the stomach to screw her, but the matron wanted him to pay almost as much just for taking her photo, so he let the girl lead him upstairs to her room. She seemed pleased with the uncertain way he entered her, taking his remoteness as a kind of tenderness. She stayed beside him in bed all night, which meant he couldn't sleep. Italians had been the enemy up to a certain hour, at which time suddenly they were friends. Other men accepted the new allegiance, but trust was hard for him even at the best of times. The girl breathed through her mouth, smelling of olives and larded sheets, but he couldn't close his eyes, so he shot her picture again and again.

The next day in Florence, he was tired and moody. The city seemed to him full of memories. The pencil drawing of the Duomo above his father's desk in Vermont had warped his expectations – somehow he hadn't expected the cathedral to be in colour. Even after all these years he felt oppressed by his father's version of history, in which the dead were the most important part of life. He hadn't heard a word from Father since Aunt Ethyl died. Grandmother wrote that even she no longer heard from Everett, who passed his days at a military base in Newark. He was one of a few art historians given a handful of thumbtacks and a world map and instructed to choose which of the world's treasures not to bomb. He was probably to thank for the Duomo not being rubble.

The Duomo has no supporting structure but floats in a harness of wood around its base; a small, round reliquary once sat on top of the dome until it was struck by lightning and rolled away; the dome is made of four million bricks and could have been built more easily in concrete like the Pantheon in Rome, but for thirteen centuries people forgot how. That's the irony of progress; we rush towards one thing and forget about something else.

Father's historical trivia filled his head, and the smell of frankincense in the basilica made Aubrey half expect to see him swinging a censer up and down the aisles. Because there were soldiers everywhere, shouting across the nave and showing no respect for the godliness or the emptiness, and because he kept imagining all those bricks falling on him, Aubrey climbed up the long stone stairwell and hid out on the roof. Over the last several months he'd become used to being alone in a crowd of men, but it was rare and sweet these days to be alone by himself. Evening lay on the terracotta city. The sun crouched beneath the horizon; the pink and green marble of the bell tower faded. Jeeps moved in and out of the palace, the railway station, down the Uffizi, over the Ponte Vecchio, which braced against the swollen Arno pouring over the ruins of every other bridge. Women and children came out of their homes to walk in the cool evening in their least tatty clothes. Aubrey inhaled the acrid fumes of his cigarette, then shot the sky. A cloud appeared in the shape of a boy; the air currents gingerly pulled off his arms and his head floated away.

Two weeks later, when his plane went down over the Italian front, he was filming the bombing of two of the last industrial holdouts in Europe: the rail diversion bridge in

Ponte di Piave and an ammo factory at Ghedi. It was April 14, 1945, the Spring Push, delayed by fog on the airfields and the news of President Roosevelt's death, delayed again due to lightning storms and the fact that the thirteenth was a Friday.

With two engines hit and spilling fuel, the pilot, in a final attempt to stay airborne long enough to cross the front line, ordered the dumping of all non-essentials – guns, radios, chairs, cameras, photo flashes – out the bomb bay. The plane gained altitude, the line came nearer, and they hung on a little longer. Then they lost height again. The crew stripped down to their underwear and chucked out their heavy flak vests and flight suits, retaining only their parachutes. But the line was not near enough. There was nothing left to throw away except themselves, and soon they'd drop too low to evacuate. The pilot, who'd try to save the plane by flying it alone, ordered them to jump.

Each man floated off in his own direction, the scene below rising up to meet him: overturned tanks, incinerated Jeeps, bodies like a cucumber harvest, foot soldiers pushing north along the Italian front. Floating down through the morning fog, Aubrey saw the crew disappearing. The white chutes of solitary men faded away into sunspots. Then, in the distance, the River Po, in turmoil after last night's downpour, and his plane crashing in the hills.

His pictures, not his life, flashed before his eyes. He wanted somehow to keep floating, to stay above the ground, where this was this and that was that and he was not consumed by chaos, not altogether lost. He held his breath as long as he could, for the whole world was a graveyard.

When he landed hard in a field, he touched his fingers to his dripping forehead and thanked a god he didn't believe in that this wasn't blood, although it was. One sign of shock was the shivering. And yet why shouldn't he feel cold to his bones, having fallen almost naked through the sky? The other sign was the total absence of fear. "The only thing we have to fear is fear itself" was crap, and every soldier knew it. But Aubrey felt no fear. It was a false fearlessness, yet he felt wonderfully alive. Though on the mountains the snow sat firm and in the hills was slush and in their dips and furrows mud, in the valley springtime bloomed. He'd fallen into a perfect world. Pastoral, photogenic. Infinite fields of wildflowers, their muted red edging into pink, chalk-white stones scattered about the blossoms. Tasting the blood that dripped into his mouth, he still didn't know it was blood. He felt more wonderfully alive than he had since he was twelve years old, wonderfully alive and happy. This was the kind of time that lovers hoped for: time outside time, when the realities of their lives disappeared completely. War didn't enter his head.

No sheep in the field. He told himself they were penned to avoid the storm, for though the day looked perfect, he could hear the thunder clearly, and it was coming closer. He tried to gauge the distance by counting the seconds between thunder and lightning, but there wasn't any lightning. And it was strange there were no clouds.

He followed a low stone wall along the perimeter of the field, ran his hands along the sharp flint edges, sat down on the wall and pulled thorns from his bare feet. When blood slipped into his eyes, he imagined he was crying with happiness. When the blood fell onto his hands, he fingerpainted his name onto the stone wall. Then he moved through the landscape, signing his name on objects he could barely recognize. A wall. A burnt-out car. The world was coming slowly into focus. He first saw the blackflies on the ground. Then something else: a torso sat upright in the mud. Parts of men were everywhere. He'd mistaken them for flowers and stones.

He walked naked through a pasture of body parts. Heard artillery fire over the hill. He counted fourteen corpses, but only twenty-seven hands. If no other hands were to be found, he reckoned there were *thirteen* men. The next sign of shock. Why assume there were fourteen bodies because there were twenty-seven hands? Why not assume one guy had three hands to start with? Or maybe there'd never been men here at all, just body parts. Just pieces of humans. He knelt in the mud and didn't move for hours.

Only as the sun was setting, when he felt his own body sinking beneath some dangerously permanent horizon, did the will to live kick in. A white man, he shone like a snowshoe hare in the dark, which made an easy target. So he camouflaged his skin with mud.

He ran from the gunfire over the hill. But whether he ran uphill or down, he met gunfire again. He ran like those men in the Escher painting, up and down interweaving stairs, going nowhere. The mud kept him warm. Someone had told him mud could do that, and though there were few thoughts in his head, just simple commands that seemed to come from outside his head – run, stupid; hide; shut up; breathe; go faster – it bothered him that he couldn't remember who had told him about the mud.

In the cocklight, he saw a farmhouse. The sun was returning dismally. The fluttering of birds was the sound of a mortar before it hit, while the real birds were shouting at the morning. Something sweet in the air pinched his lungs – pollen from some deadly flower. Aubrey gasped for breath. Maybe he was winded from running. Or maybe he'd die of common asthma, die as pathetically as he'd lived, die for no reason at all. He stood panting with his back to a wall, terrified to open the door. When he inched it open, he found a dead German gunner hanging his broken neck over a blown-out wall.

Red tiles shifted from the roof and fell against the German's head. A stairwell led to the sky. The top of the house was blown away, and the kitchen wall was down. But a deck of cards sat undisturbed on the solid kitchen table where men had carved their initials in the wood. On the playing cards, the King of Hearts jammed a broadsword into his own brain – one of those injuries where the blood doesn't flow until the weapon is extracted. Aubrey told himself to keep his head: it was only a picture. He put down the cards and wrapped the cut on his forehead in a dirty dishcloth to stop the persistent bleeding.

He found cheese, wine and turnips in the cupboards. Yanked the stiff cork in the wine bottle out with his teeth. He drank till he could see straight again and warmth returned to his skin. His sweat had dried, and the mud tightened against him. No stairs up to the bedrooms meant no sheets or blankets to wrap in. Nothing to wear except an enemy uniform. The German hung his head over the rubble as if he were dreaming of a girl. So Aubrey let him be. He couldn't sleep. He couldn't even dream of sleeping. In his undershirt and boxers, he played solitaire at the kitchen table. Though the sound of gunfire was dying, silence was equally dangerous: out of it anything could come, and eventually it did.

A soldier like an unholy wind threw open the door and emptied his rifle into the ruined farmhouse. But Aubrey was lucky. The soldier recognized government-issue boxers and in a split second had the self-possession to shift his aim away. Only the wine bottle blew apart.

"Jesus Christ! American? Regiment? Where are your clothes, soldier?"

A dozen men in combat uniform poured in. They wiped mud and blood off their lips and leaned on the kitchen cupboard, eating the turnips Aubrey had found inside it and drinking what was left of the wine. Like a cocktail party in hell. Their lieutenant entered and unrolled a map on the table. On it, hills with no names, designated only by elevation. Aubrey was shunted into the corner until at last the lieutenant fed the map back into a hard plastic tube and said, "So?"

"11068643, Private Aubrey Brown, 5th Reconnaissance, US Air Force. Plane went down over the Po, sir."

"Duty?"

"Photographer."

"Photographer?"

"Yes, sir."

"You're a goddamn liability."

The lieutenant of the 10th Mountain Division slung the strap of the map tube over his shoulder. He said, "What the hell are we going to do with you?" Not waiting for an answer, he walked to the door and shoved it open as if its presence were yet another nuisance. The door open, Aubrey in his confusion thought he was being directed to leave, but when he took a step forward the lieutenant put out his hand to stop him. "Well, Brown," he said, "lucky for you your dad's here."

It was meant as a joke. The lieutenant was tired to death: it was a slap-happy whim, putting Brown and Brown together.

"Everett Brown, get the hell over here!" the lieutenant called into the farmyard. "From now on, this kid's yours. Find him some clothes."

A mos took one step to Aubrey's two. Aubrey kept saying Amos's name, he couldn't think what else to do, but Amos didn't say much. Aubrey didn't believe in God or fate: everything was luck and sourceless miracle. The fact that he, instead of one of the millions of other possible arrangements of human genes passed down through the Shaw Browns, should be standing here on earth at all, even if this place was hell and a person was reborn here by perpetual terror, the fact that this person was him, this person was *Aubrey*, was already absurd enough. So he didn't know what to say, except Amos's name.

Outside, Amos found a dead Yank of about the right size and stripped him down as if he were skinning a rabbit, then gave Aubrey the kid's uniform and K-rations and gun. Aubrey noticed that Amos carried an axe, which wasn't Army regulation. The troops were moving out, no time to think or talk, but Aubrey kept saying, "Amos."

The ski troopers were taking Hill 814 without skis. They were taking Hill 931 without ropes, but were repelled downhill again. Sent to the front in khakis, not whites, without skis or ropes, the ski troopers were chasing the Germans into the Alps like ordinary foot soldiers. Amos hauled a soldier, possummed into a ball in the mud, up to his feet and shouted over artillery fire, "You wanna ski Big Dome again?" The soldier held out a severed right arm, and a blast threw Amos backward, clutching the man's elbow, while the skier took shrapnel through the neck and dropped dead into a ball once more. Amos stuck the upright arm in the mud like a totem pole. He dug into the mud as if he could dig his way home and dragged Aubrey down beside him, then dragged him up again. Aubrey, like a bird with one song, said "Amos" again and again. Up the hill, a cow tied to an ancient chestnut tree mooed loudly. A mortar round: the chestnut cleaved in two. Amos ducked his head into the dead cow's belly, heat pouring out of its organs, and he pulled Aubrey down there with him. This was the end, the last offence for Italy, and the lieutenant had said take trophies: cigarette cases, watches, crosses. "He didn't say cows," said Amos. It was one of the only things he said that day.

Lale Andersen sang "Lili Marleen" across the foxholes. Someone had found a record player in a German dugout and was taunting the enemy with their own favourite song. An explosion, and Andersen shut her mouth. War was a sound inside Aubrey's head, inseparable from it. The only relief would have come if his head were taken off completely. But he wanted to be alive. It was the first time in a very long time that he wanted to be alive. Over the maul of gunfire, he heard someone cry out for his mother in English, someone else in German. Amos's one eye stared down his gunsight and, already monocular, his aim was perfect. But Aubrey missed and missed again. He hadn't shot a rifle since basic training. "Shoot at anything," Amos commanded, and so Aubrey shot at the light on the horizon and the waking sorrow of birds. Amos ran, crawled, killed anything in sight, and Aubrey followed and tried to do whatever Amos did. Fog burned off like a fever off a corpse. In the dawn, the dead were everywhere. The war moved slowly into the distance. Mortar rounds like wandering minstrel song were audible over the next hill, and the birds were screaming bloody murder. Aubrey again said Amos's name, but when Amos said, "Not Amos. Private Everett Brown," Aubrey saw for the first time the blood dripping into Amos's mouth or falling to tan his hide boots.

A German corpse lay down in a dugout. Amos jumped in and lifted the rotting body over his head and threw it away. "Jesus, he stinks!" cried Aubrey, and Amos shouted, "Everything stinks." Amos pulled Aubrey in beside him. The Luftwaffe churned up the earth around them while they buried their faces in the dirt. Amos asked, "You smell the garlic growing underground?" How could anyone smell anything under the stench? Amos took a bullet to the head; his helmet deflected it, and he didn't seem to mind. Amos took what came, the way an animal accepted the weather. Aubrey remembered a skull on a desk. What does Amos see? Then the shelling stopped.

Sudden quiet, not peace and quiet, and not the lull before a storm or the tedious moment before something, anything – a turd, an orgasm, death – finally happened, for everyone was in the eye of the hurricane already, and the eye was strangely calm while in the quiet both sides waited. Aubrey was trembling. The earth had trembled for hours, and now that it was still, Aubrey wasn't. Amos said, "You got worms inside, shaking cause they're scared of dying. It ain't you shaking. You gonna learn the difference." He said he could hear the worms digging deeper into the – "what did you call it, Aubrey?" – substrata. "Worms digging into what you called it, getting ready for the planes."

The sound of the planes came first. Then the planes themselves, pounding the dead out of the earth. "Ain't no one gonna want this earth when the war's done with it," Amos yelled. Aubrey yelled back, but the words were wrong, he knew it, like bleeding someone else's blood. "My uncle says," he yelled at Amos, "the earth's like a woman. She might not appear to be what you're looking for, but if you grope around enough, you'll find something you want." Amos frowned, which made him doubly ugly. When the planes departed and the quiet returned, Amos, still frowning, had nothing to say to Aubrey. Aubrey felt afraid of the silence. Amos bowed his head between his arms and straight away started sleeping. Aubrey wanted to sleep, but he couldn't. He squatted, but he couldn't shit. He hadn't defecated in days, and his urine was so dark he could write with it, if his hand would only stop trembling. It wasn't just the worms anymore.

They were marching. Smoke and sulphur tormented the moonlight. Blind men walked into pillboxes and strode over corpses and fell over precipices. Someone drowned in a pond. Knocking his fist against a dry block of dirt, Amos said, "It's been boiled till it assholed," which meant something about turning maple syrup into candy. "You ever got to Vermont since your ma died?" he asked. Aubrey didn't answer. He was far away, though he was marching next to Amos. Everything in war was too close: you couldn't get any perspective. So Aubrey's mind receded into a corner of his brain. Amos asked again, "You ever got to Vermont since your ma died?"

Aubrey answered, "No."

"How's your dad?"

"Fine."

"Fine?"

"Yeah, he's fine. I wouldn't know, but I guess he's fine."

Because Aubrey was talking from the bruise in his head, Amos chucked him in the arm, making the bruise rise to the surface. "Goddamn, you been raised on sour milk," said Amos. Aubrey rubbed the spot, and his cursing relieved the pain.

Aubrey said, "I saw a man on fire, riding a horse with three legs today. I think that's what I saw. I don't know what anything is."

"You believe in prophecy and dreams?" asked Amos.

"I don't know what I believe in," said Aubrey. Though Aubrey didn't believe, he prayed to get injured if only to get a bath, he prayed for sleep, prayed to live another day, prayed tomorrow wouldn't come. He prayed for everything just to get over and done with. But even as he prayed to get the hell out of Dodge, he was happy he was here with Amos. Half happy, and half not believing he was even here at all. He said to himself he didn't give a damn if his prayers contradicted each other.

"Take twenty," shouted the lieutenant, and Aubrey sat down in the dark. The moon was gone, and the stars were missing from the eyeless sky. Aubrey had a full twenty minutes to linger in the wet, deep hole where he plunged his hand. He could smell that it was rancid and imagined

275

it was chewy. He was sitting on it; he couldn't stand up out of it, for the thing had hold of him, but in fact he had hold of it. He was clutching a trachea where a head should have been, and he was melting into the fleshy rotten fruit of the ground until Amos lifted him off of the mutilated corpse.

Aubrey washed his hands in mud puddles, streams and gasoline, but he couldn't get them clean. He couldn't get his eyes clean, either. A Punjabi Indian in another squadron lent him an eyecup, a tiny glass vial suctioned over the open eye to flush out impurities with water, but it had no effect. The Indian fell under a tank, which made his eyecup a gift, not a loan. "Stop washing them eyes," said Amos, as if it were simple. "Ain't you hungry?" he asked. The sky was a hard, bright blue, which made Amos hungrier, but Aubrey couldn't swallow. K-rations – cold, stale food too old to taste.

Maybe he was losing his mind. He was sane enough to wonder that. He'd lost everyone else he cared about. One day it was bound to be his turn: he'd lose himself. That was okay, as long as he didn't lose Amos.

"Clean up!" shouted the lieutenant, and they stormed into a house and shot two wounded Germans. Amos said, "Check upstairs," but when Aubrey opened the door upstairs, a

Kraut knocked the gun from his hand. The gun, more observant than him, lay on the floor watching Aubrey die. Blood poured into his mouth, making him high, and voices pounded in his ears. *Pay attention. Keep your eyes open.* He felt better closing them. When he closed his eyes, he was dancing again with Aunt Ethyl; he was grinning at a boar's head; du Pont was smoking with a blackened man in the furnace light; Jack was swinging on the parallel bars as someone hummed *"La Marseillaise"*; the ground was made of water and the water was forged out of molten iron. Aubrey opened his eyes in terror of slipping away. He saw a blonde head bob up and down above him, the enemy's green eyes as green as moss on a grave, his own head smacking against the floorboards. And though he was trying to pry the fingers from around his neck, his strength lightened into chlorine gas steaming off a heated swimming pool.

Then he was bathing in a shower of warm blood. Above him was Amos, an axe in one hand and a severed head of golden hair in the other. Amos threw the head across the room and held up his huge, red hands and said, "They're dainty next to *my* daddy's. He was a scrapper and a drinker and a hard man like you wouldn't want to meet in the goddamn dark. That boy was only a goddamn baby. Betcha he was younger than you. I gotta stop swearing. It sets a bad example." When Aubrey looked towards the head in the corner, Amos said, "Don't look. What's done's done." And while the medics inspected Aubrey's wounds and pronounced him "okay," Amos sat in a window, the sun against his big back, delicately pulling tobacco and a piece of cornhusk from a buckskin pouch. Wrapping the tobacco up in the husk, he lit it and sucked on the tip with the innocent avidity of a newborn.

Aubrey looked out the window at the squadron resting underneath the trees. "Do you know what your name means?" he asked. "Amos was a prophet in the Bible. He tended the trees and championed the silent and weak, because the rich people made them grow grapes and oilseed instead of food for their children and made them chop down the giant cedars to build the roofs of mansions and pave the palace roads in oil and gold."

Amos's hand emerged through a cloud of sunlit smoke and passed Aubrey the cornhusk cigarette. "Everett," Amos corrected him. Aubrey was always forgetting.

Aubrey said, "Everett is from the Early German and means 'brave boar.'"

"How about Aubrey?" asked Amos.

"I don't know," said Aubrey. He knew so much, it seemed, but nothing about his own name. He looked about the shattered room, past the head in the corner and the body still emptying itself of blood, as if he'd find a library somewhere in this villa that would provide him with the answer. Drawing the smoke into his lungs, he coughed and said again, "I don't know."

Aubrey was learning quickly. He learned that sound preceded sight, and scent preceded sight. He learned that the eye at war was different than the eye in peacetime. In war, some visions were permanent, like cataracts falling over the eye. Other visions, equally atrocious, were impossible to capture at all – one atrocity being replaced too quickly by another. He learned from the Indian man with the eyecup, before he fell under a tank, that air was the vehicle of the eye. But he saw for himself that air, earth and water could all in an instant become fire. And it was Amos who taught him that water was equivalent to fear.

"I read once in a science magazine," Aubrey said to Amos, "that due to the physics of water, a body weighing sixty-four pounds will float in brine. I figured it out the other day: I weighed just a little more than that when I sank in a swimming pool. So if my uncle hadn't rescued me, and if the pool had no bottom, I would have gone down until the water pressure became equal to gravity, and then I would have been weightless. The magazine called it neutrally buoyant, where you don't sink and you don't float and you don't feel anything except a little movement."

He didn't expect Amos to understand; he was really just talking aloud. But Amos answered, "Water's like fear that way. Invisible and constant. Why you so afraid?"

"Why aren't you?" asked Aubrey.

Neither answered the question.

Amos finally said, "You can swim. I saw you swim some-times in Vermont."

Amos's scars woke him. He'd been sleeping squatting, his head between his knees, swaying like a nut about to fall every time the ground shook. A pocked-up door lay over the slit-trench for protection. He often moaned or twitched in his sleep like a dog dreaming, but this morning he woke shouting, "Get your rifle out that goddamn door!"

Aubrey said, "You scared me," thinking Amos was having a nightmare. But immediately three Germans chucked the door off the trench and shoved their machine guns into the hole and barked in bad English, "Put up hands!"

Aubrey, obedient, did as he was told, and when Amos reached for a gun, Aubrey panicked – he didn't want to die; if he obeyed maybe he wouldn't die – and kicked the gun away. Amos bellowed while the sky screamed. Strafed down by one of their own planes, the three Germans fell, their cold blue eyes staring unseeing at the faded moon.

Aubrey stared too. How was it possible that what was alive one moment was dead the next? Alive one moment, dead the next: it was the reality of life, not just war.

Amos was harrowing through the mud to put the door back over their heads, his one eye flaring like the war-sky. "Jesus Christ, we're goddamn lucky," Aubrey said, and Amos shouted, "Jessum Crow, you goddamn flatlander! If you ever stop my goddamn gun again, I'm sending you to the place of your goddamn ancestors!" Amos didn't speak again for days.

They were marching with no guidebook to tell them about the pretty Italian churches along the way. Aubrey had been humming "The Ants Crawl In, The Ants Crawl Out," but he'd stopped, struck by the horrible thought that they were aunts.

Though there were men all over, lots of them, marching with him, Aubrey felt alone because Amos wouldn't look at him. As if he were interested in fourteenth-century architecture, Amos was staring straight ahead at a church. To punish me, Aubrey told himself, feeling guilty and angry. Nothing was sure or consistent, the earth itself unreliable if Amos was too.

Suddenly – it was always suddenly – Amos threw him to the ground a moment before the guy behind him was shot through the chest. There was a sniper in the church's tower. They lost two more men before they took him out through a stained glass window, the polychromatic lens flying away like migrant birds.

Aubrey and Amos were marching again, in the woods, in silence. But the trees were moaning. No more snipers, no mortar fire, no cannon fire, no instant mutilation of butterfly bombs, just the moaning of trees, their charred limbs rubbing together like a man in black lifting his hand to his mouth to cough or shoot back a whisky. Aubrey said aloud, " 'The trees were on edge all day and night, wondering what kind of men it was who walked this way amongst them.' "

Amos asked, "You mean us?"

Grateful that Amos had spoken to him, Aubrey answered quickly, "It's from an Indian book called *The Ramayana*. My father had it when I was a kid."

"Kona is a Cree," said Amos.

"Not that kind of Indian ..." Aubrey began, then asked, "Who's Kona?"

"I don't got a picture of Kona, but I figure those paintings of hell in the churches are there to make you think of Heaven, so I carry Donna around." From his pocket, he pulled out an advertisement for Pears soap: a bathing beauty, with raven hair and lard-white skin, about to drop her bathrobe. "Donna's gone to Hollywood," Amos said, and tried to smile but failed. It looked like he'd stuck his finger under his lip and lifted, as if inspecting a horse's teeth. "She had a baby girl."

"A girl, huh?"

"Yup."

Both of them knew the baby was dead, had died of hypothermia on the shack floor. Something was alive one moment and dead the next, and half alive again when you said its name.

Amos said, "That baby's gonna see forests better than this one when she's a old lady." His big voice tapered away.

Aubrey figured Amos had said what he said just to believe it for as long as it took to say it. But there didn't need to be a reason, just compassion for the sorrow of it all. "I guess so," he said.

Aubrey saw an Italian family – two boys, a girl, a grandmother in thick tattered black, a father with a kerchief around his neck, a mother – in a ditch. He was hysterical. He crouched to shit like a dog, and even shitting gave him no reprieve: he was still hysterical.

"I've killed a lot of Germans," he screamed, "and I haven't been killed, not once, not even once. How is that possible? Why is it that a rock, or a tree, or you, goddamn it" – he grabbed Amos's arm, which felt so large his own hand became a little child's – "are always in the enemy's way?"

The family's slaughter was no different from usual, but each day was different inside Aubrey. Some days, his lips twitched and he shot at anything; other days, like a lovesick girl with her face in a pillow, he wanted to cry, but he couldn't. He could never cry. He clawed at his chest as if he'd find a camera there. There wasn't one, and he couldn't cry. And he couldn't go on, because no human was up to living human life, except maybe Amos. Maybe sometimes Amos.

Aubrey was hysterical, so Amos slugged him in the gut and shouted, "Tell me about Vermont!" But even sobered by pain, he couldn't. He was gazing backwards through a camera lens: he couldn't remember what his mother looked like, and there was no one sitting on the porch.

"I can't," Aubrey whimpered.

So Amos said softly, "Then ask me something."

"Have you ever written to Kona?"

The question took Amos off guard. "No." He sounded unbearably sad. "'Cause we used to draw each other pictures, and there ain't nothing here worth seeing." Amos held Aubrey tightly by the arm and was turning him away from the wreckage. They returned to rigging a booby trap from a wire and a couple of grenades stuck between two rocks. "There," said Amos, "now you can sleep, and don't gotta worry about a Kraut slitting your throat in the night."

Amos watched: Aubrey clutched a grenade and rolled towards a pillbox while a machine gun tracking him ate up another guy. Aubrey kept rolling, sweating so hard it seemed he would suck up the earth and suck up the pillboxes too, if they weren't sunk so deep in the ground. Only a direct hit from a 150-millimetre shell could crush them, so the artillery was pounding on them fiercely.

"Do it nicely," Amos muttered, as if even a slaughter had grace. Amos thought the beauty of the day was the beauty of the day even in a war, and hell was a hillside in spring where the goal was to kill what you found. He had no argument with reality today, though he himself was in hell. He'd find himself here tomorrow, too, but one day it would be gone.

Amos watched Aubrey close in on the pillbox and toss a grenade through the gun slit. The kid slithered like a snake, crawled like a dog, did what needed to be done. Two Germans died instantly, but one rushed out with his arms in the air: "*Kamerad*, no shoot poor *Polak*!"

The soldier was blonde with a hard jaw, probably a Nazi pretending to be a Pole to get off easy. The lieutenant knew better than that. He ordered Aubrey to take the prisoner to HQ and be back in five minutes. Aubrey hesitated, looked at Amos, but Amos looked away, looked down at his rifle, shiny because blood doesn't stain steel. Aubrey did as he was told.

Five minutes, the lieutenant had told him, but head-quarters was at least two hours away. Aubrey took the fake Polack into the woods and shot him.

The regiment found a cellar full of wine in an abandoned villa and Aubrey was singing loudly: "The good old Duke of York, he had ten thousand men, he marched them up to the top of the hill, and he marched them down again. And when they were up they were up, and when they were down they were down, and when they were only halfway up they were neither up nor down."

Now he spoke into his tin cup of wine. "Shooting a prisoner: right or wrong? My uncle said anything can be cleaned up. I can't even clean the shit off my ass. I'm renaming this villa Merdaiolo. Or Macello. Do you know Italian, Amos? Everett, Amos, Jesus Christ … whatever your name is. It's a relative of Spanish. Do you know Mr Einstein's theory of relativity? A train is viewed from two different inertial frames, and therefore different realities.

In a nutshell, the entire world looks different according to your relationship to light. Do you remember what Hamlet said about nutshells and infinite space? Do you ever go by 'Professor', Amos? Did I tell you what your name means? I don't actually know what anything means. My aunt used to call me into her bedroom and then act as if she hadn't. So I asked her once, 'Why did you ask me in?' She shrugged and said, 'You happened to be there, so I happened to ask you. The same reason anything happens.'"

Aubrey paused and waited. But Amos didn't appear to have anything to say; he was even quieter when he was drunk, so Aubrey filled in the words himself. "I know what you'll say," he said. "'You don't gotta fix it if you can't. You just gotta see it as it is, two sides of a terrible thing in a beautiful world, and live your goddamn life.'"

Now Amos smiled like a dog learns to smile, on one side of his mouth. He said, "Some guys can whistle in two tones at once, like the wood thrush do."

The Germans had vacated the villages and happy Italians in their doorways threw bread and bottles of wine to the Americans, who were no longer on foot but on bicycles and plough horses or in Jeeps and a Mercedes-Benz. When a stale loaf hit Aubrey's forehead, Amos reached for his rifle. Aubrey said, "Relax, it's only a loaf of bread," and actually laughed. It was good to laugh.

When a little girl gave them a half-dozen eggs, Amos ran off to the roadside, boiled them in his helmet over a fire of trash, and fell back into formation with a stash of hard-boiled eggs in his pockets. Aubrey liked that about him:

how every action had its counteraction, and doubt didn't enter in. And yet it was only a loaf of bread that had made Amos reach for his rifle.

Now an old lady planted a kiss on his ugly scar, and Amos flinched. Though the troops were giving back kisses like candy and the Italian girls gobbling them up, he was rubbing his scar with the butt of his rifle. "What's wrong?" asked Aubrey. Amos didn't answer: he didn't know. He just kept rubbing his scar.

Aubrey looked anxiously up the lane at the dark rooms behind cracked-open doorways and sunny windows with deep ledges. The lieutenant rode in a Jeep in the front, grinning and waving, with a girl on one arm and a bottle of red wine in the other. Until the Jeep rolled over a mine. Though the woman was torn to pieces, the lieutenant was thrown out alive, while his hand, still holding the wine bottle, vanished. When the hand was found in the dust, the lieutenant carried it with him on the stretcher and refused to let the medics pry it away. He shouted that his fingers hurt like hell. Though the hand was a lifeless slab, his fingers hurt like hell.

"I don't know where a man starts and stops," Aubrey said to Amos. "Maybe everyone's got an invisible hand with invisible fingers pointing at them, asking, 'Who the hell are you?'"

"You got thin," said Amos.

"It's worms," said Aubrey, "it ain't me."

Worms had tapered Aubrey's waist. Men lost fingers, arms, legs, sometimes only hair. Aubrey was twenty-one and already losing his hair. There were fewer men; there was less of men. The sky was sick to death of men and throwing down its stars. Mortar fire all night and a meteorite shower. There was less of heaven as well.

The beautiful lake was shaped like a Chianti bottle. The troops had reached Lake Garda, happy summer playground of brownshirts and *mafiosi*. From the foothills of the Alps, Aubrey imagined that Amos could stretch out a massive arm and lob a grenade into Mussolini's villa, but tonight was a silent night, almost sleepy. Who would know there was even a word for war?

Aubrey was almost happy. He felt the way he used to feel as a boy in the summers, when he couldn't believe winter even existed – the opposite of February vertigo and the horrible thought that spring would never come. Aubrey could rest easy; it was already May, the first whiff of heat in the air. His khakis, skin and gun were filthy, but the wind off the lake smelled clean. It was a beautiful lake, even if it lay in the permanent shadow of the Alps like a limbo where prayers wouldn't reach. The water crowned by the mountains reminded Aubrey of home. He knew where home was now: he and Amos would go there together after the war.

The thought made Aubrey pause, remembering the LaSalle parked in the drive, and beside it the mud-splattered horse and cart, himself in whites and Amos dredging trash from the back seat. As the memory disturbed the future, Aubrey turned away from both to look at the Alps. They were bigger and younger than the Green Mountains. Younger mountains, he told himself, full of older men and history.

Here Shelley wrote "Ode to the West Wind" and Goethe was mistaken for a spy, and though Aubrey wanted to tell Amos this, it wouldn't have meant anything to him because he couldn't read more than headlines and children's books.

The troops were waiting for the dark to descend and the amphibious boats to assemble and cross them over, so Aubrey walked alone along the southern shore of the lake, trying to retain the happiness a little while longer. Pale cows in a paddock chewed cud they'd chewed all war long.

It was past midnight when Aubrey sat down on a limestone outcrop protected from the wind, which blew from north to south, as the locals claimed it always did past midnight.

"See the bear?" asked Amos. He'd also been walking the lake alone, thinking, though his thoughts didn't rise in sentences. When he saw Aubrey sit, he joined him and pointed to the sky with his sawed-off finger. "A person was turned into a bear and plunked down in the sky. The bear lived up there happy enough until one day it got up on its hind legs to say hello to its child hunting in the woods. The frightened kid didn't know his parent was a bear, so he lifted up his bow and arrow to shoot it. But the gods didn't want the bear to die, so they turned the boy into a bear, too, just in time. See the little bear? It's a lot fainter." Amos dropped his head and dug at the earth with a stick, as if there were stories there too.

Aubrey looked between the sky and the earth, trying to see Amos's thinking. He would have asked a thousand questions if he'd known what would happen next, but Amos wouldn't have answered anyway, would have felt that enough had been said already.

When they drove into the lake that early morning, they didn't know it was only a matter of hours before the

Germans would surrender Italy. Neither the ski troopers nor the enemy that awaited them on the far shore could see the future. As the boats moved deeper into the shadow of the mountains, the night sky blossomed with shellfire and one boat after another went down. There were many boats full of many men crossing the lake that night, and Aubrey asked himself, as he often did, why it was always others who were dying, never him. But when it was his turn, he didn't want it.

The steering wheel of his car-boat erupted into splinters and the stern shot up, and the engine whirred through the air, diced the driver, spilled its oil, and the waters beneath ignited. The boat turned turtle, and Aubrey saw Amos underwater, huge like a submerged island, and saw, like a sealed heaven, the hull above their heads. Blood eased into black water. A large fish crossed the churning dark. The waves in the north wind spasmed with gunning. Dropping unconscious, Aubrey saw nothing. He was not even aware of sinking.

He was lying on a stretcher in a summer villa. The nurses were serving limoncello scavenged from the cool cellar, but Aubrey was already high enough on morphine. He remembered little, only water. He remembered swimming, and someone drowning. Had Amos put an arm around him and pulled him back like a word unspoken?

He asked the nurses for Amos. Amos Cobb. Amos saved me. Amos saved me again. Amos saved me from drowning. Amos is always saving me from drowning. Or from something. Or something.

A nurse said to another, "It's the morphine speaking." And no one knew what or who he was talking about. In his panic, Aubrey tried to stand, but the nurses pulled him down. No one knew Amos. "Amos who?" As if he'd never existed. As if everything Aubrey had lost in his life hadn't been at all. Though he opened his mouth, his words came out without meaning.

Then he remembered Amos's other name. He asked for Everett Brown. A nurse said Brown had taken off up the mountain with a pair of skis over his shoulders. "Where did he get them?" asked Aubrey, suddenly happy.

The nurse shrugged as she poured him a limoncello and stole a tiny sip herself, wishing she, too, might get drunk, swaying to the rhythm of the songs and laughter coming from beyond the tent, for the war in Europe was over.

"Over?" he asked. "Completely over?"

"I've got a sister in Baraboo, Wisconsin," she said, lost in the revelry of her own returning world. "She's having a baby this summer."

The doctors and nurses looked up at the ceiling when, as if for no reason, the chandelier started swaying. A doctor tugged on his stethoscope, then lifted his hand as if to conduct the drums. "It's nothing," he said to the high and frightened patients, who all heard the distant rumble. "Avalanche somewhere. Far away. Nothing to fear. I grew up in Colorado: these things happen all the time."

"Forget about it, everyone," said the nurse, refilling their long-stemmed glasses.

It was a real Vermont day in the Italian mountains, the sharp blue sky softened by clouds on the fractured peaks. Amos faded in and out of the woods and drank from clear streams. Everywhere was the sound of churning water from the mountain runoff. Where the snows had melted, the grass swelled plump and emerald, while farmers' fields were spangled with white stones and ivory goats. Ferns whose ancestors witnessed the glaciers laid down and the mountains lifted up unfurled their fronds and quivered in the wind. Star-shaped mosses waited for rain to fall on their splash cups and carry their essence away. Bees born in the thousands sheared the silence, and a quick red squirrel scolded the man's passing. Amos crept beneath the low branches of a tall pine onto a granite outcrop from where he could see the alpine lake below. The wind stirred whitecaps from the waters, and a sailboat swept from the eastern to the western shore so fast it seemed to touch each side simultaneously. War in Europe was over, and everyone was celebrating by returning to the world they knew.

A pair of skis hooked to his rucksack pointed to the perfect sky, and Amos raised his good eye to the mountain: just a little higher and the seasons scrolled back towards winter, Kona and evergreens. Bracing himself against a rock face, he dug his boot heel into something soft – a bird's nest – that toppled down the cliff. Weather and fault had scarped the earth. He took hold where the rock bulged or fissured and hauled himself up. Still higher, wedged ice and groping tree roots had split a sheer cleft for his feet. Pitch by pitch, he climbed up and across the snow line.

At the cliff top, he opened his pack. It was loaded with tacks, spikes and rivets – trophies of battle he'd pulled out of his own flesh or foraged from the mud where a mine had torn apart a Jeep or shellfire had blasted the nails out of a fence. Having learned a deeper silence from the war, he hushed the butt of his axe with a cloth, and when he slammed it into a tree trunk, there was only a faint thud. The tree nodded and spoke softly. Then, as if the moment could grow yet more perfect, the immaculate blue sky brightened.

Briefly, Amos was happy. There were flowers below and snow above. He saw time reaching backwards through the strata of earth and the seasons retreating ever higher up the mountain. He saw troops steaming home across the Atlantic, and Aubrey Brown swimming hard across Caspian Lake. Aubrey was a bent sapling, but he'd right himself in the sun. Amos saw, somewhere in the deep tunnel of his scars where visions appeared and passed like weather fronts, Kona's child growing big and strong, and the mother looking for the father in the Green Mountains. Even through the hard shield of a sunny day in Italy, he heard faintly the chorus of the northern lights, while a Canadian wolf howled and a wood pigeon answered. He heard a moment's peace, a temporary reprieve for the world. He sat down in the snow and smiled at the peaks above him, the bright yellow sun, the blue snow, steep and precarious.

Below him, a car sped around the lake road. And in the distance, a train. The sound of its approach carried effortlessly up the Alps, and Amos's smile faded. Frowning, he was an ugly sight made brutal by war and killing men, but no one was nearby to see him. His vision was shrouded by the simple desire to continue to be happy, to be more happy, permanently so, to pretend such a thing was possible. He was thinking of Kona: they were skating together in Bitter Valley; they were skiing over Caspian Lake. Even to great men, vision is parcelled out in small supply, and he did not see what would happen next. Though his skin twitched and his blood rushed to his scars, and though, as if out of nowhere, he felt the shudder of an unstoppable, impenetrable advancing sadness, he didn't jump to his feet and run.

The train whistled down in the valley. In and out of view, small and quick, like a toy chugging through plastic tunnels, it sped faster and faster beneath the steep snow, past the granite cliffs that cupped the lake and held it in place. Tunnels one, two and three were passable, and the train chugged into and out of them. But tunnel four – neither Amos nor the conductor could see inside – was a tomb. There the Germans, intending to blow up the railway, had run afoul of their own demolitions and dropped the cave roof on their heads. Rocks and corpses awaited the quick little train at the end of the man-made hole.

The crash echoed against the snow-packed cliffs. It could be heard even over the din of the celebrations in the far-off camp. The peaks answered with thunder. From their nests, a hundred birds took flight. The mountain sat up fast, as if it had awakened from a nightmare, and against the sky the snow slipped. Amos didn't have time to pity the dying below him, for the wet, heavy snow above was on the move. It fell to the south, gaining momentum to gather up the world like children to its petticoats, sweeping up sheep and stones and boundary markers, dropping the white sky on the sweet brown earth to plunge into the cold blue lake, Amos with it. It made no exceptions. The avalanche descended, an unfathomable power let loose. Amos lifted his eye to the mountains, and his day ended.

Aubrey vomited into a bucket. The Atlantic was fierce and hoary, and he was eight hours off of New York. He sat up in his cot and kept himself awake by staring out of the porthole until morning. He warded off sleep because of the nightmares, though he used to pray for sleep.

At Pier 88, the Hudson in summer stank of oil and excrement. Fish corpses jammed up the reedy banks and a barge pumped waste from its bilge. The humid air was thick with perfume and poisoned armpits. Seagulls arrived like the piper's rats behind the incoming steamer that had taken young boys away and returned them as ruined men. River gnats swarmed around the smiling faces of the not-dead soldiers who'd feared they'd survived Italy only to die in Japan, but who now would drive home singing, knowing they'd never see the Land of the Rising Sun.

Aubrey stepped off the gangplank and dropped his duffel on the concrete pier as a woman in whites ran by him. Watching her throw her arms around a soldier, Aubrey felt fiercely alone, but as a limousine rolled into the crowded parking lot, he cursed his uncle for disobeying his wishes.

"Don't you want me to meet you?" Jack had asked on the phone from Mexico.

"No." Just no.

The limousine, it turned out, was for some other soldier, forever done with cleaning latrines, returning to his unequal world. A little girl swung on the arms of her long-absent father, whose biceps were sturdy as monkey bars; her feet, slipping out of her sandals, wrapped around his back as the ragged soldier swung her into the car. Family and friends had driven hundreds of miles to greet the homecoming troops and whisk them off to the Bronx and the Hamptons, the Catskills and Adirondacks, even as far as the White and Green Mountains, where the gall of the earth was blooming, a wildflower that, strangely, stared away from the sun.

It was August 11, 1945, and now that Little Boy had dropped on Hiroshima and Fat Man on Nagasaki, happiness floated in the air like litter in the Hudson. Cars gunned their engines in the festive jam and a cross-breeze of fumes hit Aubrey's nostrils. A small old woman squeezed her hands together as if, by a conjuring trick, a little seed of a hero would sprout between her palms. As she looked for a son she could not find, a mushroom fell from her shopping basket and rolled into the river. The intractable water spread like tar, and the mushroom disappeared. A shadow of a bird crossed Aubrey's eyes. Under the cheers on the quay, he thought he could hear a fish die. They drowned, as it were, inversely, floating to their deaths.

The city bus to the train station was slowed by celebrations in the streets while the drums of a parade resounded against the skyscrapers. Aubrey listened to the bus radio rehash the news: "The force from which the sun draws its power has been loosed against those who brought war to the Far East. A new era in man's understanding of nature's forces has begun."

On the marble floor of Grand Central Station, Aubrey stood beneath the astronomical ceiling on which a starry sky was painted backwards, as if from the perspective of God. A blonde woman with a pug nose, her suitcase papered with stickers from faraway ports, paused for a moment beside him and mused aloud, "I guess God is the only New Yorker who can see the stars anyway." When the flaps on the departure board shuffled like cards, the pretty lady wandered away to her platform. Aubrey lit a cigarette, slumped into a crisp vinyl waiting-room chair, and from beneath his cap watched the people in the charged air rushing for their trains.

As passenger trains no longer ran as far as Hardwick or the Bend, he disembarked at the state capital and hitched a ride with a farmer who, having sold his farm, drove a four-door sedan. The farmer's thick Vermont accent sounded like a jug of turning milk sloshing between his molars. Aubrey watched the view through the car window. The highway was newly paved, and the automobile moved fast enough to kill a deer. He saw a hard, slow tortoise desperate to cross the road.

After the car turned north up Route 15 and east up 16 to the Bend, it came to a stop by the hill to Greensboro and Aubrey got out. Throwing his duffel over his shoulder, he set off up the last hill he ever intended to take. Sweating, though he was neither hot nor tired, he'd walked only a few steps before an old Model-T laboured past and misfired. He hollered and dropped. He reached for a phantom gun and rolled towards the ditch. Huddling in a runoff stream, he covered his mouth with one hand clamped over the other to force the screaming back inside.

Beneath him was the Bend, where a freight car waited in the station, though most freight went by truck. The Railway

Inn had closed when the passenger train was discontinued, and the junction sat inert in its frigid valley. Hardly an enterprise was running, except the pulp mill.

When he finally reached the lake road, he was glad to find it wasn't tarred. Muddy streams dashed along on either side and worms lay in the potholes, indistinguishable from the worms of his youth. He stopped at a large new granite monument where a herd of cows leaned their heads over a barbed-wire fence. Though he read silently, his tongue moved and his jaw hurt: "1771, near this spot, guarding Hazen Road, two scouts, Constant Bliss and Moses Sleeper, were killed by Indians and buried where they fell. Lest we forget the pioneers, this memorial was erected, 1941." It had been carved on the eve of America joining the war.

The first view of the lake was dark with the threat of an imminent storm, though over these hills, a heavy sky might drag on for days or alter in the upstroke of a hummingbird. He sat on the roadside, smoked a cigarette, breathed deeply. There was peace on earth, in places. There was sameness in the sweet summer air. He heard the wood thrush sing two delicate synchronous notes. But when a man with a flamethrower dodged behind a rock, Aubrey pressed his fists to his eyes. He stood up and ran the final mile.

He found the cottage eyeless, for it still wore its shutters. His father had abandoned Greensboro after the summer of 1939, and only a week ago, shortly after the first atomic bomb was dropped, Grandmother had died of heart failure in a Princeton nursing home. That she'd neglected to wait for his return didn't particularly hurt him. If he felt anything, he felt spared from having to witness yet another death. Her last letter: "My dear friend Mr Einstein is grief-stricken over recent events and insists that he should have been a shoemaker."

Aubrey entered through the kitchen door, where the coffee machine sat amongst mouse droppings. Though Uncle Jack had inherited the house, with its small plot of land leading down through the blackberry bushes to the lake, he had never come here. And Delia hadn't been there to clean it; she and her husband had sold their farm and moved down south.

Though he had at last arrived, Aubrey found he could not sit still. He paced from kitchen to dining room to living room, in and out of his childhood bedroom, his father's study, the dark room where his mother slept through the afternoons, while in every chamber the doors and floorboards creaked with ghosts. He walked out to the porch and leaned over the rail, where the air was sharpened by the incoming storm. Something fell over the railing and was gone. He rocked his mother's rocker back and forth, slowly at first, then hard.

A sudden squall rushed through the inlet, and opposing winds baffled a neighbour's American flag. Clouds slashed through the monotone sky. Black swallows skimmed the chaos. The sunken shark-finned islands vanished in the waves, and the buoys that marked their hidden shallows disappeared as ragged scud clouds ushered in the first break of thunder. The mountains were gone behind a mask of rain. The woods were gone. The steeple and cupola of the village were all gone too. The shore, with its ring of pines and fields and cows and cottages, gone. Lightning hit the hills, as if God had snapped a picture, and for a moment the world returned by flare light. Aubrey stood on the porch and screamed. His screams were carried by the water to the cottages across the lake, and he knew he frightened children far away in their beds.

Mrs Irwin, who lived down the lane in the only cottage that had a phone before the war, was on the party line when Aubrey picked up the receiver the following morning. He was trying to call in a liquor delivery from the general store, as he had no desire to stand in line and be gawked at by curious neighbours. Thankfully, more phones had come to Greensboro, but Mrs Irwin – who was now referred to as Old Mrs Irwin – informed Aubrey that the store no longer delivered. Shouting down the receiver as if she were calling across the field, she invited him to a picnic, which he declined, after which she expressed her regret at his grandmother's death and asked after his father. Aubrey supposed his father was fine and suggested she get on with her conversation with whomever else was listening.

He walked to the store for provisions: cigarettes, a little food, rain gear and something to help him sleep. Reaching for a gallon of cheap whisky in the liquor aisle, he kept his gaze on the linoleum floor. Whisky would get him through the days and rock him to sleep at night, stop his hands from shaking. Not to think, not to know, not to remember, not to imagine the day after tomorrow, it helped with all of this. He filled his duffel, took his change, marched home.

It was blackberry season, and Aubrey's pale skin burnt in the sun as he picked the berries. He made black jelly, but it didn't set. He sat quietly on his mother's rocker and saw the children swim past, swimming laps between the Carters' raft and the Smiths' buoy. There was often a youthful fisherman puttering by at dawn. He sat in his grandmother's chair, looked staunchly away from the lake and read his father's books on faraway times and places. When he picked another bucketful of blackberries, he left them too long on the counter and they began to produce white mould. And when, one warm night, a squadron of kids ran past the cottage playing flashlight tag, he shouted. He didn't mean to. He was unable to control his mouth. And now the kids played elsewhere.

In his father's study he removed all the drawings from the wall – the sketches of monuments men had erected to themselves – and stuck them beneath the paperweight so they were a mere three inches high. His mother's photograph he moved from the nail above his father's desk to the nail above his own bed, where it belonged. Other than the loose jam, he hardly ate.

Jack phoned and said, "I can't get a word out of you." When his uncle announced that he'd phone again soon, Aubrey stopped picking up on the double ring.

Mrs Irwin dropped by to say, "You know that when it rings twice, it's for you?" She looked worried as she went home to the large cottage where she'd summered all alone since her children had grown. She'd lost her husband in the Great War, which her generation had presumed to be the final war but was only the first of its kind. Aubrey watched her retreat down the lane in her new white rubber-soled sneakers, which the old folks had taken so sensibly to wearing.

A letter arrived in the communal tin mailbox and sat there a week before the old lady determined to deliver it to Aubrey's porch. She brought him a rolled-up *New York Times*, plunking it on the wicker table, declaring, "We must all keep up with the world." Then she waved an envelope in front of him and said, "From your father!"

It was a formal letter, suggesting that Everett secure his son a place at Princeton to pursue a bachelor's degree. Aubrey read it again and again, looking for a sign of the man in the handwriting. Everett had written, "Sincerely, your father." But Aubrey, no matter how hard he looked, could find no trace of him on the sheet of paper.

He understood his father too well now, and he didn't want to be his father. Aubrey buried the letter with the drawings under the paperweight and wrote back to decline the offer. He was glad not to have to walk to the village post office, for he could lift the tin flag on the mailbox to alert the mailman to the outgoing letter, and there were sure to be postage stamps in Grandmother's roll-top desk. His hand was firm and his writing was steady until he signed his own name. He attempted to control the shaking by seizing his right wrist with his left hand, but the signature was an ugly scrawl, and he blotted it out with white zinc pigment, which he found in his father's study. He'd send the letter nameless.

He needed air and a cigarette. Out on the porch, the wind was scented by a sea of goldenrods leading down the hill to the lake. The sun struggled to warm the day. The high, cold mountains were spotted with red, and even along the shore the weakest maples had turned, but the strong ones still insisted it was not yet autumn. As he smoked, he eyed the rolled-up newspaper still on the wicker table. Carrying it into the house, he turned it round and round in his hands, trying to read the headlines. When he cut the strings with a knife, the newsprint pages flopped open, revealing the picture on the front page. A black-and-white photograph of Auschwitz-Birkenau flashed into bloody colour.

He didn't read it. But he heard it say, *The world is divided into three kinds of men: those who are dead, and those who are not dead yet, and the living dead left over.* From his grandmother's open roll-top desk, the stench of a mass grave poured out. Aubrey dropped the paper and vomited into his hands.

The evenings were growing cold, and that night he used the *Times* to light a fire. But unwilling to burn the dead, and not knowing how to dispose of the evidence of over a million murdered Jews, he folded up the front page and lay it beneath a rock by the side door of the cottage. The news of the death camps having reached Vermont, no one would call their cottages camps anymore.

Aubrey wrote a letter to his uncle informing him that the cottage was in disrepair and requesting that Jack consider selling it to him for a nominal sum. But a week later, when the phone rang for him repeatedly, he couldn't bring himself to answer.

"From Mexico!" Old Mrs Irwin cried, delighted by the Aztecs on the postage stamp, when she delivered a fat package to the door. She lingered on the porch to hear the news.

Aubrey obliged her by opening the accompanying letter and reporting, "The government has dropped the charge of treason against Standard Oil. My uncle is very pleased."

"I'm so happy for you!"

"He's going to hell."

"Aubrey Brown," snapped Mrs Irwin, "he's your uncle!" The tone in an old lady's voice was unaltered by the war.

As to the lake house: "Happy to sell if it makes you happy!" Jack wrote. "What's up with the phones in Vermont?"

Aside from the letter, the package was stuffed with legal papers needing signing to confirm the sale. It also contained the photo album that Aubrey had left in Mexico. He skimmed through the first few pages, then dropped it on the floor, ashamed of what a child he'd been, as if it were wrong to have been a child.

He said to Mrs Irwin, "Can I borrow your car?"

He drove up Barr Hill and parked below the hay elevator. Finding the door to Delia's kitchen unlocked, he entered, and a blast of hot air and wood smoke smacked against his face. Her stove had been smoking for over a hundred years. Boiling water rattled the lid of a pot on the stovetop where plums were canning, and his heart battered his ribs. Like a bear, he smelt the wet, stringy plum pits on the chopping board. He saw a farmer's socks hanging from the flue pin, and a child's and a toddler's underclothes drying over a chair back. A woman stepped round the house onto her porch and the laundry in her arms slipped to her feet.

He said quickly, "I used to know the woman who lived here. I used to play in the barn as a child. We were going to park under the hay elevator. We never did."

He knew he sounded absurd, but it didn't matter. The woman had sized him up: everyone had sustained losses in the war. Maybe hers was her eldest son. Being a Vermonter, she said only what she was thinking.

"Where were you stationed?" she asked.

"Italy."

"My children are playing in the barn. Don't scare them."

In the barn, two small faces peered out from behind a hay bale. A young girl and boy lifted their fingers to their lips to silence him, then pointed at a teenage girl leaning against the haymow down the nave. Light from the high-drive downlit the red in her long brown hair. Swallows flew catercorner between their dark spittle nests and the sky. Her eyes were shielded by her hands as she counted to one hundred. Her speech consisted only of numbers, and yet it was somehow more powerful than the vertical sunshine, as if counting in self-imposed blindness were the only order in a chaotic world. Seventy-eight, seventy-nine. They pointed at her and said, "*Shh.*"

The children were happy. For them, there was happiness only. The sun was busy lifting the asphalt off the roof, carelessly peeling the red paint from the west side of the barn. Light dropped through the cracks in the eaves. Yet happiness judged in an instant was eternal and judged over time was unhappiness. Aubrey backed out of the barn and left the kids to their games, glad that at least he hadn't scared them.

He climbed farther up Barr Hill. Over siliceous marble, phyllite, quartzite, white mica, black mottled slate, his feet on lichen and fern, liverworts and hornworts, maple and oak root, walking over pollen cones and ovulate cones, over oak bark that a stud deer had skimmed with its antlers and birch bark that the children had peeled off for paper. He passed the picnic area, the charred wood in a fire pit, a Coke bottle forgotten in the chokegrass. He slid down the granite rocks that led to a pond that, being too ugly for men to have named it, bears sought for its seclusion. No human would think of swimming amongst the weeds and water snakes or picnicking on the anemic shore, where flooded and lifeless totems stood in the murky shallows.

Two deer bounded through a thicket, their necks twisted towards the spook behind them. Something was coming up the back side of the hill. It emerged on the limestone ridge. It shuffled on its short hind legs a moment, then rose up to seven feet tall to sniff the wind. An American black bear swung his head from side to side like a constellation lolling in the ether.

He woke in a sweat.

He had dreamt that Amos came up the back side of Barr Hill and the birds sang in dialect, that Amos was breathing the rich high air, the good air that had rushed into him before his mother's milk. If Aubrey had dreamt it was winter, there would have been skis on Amos's feet, for Amos was moving quickly. He was free; he was running. Running past Delia's red barn and white farmhouse, he took the cow pasture in ten massive steps, jumped the brook, leapt across a stone wall, stumbled over an irrigation ditch and rose again from the brambles. He disappeared into the dark shade of the woods moments before a limousine drove up the dirt road and Jack alighted: Jack and Aubrey were going bear hunting.

Rifles over their shoulders, they walked through a clearing where a marshy lowland watered like an eye in a circular field and forget-me-nots blossomed in the wallow. Aubrey raised his hands to his mouth and offered up to the air the squeal of a rabbit in distress. "Bear calling," he said. "When I was a boy, our handyman taught me." Even dreaming, he wouldn't say Amos's name in front of Uncle Jack. "The bears think you're a rabbit dinner. You can count on them being hungry." He raised his hands and shrieked again, imitating a small and desperate creature.

Though the sound was muffled by the trees, the granite boulders in the woods offered back an echo. Aubrey slid down the rocks that led to a pond where mosquitoes bred in stagnant water. As a bear emerged on the ridge, he cried out again. Looking down his gun he watched the creature, astonished by the swiftness and lightness of the tonnage that flew down the hill as if it would lift off into the sky.

"Shoot!" Jack commanded.

Aubrey tried to wake himself but could not do so in time. He shot the bear. He shot the bear, but what died was Amos. The bullet, speeding through Amos's one good eye, journeyed out of the back of his head and into the tree beyond, and Aubrey awoke.

He woke in a sweat and shivering. He was both hot and cold. Aubrey poured himself a whisky from the stash on his dresser and walked down the hall to his mother's room, where a trunk held extra blankets. He put down his drink, leaving a cold, wet ring on the floorboards. He opened the trunk and the smell of mothballs overwhelmed the room. When he shook the mothballs out of a quilt, they rolled down to the trunk's bottom. Under the quilt was a package: the return address was "Everett Brown, Princeton, New Jersey," the mailing address "Everett Brown, Greensboro, Vermont," but the packing tape had never been broken. He slipped a nail file from his mother's vanity into the taped edges.

Inside, he found her jewellery case. In it were her wedding ring, the Bakelite necklace she never wore, the string of pearls that had once had a pair of matching earrings, and the pretty but worthless pebbles that he himself had picked out of the lake and given her as a present. And a pile of photographs. Father had developed Aubrey's film from his final summer in Vermont. There was Garbo. Though her breasts were overexposed, the camera had captured the instant her smile changed into a scowl.

With heavy blankets draped over his arms, he balanced the tumbler of whisky in one hand and clutched Garbo's photograph in the other. If he was to use the quilts, he'd need to air them. He'd hang them over the pine trees. Descending the stairs, he stopped at the big picture window on the landing and stared at the crowded sky. There was Cassiopeia and the Big Dipper and others he couldn't name. He wondered what the Dipper was full of, whether it was pleasant or poisonous. He was full of something too. It was overflowing. As he leaned his head on the cool glass, sweat dripped down the window. He laughed at the thought that he was raining. Then his knees buckled beneath him. The drink slid out of his wet palm; ice cubes clinked down the steps. The glass rolled down and shattered, and the cubes began to melt against the album on the floor. The muzzle of a tank gun emerged from the curtain drawn across the closet.

Crouching mid-stairs beneath the mound of quilts in the naphthalene-heavy darkness, Aubrey pinched his hands under his thighs to stop them trembling. But when his hands couldn't move, his jaw convulsed.

"Worms afraid of dying. It ain't you," said Amos.

"Nothing's goddamn me!" Aubrey screamed over the shelling. He hit himself in the gut, tried to wake himself out of hell. He closed his eyes.

"Ain't you seen it's all you? Open your goddamn eyes! You can swim, can't you?"

"So what? So what the hell? What in goddamn hell does that matter?"

"I can't. I can't swim," said Amos.

Aubrey opened his eyes. The shelling continued, but now the memory returned. On Lake Garda in Italy, so much like Caspian, it was Aubrey who had reached out his arm and pulled Amos ashore before dropping unconscious himself. It was not the other way round. It was Aubrey who had known how to swim.

Now he peeled the blankets away and, with Amos covering him, crawled to the closet. Aubrey was staring down the nose of the tank, his light touch on the pin of a grenade. Amos yanked back the closet's burlap curtain and a fishing rod fell out.

In the closet Aubrey sat and cried. He missed Amos, his mother, his father, his aunt, his grandmother. He missed his childhood. He lay down and pressed his cheek into the floorboards; he was deadwood like them, over which so many people had walked. He pulled his knees up to his chest and could feel his heartbeat against them. It seemed only his knees were his, but sometimes it seemed his heart was too.

In the sharp-angled dawn, he opened the flimsy lattice door to the empty space under the house where his rowboat and Father's sailboat were stowed. Until recently, they'd sat undisturbed for years. The sailboat proved beyond repair – frost had split the hull and the sail had been used as nesting material by raccoons and field mice. But although the rowboat had tipped off the logs that kept it off the earth and the bow had rotted, Aubrey had fixed it. Testing the new fibreglass patch, he found it was solid and dry. He hooked the oars into the oarlocks and folded them into the hull before dragging the boat out from under the house. It crushed the stiff goldenrods on the way down to the water. All summer, Aubrey had neglected to put in the dock, and the rowboat's bottom scraped against the rocks. Despite this, the mend held.

A jet vapour trail hung in the sky, undisturbed by the wind, for there was none. The lake was glassy – no motor-boat today. But the sun rose just as it had on that day when he was twelve. He still thought of the far shore as belonging to Garbo, but he didn't expect to find her, or anyone in fact, in the cottage by the granite bank. Sometime during the war the house had changed hands, and the new inhabitants drove up from Boston each weekend, remained Friday to Sunday, then drove back down again. Midweek, the cottage would be vacant.

He rowed across the lake.

No one saw him tie his boat to the wiry tree on the rocky outcrop and walk straight up to the craftsman-style cottage whose two big windows were placed like eyeballs on either side of the mouthy porch. No one saw him walk around back to the forested side of the house, half blind in the dawn light, the morning redarkened with overhanging trees. The place, though it was empty, seemed emptier in the early hour. Forgotten sheets on a laundry line, destined to be rained on, transformed into motionless ghosts. Dawn fought the dark in the canopy of pines.

One cottage was much like another, and Aubrey easily found the downstairs bedroom: a small private porch scattered with pine needles, French doors letting in scant light and no view. The room was dark enough for someone to sleep there late into the day. This was where she had slept in 1938. Aubrey peered through the glass: there was a single bed, heavy with quilts, a cedar chest at the foot, a painted vanity with an old warped mirror, and beside it someone's amateur painting of Caspian as seen from the cottage. In the painting, he could just make out his own house across the lake.

He sat down in a patch of wild mint, his back against a sappy trunk, and pulled out his Lucky Strikes to smoke the remains of the pack. When he'd butted out his last cigarette, he pulled her photograph from his pocket. He stood and peered through the glass once more, slid Garbo's picture into the crack between the doors, and returned to his boat. Lake Caspian was disquietingly calm.

While the autumn sun was shining on the porch, Aubrey was inside, emptying the burlap-curtained closet of its contents, dragging out mildewed life jackets, mangled nets and crushed crayfish traps. The trash cans in the lane overflowed. In the back of the closet he found a pair of old skis, though he had no memory of anyone coming up in winter, when the thin-walled cottage would have been unbearably cold. The skis he placed on the porch.

Aubrey divided the empty closet into a wet side and a dark side. From the dining-room cupboard, he took four salad bowls – the first for the developer solution, the second for the stop solution, the third for the fixer, the last for the bath – and four salad tongs from the cutlery drawer. He removed the laundry line from the kitchen porch and attached it to the walls of the closet. He ran black tape along the bottom of the burlap curtain. Then he sat down by the phone. Mrs Irwin was not on the line, for she had already returned to her solitary home in Rhode Island. But he sat there anyhow, waiting on himself.

While the busted second hand on the wall clock jerked noisily back and forth, the minute hand moved diligently forward. He tapped his sternum, where his heart was and his camera soon would hang. He waited, not certain what he was waiting for, but knowing he'd recognize it when it came. Finally he felt it was possible, and he picked up the receiver. Phoning the operator to get the number of Black's Photography in New York City, he made an order and waited again, this time for weeks.

The days continued to shorten. At night, fewer lights on the lakeshore. The last summer folk were leaving, the trees were changing, but the two great pines were timeless, being dark already. When his photographic equipment arrived, he'd spend the winter inside the darkroom, where the safelight cast everything in red.

Winter. The mornings were so cold, if he did not rise, he never would. The chimney sucked down the arctic winds and drove out the fire's heat, and the snow shovelled up against the shingles held little warmth inside. Quilts were nailed to the walls as insulation, and Aubrey jumped from rag rug to rag rug scattered on the floor. A small electric heater kept the darkroom chemicals from freezing.

Pulling on the ski boots he'd found under the stairs, skis over his shoulder and camera around his neck, he walked out the kitchen door and through the knee-high snow down the lane to the lake road. The village had ploughed it, but for little reason: cars came this way infrequently in winter, and though the occasional farmer still milked by hand in the hardscrabble hills, no one since the arrival of the refrigerator came to the lake to cut ice. At the end of the lane, at the mailbox, Aubrey stopped to take a picture.

He felt an uncertain peace whenever he raised his camera. He was over here with his body, but over there with his eyes: the snow-capped mailbox, the lane to the cottage and the aspen onto which was nailed a hand-painted sign of a child with a ball, meaning drivers should go slow. Standing still enough to frame his world, he too became crowned by snow. Standing still enough to see, he saw the surprising way the light shocked the ice, and he watched the unsteady wind elevate the fringes of a snowdrift. When he raised the camera, he froze the moment: shadows were shadows and light was light, and of the two, he found to his relief he had no preference. He and his subject were just as they were; there was no more to be said about either. We fill in the rest with doubt, which from blind habituation we call certainty. We hurry towards happiness and death as if they were our answers, knowing neither is.

As his camera captured the absence of people and the overbearing weather, Aubrey's thoughts drifted away, not even a bird to hear them. He was going to the graveyard to see his mother. All these months, and he still hadn't been there. It was marked by a white picket fence along the road and a frozen creek separating the graves from the fallow winter fields. In the back, in the more recently dug ground where a tall man had a view of the lake, Aubrey found her stone, a grey slab of granite carved with a weeping willow and a quote from Emerson: "I become a transparent eyeball; I am the lover of uncontained and immortal beauty."

Father's name was already engraved beside Mother's, and so was the date of his birth, followed by a dash and an empty space. He might never visit Vermont again, but he wanted to be laid down with his wife. Aubrey clicked the picture. He couldn't say shoot anymore. He opened the aperture to let in more light. The graveyard's wild summer roses had transformed into winter's withered rosehips. He caught them in his lens in their various stages of decay: life making life and tearing it down to make it all over again.

The earliest graves, of settlers and pioneers, were black with age, but every stone in the yard was topped white with snow. The tiniest gravestones were submerged completely. Clearing the snow from the little markers, he took a series of photographs. No given names, just "Baby"; "Ba –" the rest covered in lichen; "Our baby." Then, "Maple Cobb, 1940." Here, beneath the mountains that raised him, was something of Amos. And someone, probably Delia, had named his daughter for the trees. Aubrey smiled and focused as tightly as he could.

When he left the graveyard, he walked towards the schoolhouse, where he sat on the stoop and hitched on his skis. He skied across the fields into the woods, which themselves were cradles and graves. In the forest, he attached a telescopic lens. The earth was bare of snow under the heavy-set pines. The frost forged worlds out of coldness and light in equal measure. He clicked the dying mosses shining. He clicked the patient limbs of trees, and the puckered frozen toadstool, poisonous to a man but edible to a bear or white-tailed deer. He was in love with the weird grandeur of its frozen gills beneath the stalwart canopy. He was in love with the burden of ice bending down a tragic sapling. In love with the signs of wilderness as well as the signs of man, and the terrible, inevitable distance and dance between them. In love with the silence after all brief things had had their moment and were gone. The northern darkness of a gnarled apple tree, proving the existence of a forgotten ancestor, and the ever-returning fruit strewn over the winter ground in the undemanding colour of rot.

Spring arrived, though in its absence Aubrey had doubted it would ever come. When it did, he failed to capture it on film. No one could frame the spring. It was shy, hysterical, ravishing, deceitful, bold, belligerent and uncontainable all in one day. The cauterizing winter was gone, and what followed was change upon change. The sun dispelled the cottage greyness and melted the snow into snake holes and rabbit holes while cars got stuck in the mud. The earth had become so soluble that Aubrey imagined the rocks would melt and his prints would never dry. And when the ground burst forth, an even truer spring erupted. When he sought to frame that too, it also was elusive. It spread and conquered and rose into summer and brought the summer folk.

The dragonflies droned and the motorboats droned. The dark hours were alight with fireflies and the string of electrical lamps around the shore, which, with very slow film and patience, Aubrey replicated on photographic paper. He snapped a photo of Old Mrs Irwin, a year older, still in her rubber-soled sneakers, delivering his mail. Mornings he spent in the darkroom, afternoons in the woods and fields. In the dusk, in the silence, he returned home, content.

To his sorrow, the children still stayed away, for though he no longer screamed, they remembered. And so he was bewildered to see, on his return from taking pictures one day, a solid little boy of dark complexion with wet black hair and dirt in his fists running naked around the side of the cottage.

"Hello," said Aubrey. "Who are you?"

Aubrey was afraid he'd scared the boy, for the child didn't answer but raced up the steps, vanishing around the corner. When Aubrey followed him onto the porch, he found the boy's mother seated in the rocker. The boy buried his face in her lap, and she smiled and ran her hand over his big wet head. He was a monumental child.

"He's been swimming," the mother said. She smiled at Aubrey. "I'm looking for Amos Cobb. He work here?"

Unable to take his eyes from her face, Aubrey stared at the Indian woman. "Yes," he said, then "no." He floundered. "It was long ago," he said. "He was our handyman."

"Hear that?" she said to her child's head in her lap. "Someone knows your daddy." Then, to Aubrey, "Up at Delia's farm they ain't even heard of Delia, let alone of Amos."

"Yup," he said.

She nodded. She pinched a lock of her son's mop of black hair and wrung the water out. The boy did not look up. "He's shy of strangers," she said.

"That's okay," he said.

She asked, "You seen Amos?"

There was no right answer. Aubrey looked towards the lake and the mountains, hoping to hear his own reply, then back at the beautiful woman. He waited for speech, and she waited with him and didn't seem to mind his slowness. He saw her beauty. He lit a cigarette and watched the smoke rise freely.

Finally, he said, "I recognize you. I've seen you before."

Kona turned her face towards the submerged islands.

He said, "Amos was always thinking about you. He didn't talk much during the war, but I know he was always thinking about you."

Kona looked back at him, looked up and down him, her eyes like a bird about to land in fire.

"Amos was killed in the Italian Alps," he said, "when he was spiking trees."

She was gazing out at the lake again, and the mountains bruised purple in the dusk. She was real, solid, lovely; she would not disappear when his vision cleared; she would not vanish whenever he awoke, but she withheld herself as truth does, and only her hand kept moving over her child's head.

Time moved slowly forward, until finally the little boy lifted his eyes and looked at Aubrey, and Aubrey said, "I bet you're hungry after all that swimming," and Kona, beneath her grief, smiled.

They would sit on the dock with their feet in the lake, while Amos's child paddled like a puppy. They would sit on the porch while the sudden squalls came in, while the rain came on, passed over them, and left the grasses gleaming and the water colder. They would lie in the woods, on the mosses, where pollens gave life in the speckled sun and the child played hide and seek; lie by the fire at night, when the northern nights fell frosted to the earth. They would speak and not speak, and sleep and not sleep, while the Great Bear lumbered across the sky searching out a place to lay his head, while the little boy went upstairs to his bed or rested in the hammock, his eyes wide open, observing the silent pattern of the stars, while one by one the electric lights extinguished around the shore and the nights grew colder and the lake grew colder, and the first ice shuttered down on the surface of all things, while the fish and the bears lived without words but also without fear, awaiting the rising of certain spring, sure of the sweet, free summers.

Aubrey knew the future, what little of it was written. We live. We live. We die. We die. A big man reaches up for the sun and carries it across the horizon.

NEW FROM PERISCOPE IN 2015

PRINCESS BARI
Hwang Sok-yong; translated from the Korean by Sora Kim-Russell
'The most powerful voice of the novel in Asia today.' (Kenzaburō Ōe)
A young North Korean woman survives unspeakable dangers in
search of a better life in London.
PB • 204MM X 138MM • 9781859641743 • 248PP • £9.99

LONG TIME NO SEE: A MEMOIR OF FATHERS, DAUGHTERS AND GAMES OF CHANCE
Hannah Lowe
Acclaimed poet Hannah Lowe reflects on her relationship with her
late father, a rakish Jamaican immigrant and legendary gambler.
PB • 204MM X 138MM • 9781859643969 • 328PP • £9.99

THE BLACK COAT
Neamat Imam
Months after Bangladesh's 1971 war, a simple migrant impersonates
the country's authoritarian ruler – with shocking results.
PB • 204MM X 138MM • 9781859640067 • 240PP • £9.99

THE MOOR'S ACCOUNT
Laila Lalami
'Brilliantly imagined ... feels very like the truth.' (Salman Rushdie)
The fictional memoirs of a Moorish slave offer a new perspective
on a notoriously ill-fated, real-life Spanish expedition in 1528.
PB • 204MM X 138MM • 9781859644270 • 336PP • £9.99

DRINKING AND DRIVING IN CHECHNYA
Peter Gonda
A disaffected Russian truck driver winds up at the centre of the brutal
bombing of the Chechen capital, forced to engage with reality as never before.
PB • 204MM X 138MM • 9781859641057 • 240PP • £9.99

THE GARDENS OF THE IMAGINATION
Bakhtiyar Ali; translated from the Kurdish by Kareem Abdulrahman
A group of friends search for the bodies of two murdered lovers in this
haunting allegory of modern Iraqi Kurdistan.
PB • 204MM X 138MM • 9781859641255 • 448PP • £9.99

A MAN WITH A KILLER'S FACE
Matti Rönkä; translated from the Finnish by David Hackston
A detective's orderly life is upended when a missing-persons case draws
him into the Russian–Finnish criminal underworld.
PB • 204MM X 138MM • 9781859641781 • 288PP • £9.99